For all those who seek

Heidi Jean - You are a woman of noble birth - a daughter of the King, the Most High, who is gracious towards you and Who is working all things together for your good!

May He continually fill your life with good things!

Revelation 1:3

D1602728

ONE
WILL BE TAKEN

DAWN MORRIS

RELIQUUM PUBLISHING

ONE WILL BE TAKEN
Second Edition Trade Book, 2014
Copyright © 2012 by Dawn Morris

All rights reserved. No part of this publication may be reproduced, stored in a retrieval system, or transmitted in any form by any means—electronic, mechanical, photocopy, recording, or otherwise—except for brief quotations in critical reviews or articles, without the prior permission of the publisher, except as provided by U.S. copyright law.

Some Scripture quotations and words of Jesus are taken or adapted from the New American Standard Bible, ® Copyright © 1960, 1962, 1963, 1968, 1971, 1973, 1975, 1977, 1995 by The Lockman Foundation. Used by permission.

This novel is a work of fiction. Names, characters, places, and incidents either are the product of the author's imagination or are used fictitiously. Any resemblance to actual events, locales, organizations, or persons living or dead is entirely coincidental and beyond the intent of either the author or the publisher.

To order additional books:
www.amazon.com

Visit Dawn Morris' web site at www.DawnMorris.net

Published by Reliquum Publishing

E-book also available

ISBN: 978-0985457884
Editorial: Arlyn Lawrence, Inspira Literary Solutions, Gig Harbor, WA
Book Design: Carrot Stick Marketing, Gig Harbor, WA
Printed in the USA by Lightning Source, Nashville, TN

Acknowledgments

Most of the novel you are about to read is purely fictional, though it is inspired by the prophecies written throughout the Bible concerning the events and persons of the End Times.

First of all, I would like to thank my husband, Dennis, who has read every version of this novel, including the first one I wrote seventeen years ago. He was my first editor and I appreciate his truthful evaluations of the characters and scenes.

I would also like to thank my family for putting up with me while I write!

I'm grateful for my editor and friend, Arlyn Lawrence. She has a graceful way of balancing constructive criticism with encouragement.

Finally, I would like to thank the Lord for the truth of His Word. From the beginning of my faith journey, I have been awed by the fulfillment of prophecy in Scripture. If you want to look to what the future holds, I know of no more certain place to find it than in the Bible.

1

GEORGETOWN
WASHINGTON, DC – 2000

Arturo stood at the window and stared out at the well-manicured garden. As the wind bent the heirloom roses, a few petals danced in the breeze like confetti. He noted, with a frown, a few weeds the gardener had missed. He sighed in annoyance. The Federal-style mansion in Georgetown was adequate to his needs, but was not to be compared with his ancestral home in Rome. There his servants were well-versed in caring for him, and they knew the consequences of not measuring up to his standards.

He was here for several reasons; the most important one was not to be made public for many years. He had a vested interest in keeping that one secret. The other was the expansion of his medical practice into the United States. Unfortunately, irrational laws kept him from practicing his specialty legally here, but he had a team of lawyers, lobbyists, and doctors working to change those laws. Everyone had a right to reproduce; infertility was something that could be overcome with modern science, for those who had the funds. He was frustrated by the medieval mindsets that kept him from bringing the fruit of his research on embryos to the United States.

A side benefit to moving here was that he could spend more time with his daughter, Teo. She was eleven years old now, and he had missed a great deal of her childhood by living in Rome, only being able to see her for short visits in the summer and during an occasional holiday. Of course, she wasn't the son he so desperately desired, but things were looking promising in that direction.

He glanced at the clock, expecting Stephen, his assistant, to arrive any minute bearing the results of their latest experiment. After their initial success in taking the DNA coding of eggs harvested from the ovaries of young women, he and Stephen had begun to look at recoding DNA. While Arturo was a medical miracle worker, Stephen had an uncanny ability to see what no one else could see—and a staggering intellect that could overcome almost any roadblock they encountered.

No longer would people have to leave to chance the sort of progeny they produced. Now, select clients could decide for themselves the level of their children's intelligence and attractiveness, along with hair and eye color. Arturo had used his own DNA to attempt to produce the son he had always wanted. The failures had been dismaying, although now it appeared they had the process under control. They had found it necessary to complete much of their research in secret, but he felt certain his life's work would one day make him famous as a scientist. Science was his religion; he put no faith in dogma touted by weak-minded people who could not think for themselves.

The doorbell chimed pleasantly. A minute later, his study door opened as the maid let Stephen into the room. Arturo smiled as the handsome older man strode quickly over to shake his friend's hand. "At last! I have been waiting to see the results, Stephen."

Stephen grinned. "I actually brought the results with me." He turned to the doorway where a lovely girl of about eighteen stood waiting for an audience. "This is Serena. She is a freshman at Georgetown."

Arturo looked at the young woman in front of him with appreciation. Her smile was demure yet confident. Her honey-blonde hair curled in masses, framing her deep brown eyes.

"It's an honor to meet you, sir. My parents are thrilled about my opportunity to help advance your work. I am pleased to tell you that the process was successful. I'm past my first trimester, and all test results show your son to be in perfect health." Serena's dark eyes flashed with emotion as she shook Arturo's hand.

Arturo responded by pulling her into an enthusiastic embrace. "I have waited for this for years! Please sit down, Serena!" He led her to the lush aniline leather couch in the center of the room.

Stephen seated himself beside her, draping his arm across the back of the couch almost protectively. "Everything is perfect, Arturo! Serena will deliver the child via cesarean section in March. Nothing will be left to chance. Biologically, this child is only yours. The moment the child is born, Serena will sign the paperwork and her financial remuneration will be wired into her account in the Grand Caymans."

Arturo noticed how Serena's blonde hair framed her oval face perfectly, like a Madonna painting by one of the masters. *How fitting that this leap in evolution should be carried in the womb of a virgin,* he thought to himself, scoffing. *Religion—superstitious nonsense.*

"Yet, there is a certain appeal to the symmetry," he mused aloud quietly, to no one in particular.

Stephen continued his congratulatory monologue. "This technology may well prove to be the answer to the world's problems. Certainly we can find the means to design children who are not just intelligent beyond our imaginings, but who will also lead humankind to the next level of evolutionary development."

"Yes!" Arturo waved his hand emphatically, his voice rising with passion. "We need peace and prosperity in the world. Certainly it is within man's ability to use the knowledge we have gained to take this next step in evolution."

Serena smiled, a dimple flashing for a moment on the left side of her perfectly shaped mouth. She was pleased with how things were turning out for her. Not only was she integral in Arturo Giamo's successful experiment, she also was going to be set for life financially. Now medical school would be no problem. She was also hopeful of future employment with Giamo Infertility Associates when she graduated. All the months of preparatory shots and the nine months of pregnancy were not too great a sacrifice for the advancement of medicine—and her own career. She was truly happy to help science, which she loved, and her own future at the same time.

Arturo walked over to the bar. "I've been saving this, Stephen, for just this moment." He opened the 1926 Black Bowmore scotch reverentially, carefully pouring a measured amount into two tulip-shaped glasses. He handed a glass to Stephen, and they toasted one another and Serena.

"Do you have a name picked out for your son?" Serena asked.

"Of course. He will be named Luca Romano Giamo. Luca means 'bringer of light.' It is my hope that my son will help usher in a restoration of Italy's former glory. Hopefully, he will be a man of vision as well—a leader in the new world about to dawn with his birth."

The Giamo Estate, outside of Rome – 2013

Arturo smiled as he watched Luca ride his new horse. He rode well, even after just a few lessons. Luca did everything well. He was a good-looking boy with blonde hair and blue eyes. His wide smile caused dimples to crease either side of his mouth in a most appealing manner, and the cleft in his chin set just the right touch to his strong jawline. His shoulders were broad, and his muscles were already well defined, despite his youth.

The boy cantered his horse around the arena, whispering something as he rode. *Probably translating from Greek to Latin,* Arturo thought with amused pride. Luca had three private tutors, and they could barely keep up with him. He already spoke five languages fluently. He was just finishing calculus; he wrote well and read extensively. In short, Luca Giamo was an amazing child. He had very few, if any, peers.

Arturo sometimes vacillated about keeping Luca's origins secret. The technique Stephen had developed had been successful

4

no big deal, Teo. I think a lot of mothers and daughters have a hard time. But I like your mom. She's very sweet. The religious stuff isn't for us, but she believes what she believes, and that's what this country is all about. It's not like she tries to convert us or anything. She just expresses her opinions."

"Yeah, but her opinions come from some medieval superstitious system of Christian, mind-numbing—" Teo cut herself short. "Well, you know what I mean. I don't have time to discuss that ridiculous ideology. I have to get to work. My father has invited us out to his home in the Hamptons this weekend to celebrate. What do you think?"

DC nodded and gave her a kiss. "Sounds good, babe. I'm going to get a quick shower and get going."

Alexandria, Virginia

Elena Giamo got up from her bedside, rosary in hand. She had faithfully prayed each morning for as far back as she could remember. Today, though, she had no peace. Many years ago, she had endured the traumatic ending of her marriage to Arturo Giamo, and now her only child was his ally, actively pursuing the same agenda that had destroyed her marriage. Teo had succeeded in opening the door for Arturo to practice his atrocities in the United States.

Man would play God. Elena sighed.

The weather was awful, and had been all week. She'd been stuck inside her small townhome for days. She picked up her phone and scrolled through her call log. She had called Teo several times and left messages, but Teo had not called her back—or responded to Elena's e-mails. Elena felt dejected and distraught.

I've lost her to Arturo, Elena thought bitterly. Just thinking of Arturo filled her heart with anguish. She had loved him so passionately once. They had met at a party at the US embassy in Rome where her uncle had been the executive assistant to the US ambassador. Elena's parents had, as a gift for her college graduation, flown her there first class pay a visit to her aunt and uncle, who had made sure Elena attended as many social events as possible during her visit. They had also taken her on several lavish shopping trips to ensure she was dressed appropriately for the occasions.

Elena had been bored out of her mind listening to the inane ramblings of an urbane socialite when Arturo had walked into the room. She'd never seen such a handsome man in person before! He was tall and well built, his clothes obviously expensive and tailored. She couldn't believe it when his eyes met hers and he immediately made his way across the room to her side. They'd been inseparable from that moment on. He was charming and intelligent—and smitten. He had respected her strong faith and had not pressured her in any way that would have offended her. After one short month, they were engaged, and married two months later. It was absolute bliss.

Elena sighed nostalgically. She had truly loved Arturo and thought he loved her, too. She was sure he had, at first. They had made their home in a stylish and comfortable apartment in the city—a wedding gift from Arturo's wealthy family. His family was aristocratic but kind, and they had welcomed Elena with open arms, thrilled with their son's new bride.

To everyone's delight, she had become pregnant very quickly. Arturo was elated. As a young doctor specializing in obstetrics, he had taken keen interest in every aspect of the pregnancy. It had made Elena feel cherished.

Because I did not know the real reason for the interest, she thought sadly. It was the child Arturo had been the most interested in, not the mother. But ignorance had kept her in bliss, a bliss that had erupted into pure joy when she heard their baby's first cry and held the squirming newborn in her arms. They'd named her "Teodora," which meant "gift of God," although, ironically, her father's belief system did not acknowledge a personal divine being. They immediately shortened it to "Teo." Arturo had expressed his happiness

"Look, I've examined it," Father Martin retorted. "I had a class in seminary on prophecy. The Church has taught that the apocalyptic events talked about in Revelation are symbolic revelations meant simply to encourage the Christians of the day who were being persecuted."

"You'll excuse me, James," the old man interjected candidly, "but I have never been one to accept what any organization told me. I have always been one to question and to search for myself. It was my birthday that first made me curious about prophecy, you see."

Father Martin took a sip of his warm coffee. "Your birthday?" He'd wondered exactly how old Joseph was, but had never felt it polite to ask.

"Yes, I was born May 15, 1948."

Rapidly calculating, Father Martin figured that made Joseph seventy-two years old.

"I am not sure what your birthday has to do with Bible prophecy, Joseph."

The old man smiled. He was profoundly endearing. "It's quite an important historical date, especially for my people. Don't you know its significance?"

Father Martin thought, but came up blank. "No. That was a long time ago. Did it have something to do with World War II?"

"It was the day Israel was reborn."

"I thought you were a Christian, Joseph." Father Martin was confused.

"So I am," Joseph responded knowingly. "A Hebrew Christian. I thought you would know from my last name, Levy. But young people today have little care for such things, too busy on their phones and computers. I was born the exact day Israel became a nation again, seventy-two years ago."

He paused for a moment to sip his tea and wipe his mouth. "The prophecies of Isaiah and Ezekiel spoke of such a time, when Zion would be born in one day. When I heard about it as a young man, I had to know more. It started me on my path of faith, James.

Those prophecies led me to other prophecies, which helped me realize that the Messiah had already come. Through the guidance and mentorship of a believer who took time with me and the Word of God, I came to put my faith in the Lord Yeshua."

Father Martin felt uncomfortable and was a bit taken aback. He really liked Joseph and did not want to offend him in any way, but taking those "prophecies" literally was absolutely ridiculous.

Joseph stood up and put a hand on Father Martin's shoulder. "I know it's difficult to question what you have always been told. I think it was the Bereans in the book of Acts who were commended for their study of Scripture. They didn't take even the Apostle Paul at his word, but examined the Holy Scriptures to see if what he said was true. Perhaps instead of agreeing to disagree, you would do well to examine Scripture for yourself?" He gave Father Martin's shoulder a squeeze, put on his coat, and said good-bye with affection in his voice.

In the short time Father Martin had known Joseph, the priest had felt encouraged and challenged in his own faith. He had begun his time at Holy Apostles by calling his new congregation to read God's Word for themselves. He loved the Scriptures, but the thought had been nagging at him lately that he only loved the parts he was comfortable with. His heart was beginning to feel conflicted. Father Martin flipped through the section of his Bible that held the Major Prophets. Except for the portions in Isaiah that spoke of the "Suffering Servant," the rest had no notations, no underlined verses, and barely any wrinkles in the page. He'd hardly even opened that part. He turned to Revelation, already knowing it, too, would be devoid of marks, and asked himself why he had never turned through its pages. A verse caught his eye: "Blessed is the one who reads aloud the words of this prophecy, and blessed are those who hear it and take to heart what is written in it, because the time is near."

Father Martin sat down and pulled the great book close. The phrase he'd just read reverberated in his mind. Maybe it was time he looked for himself, studied what the Bible had to say for itself, and didn't listen to anyone but the Word of God. He bowed his head and asked God to help him understand, and then he began to read.

Georgetown, Washington, DC

The morning air was crisp. DC smiled as he saw the unmistakable sign for Susie Q's. The oversized neon mug of steaming coffee blinked like a beacon to the shop's customers. He wished he were meeting Elena for lunch instead of breakfast. Roasted turkey and sautéed onions with Swiss cheese on rye was a favorite.

The bell jingled softly as he pulled the door open. Susie Q's was small and quaint, so it took no effort to spot Elena at a table, sipping her coffee. She looked so much like her daughter, DC had to smile. It astounded him that the two women were so alike on the outside, but completely different on the inside. Teo was all drive, ambition, and hard edges, while Elena was peaceful, quiet, and fragile.

His thoughts were interrupted by Elena's gentle smile. Smiling back, he made his way to the table and sat down. The waitress quickly appeared with a mug of coffee for him and took their orders before he could say more than hello.

"Thanks so much for meeting me before work, DC," Elena said. "I know you're very busy."

"I'm happy to meet you for breakfast, Elena," DC said as he took an appreciative sip of his coffee. "I'm glad we finally live close enough to family to do stuff like this."

"How are your parents doing?" Elena asked with genuine care.

"Great. You know the construction business is full of ups and downs. But my dad knows the business so well that he plans for the lean years. He branched out about twenty years ago into government construction, and that has been the backbone of the business ever since." DC shook his head in disgust. "Washington never runs out of money to spend."

"How are things going for you, DC? Do you like working for General Stanton?"

General Stanton had been the thirty-seventh commandant of the Marine Corps. An old Marine aviator, he was tough but fair. He'd retired from the Corps and taken a job in the State Department overseeing the Bureau of Diplomatic Security. His task was to ensure a secure environment for conducting US foreign policy, and DC had been handpicked by the retired general to be his assistant. As a former Marine himself, DC felt honored to be at the general's side.

"You know, I like working at the bureau, though I don't see a lot of the general. I've just been tasked with overseeing security in New Babylon. We'll be sending an ambassador there soon, and so will other world nations, so the US is heading up the security task force."

Elena's eyes lit up. She had read a whole series of books many years ago that talked about the end of days, and there had been something in them about Babylon. It had been so long ago that she could not remember much about the plotlines, but she recalled they'd fascinated and distressed her at the same time.

"I think it's amazing that an ancient city is being rebuilt according to its ancient designs," Elena responded with interest. "There was an entire section about it in a magazine I read last week. Are you going to get to go and see for yourself? I've heard the UN has restricted access until it's finished. It's hard to see images even on the Internet."

"Yes, they're going to great lengths to keep it under wraps. The opening ceremony will be elaborate. There are so many world leaders planning to attend, the security preparations require supreme secrecy. Archaeologists have been involved every step of the way to insure historical accuracy, along with technicians who have added modern amenities." DC paused mid-conversation as the waitress brought over their food. Breakfast was sounding good after all.

3

GEORGETOWN,
WASHINGTON, DC

DC walked into the house from the garage. The Federal-style row house in Georgetown was far above his own budget, but his wife had deep pockets and high aspirations. Personally, he would have been happy with a little condo in Arlington. Their five-bedroom home was more than they needed, and the amount of time and money it had taken to restore it to its 1812 grandeur still amazed him. But Teo wanted it, and that woman always had a way of getting what she wanted. Since she was usually pleasant about it and took care of the details herself, DC didn't mind. *As the old saying goes, "Happy wife, happy life,"* DC thought to himself.

He plunked his keys on the kitchen counter, opened the refrigerator, grabbed a Coors Light, and sauntered into the family room. A high-definition television hung over the fireplace. He flipped it on with the remote and sat down on the couch. Teo would not be home for another hour or so, so he cruised through the news channels before settling on his favorite, Fox News. They claimed to be fair and balanced, and he liked that they were pro-military.

One of the commentators was talking earnestly, and a banner scrolling across the bottom of the screen proclaimed breaking news. Interested, DC turned up the volume. The host had a grim expression on his face as he described an attempt made by a suicide bomber in Babylon. The would-be terrorist had tried to detonate his bomb in front of the Ishtar Gate, but thankfully his efforts had failed. Turning to the elderly gentleman next to him, the commentator introduced an expert from the World Monuments Fund, or WMF, Gabir Hakim Hussein.

"Mr. Hussein, you have led efforts in the collaboration of the WMF and United Nations to complete the work called for by the master plan of the New Babylon Project. It's been nine long years since the Obama administration granted funding for the project to restore this ancient city as a symbol of the new Iraqi democracy. That initial objective has expanded, and now New Babylon is to be a Millennial City, the first of its kind, a highly technological and safe city. What does today's bombing attempt do to those efforts?"

The white-haired scholar tilted his head slightly as if to consider the weightiness of the question. DC rolled his eyes. He knew the failed attempt had no effect on the completion of New Babylon. He did like Fox, but they had an irritating habit of using "experts" to pad their stories.

New Babylon was one of the safest places on earth. DC's office had known of the attempt almost immediately. It had failed not by chance, but because of technology the US government had purchased at great cost from a small defense firm, SavTec, in the Badlands of South Dakota. This new technology was to be used to defend and protect citizens in the ultimate city. Babylon was not just an ancient wonder rebuilt; it was a new world wonder, too. Teams from every nation had competed for the lucrative contracts awarded by the United Nations. Only the very best experts were able to plan the city and then implement those plans. Every technological advance known to mankind was used to completely rebuild Babylon, the first "smart city" in the world.

The world had changed dramatically after 9/11 and asymmetrical warfare had become the norm. Now an individual, not just an army, could inflict massive destruction on an enemy. SavTec provided defense against such enemies and had developed multilayered technologies that stopped interactive explosive devices, known as IEDs, before detonation. The company's facial recognition software was just part of the layered package the United States had invested in and implemented in New Babylon.

As he continued to watch the news coverage on television, DC was impressed with the brilliance of the SavTec team. Not only had they developed advanced technologies to aid in the war on terror, but they were also experts at training others to perform the work necessary to hinder terrorists before they had a chance to attack. Prevention was the key, and the people and technologies SavTec provided were highly successful. The bomber never had a chance. Of course, DC was one of the select few who were privy to this sort of information. He smiled to himself as the WMF expert pontificated. DC had to admit, it was fun to be in on the secret!

The soft chime of the door alarm interrupted his thoughts. It was Teo. He stood up and stretched his six-foot frame quickly, cracking a few vertebrae as he did so. Picking up his beer bottle, he walked into the kitchen. He expected a hug and a warm greeting, but instead he found his wife slumped over the kitchen island in despair. Teo looked up at him; her eyes were red and full of tears. DC rushed over to her and folded her into his arms tightly.

"Are you okay, babe?" he asked. She leaned against him and started to sob again. "What's happened, Teo?"

She continued to weep for a few moments, struggling to gain composure. "I had . . . results." She sobbed softly into his shoulder again.

DC sighed deeply. Teo had been expecting the test results from her father's infertility diagnostic team. He was not as invested in the whole baby thing as Teo was, but Douglas Charles Bond was a true Marine—loyal. If it was important to his wife, it was important. Period.

"What did they say, Teo?" He couldn't bear to see her in such pain.

She pulled back from his embrace and looked at the floor. "My uterus is damaged beyond repair. There is no way for a fertilized egg to grow and thrive." Her voice broke as she sobbed again. "If I had only known that this could happen! Now I'll never have my own child!" She staggered to the kitchen table and sat down in one of the chairs, sorrow overtaking her. DC felt helpless. He crossed the room, knelt beside his wife, and did what he could to comfort her.

Arlington, Virginia

Elena felt uncomfortable. It was not the hard metal chair she was sitting on so much as the ease and familiarity she lacked with the women around her. She hardly knew anyone because she had not socialized much the last few years. The long room on the second floor of Arlington Community Church was dark but cozy. Couches and chairs were arranged invitingly in small groupings, and on the tables were retro-style lamps reminiscent of those Elena had seen in the library as a child. At the opposite end of the room from where the women sat were a couple of pool tables and a Ping-Pong table. A new friend she had made at Holy Apostles had invited her to the community Bible study. Margaret. Margaret was such a kind woman. She'd introduced herself to Elena one day after Mass while both of them were waiting to talk with Father Martin. She'd asked Elena to join her for lunch, and that had been the beginning of their special friendship.

Elena caught Margaret's eye. Margaret gave her a quick wink and a sideways grin as the group leader began to speak.

"Good morning, ladies!" The woman's voice rang sweetly. "It is so good to have each of you here. We have a few new people in the group today, so let's all go around the table and introduce ourselves. How about you tell the group where you were born?"

Elena was relieved when the woman to the leader's left went first. This made her last and gave her a moment to compose herself. She had been quite a recluse since her divorce. The anger and bitterness she felt against Arturo left her with little desire to form friendships—until lately. Recently, she'd begun to feel that she'd wasted too many years in the emptiness of her small townhome. She longed for someone she could really talk to. Then Margaret had come along. Being in a large group like this was outside of Elena's comfort zone, but the fact that Margaret was here gave her courage. Elena smiled and looked shyly around the table as the woman next to her finished her introduction. Then Elena gave her own. "My name is Elena Giamo," she said. "I was born in New York City." Others in the group smiled in welcome.

"Okay ladies, I am Marisol Jameson," said the group leader. She had gray curly hair and wore glasses with a beaded string attached. "Today we will begin our study of First Thessalonians. It is one of the oldest books in the New Testament, written about eighteen years after Jesus's death and resurrection. It's one of the shortest books too, easily read in about half an hour. I would love each of us to read through the book once a day as we go through this study." Marisol glanced around the circle of women.

"We are going to look at this important book of Scripture inductively, so I have bound copies here—they've been double-spaced—you can mark in them as you study. We'll get more into the 'hows' later on, but right now I'd like to discuss the basic question of this study. What does it mean to be a Christian?" Marisol's eyes lit up as she spoke. It was obvious she was passionate about this. "To many, it means that you belong to a particular church, whether it is Lutheran, Baptist, Catholic, or what have you. To others, it is simply a default identity, because they are not Buddhist or Muslim, and so on. As we study First Thessalonians, we will look for the Lord to show us the answer to that question, through Scripture."

Marisol spoke for a few more minutes before praying for the group and handing out the packets. Elena thought the whole process was interesting. It was like going to school. *This might make Father Martin's challenge easier,* she thought. She had tried to read her Bible every day as he had asked, but it was too overwhelming. She did not know where to start. *This makes sense. Why wouldn't I study the Bible like a student studies a textbook? It's been so long since I finished college. At least it will be good for my mind to work on this.* Listening intently as Marisol explained the process of study to the group of women, Elena determined she would come back again next week with her homework done. She caught Margaret's eye and smiled. She was grateful to be here.

The Giamo Estate, outside of Rome, Italy

Luca felt the heat of anger rise in his chest as he read through the legal papers he had just found in his father's safe. Years ago, his father had revealed some of the details of how Luca had been conceived and born. Now Luca saw that his father had not been exactly honest about how it all came about. A science experiment was all he was, despite his father's insistence that he had moved heaven and earth to find a way to have the son he'd always wanted. Luca read the pages of complex legal statements easily. For a large sum of money, his birth mother had sold him to Arturo Giamo, who was not legally the child's biological father.

A scientific manipulation of an egg from a prepubescent female, a mature egg from the young woman, Serena, and a proprietary process that was the intellectual property of Giamo Infertility Associates were the "birth parents" of the male child. The papers went on to request formal adoption of the male child by Arturo Giamo.

Luca's father had explained to him the basic story of his conception, thinking it would make him feel better about his mother's abandonment. Arturo had not realized as he spoke with pride at his scientific accomplishment that the brilliant child sitting next to him was sinking into greater hurt, for the boy had thought Sylvia was his mother. With his father's words, Luca absorbed the harsh realization that she was not. His real mother also had apparently abandoned him. As his father had droned on about how unique Luca was, all the boy could think of was that his mother had not wanted him. Neither of his mothers had wanted him.

Luca shoved the offensive papers back into the safe. Not only had his mother not wanted him, but she had also sold him like a commodity. His birth mother had not loved him, nor had the woman he had thought of as his mother. As he pushed the hurt down deep into his spirit, anger and rage built inside of him. It gave him a feeling of strength; somehow it felt good to be angry, to hate both of the women who'd betrayed him.

Luca thought of what his father had told him about his conception and birth, and he realized that although Arturo truly loved him, the man was not his biological father—at least not as other children had biological fathers. It would be more accurate to call Arturo a manipulator of genetic coding, or his creator. His spite grew as the gravity of the truth hit his brilliant young mind—he was not like other people. Not because he was so highly intelligent, but because he was not human in the same way they were.

He gripped the sides of the mahogany desk in Arturo's study as his mind raced, one thought chasing another, the emotions escalating in his heart and threatening to choke him on their virulence. How could any God allow him to go through this? He thought of Augustine's Confessions and the ridiculous quote that had touched him as a boy. "I hate!" he whispered. "I hate! I hate!" His voice rose. Tears rolled down his handsome face as the anguished expressions hardened. *"I hate you!"*

Amazingly, his pain ceased as he spoke those words. He felt instead a sense of well-being as comfort instantly invaded him. He wiped away his few tears with the back of his hand and slowly stood up. Suddenly, Luca sensed someone was in the room with him. He cautiously looked around the large study, but it was empty. Nevertheless, he still felt calm and at peace as if someone had come in and comforted him.

Just then, the door opened, and Arturo's associate, Stephen, came in. Stephen noted the expression on the young man's face— wonder and strength. *So, the time has come,* Stephen thought. Smiling triumphantly, he walked across the room to stand beside Luca.

"You have begun to know who you really are, Luca. I have been waiting for this day for a long time. You have a destiny like no other human being has ever been offered." Stephen put his hands on the young man's strong shoulders. "It is yours, just waiting for your hands to grasp it. Through the centuries there have been others who thought they could take it, but this destiny is your birthright and yours alone. I have been chosen to lead you to the source of your power and to the future that awaits you."

For some reason, these words were not shocking to Luca. They simply felt right and he was incredibly intrigued.

"You are the savior of the human race, Luca. You will lead us to a truly new Millennium. Arturo loves you, but he is not your true father. I serve your true Father, and I serve you." Stephen knelt in front of the boy respectfully.

It struck Luca as strange that this act of reverence seemed fitting to him. The words Stephen spoke were like water poured onto his dry, parched heart. Within himself he felt the truth of each of those words spoken over him like a benediction. This was his destiny. His fate. Finally.

Arlington, Virginia

Joseph Levy pulled himself up, finishing his hundredth sit-up. He still practiced the workouts he had learned as a young man. *But not with the same fervor,* he thought to himself as he chuckled. Long ago, he had served in the Israeli Defense Force, or IDF. He had been so young and so strong, still a teenager.

He stood up and picked up the towel he'd left on the back of the chair. He quickly glanced at the picture on the side table. Natalie, his bride, smiled out from the delicately scrolled silver frame. She'd always teased him that he had joined the ground forces because their olive-green uniform brought out the green in his hazel eyes. Joseph never told her the horrors of the battles he endured. He had been part of the force that crossed the Suez Canal and cut off Egypt's Third Army during the Yom Kippur War. It was a necessary war, though, especially for his people. What Joseph had seen and done were essential to their mission, but the guilt of his actions had started him on a deeply spiritual journey. The Lord had used Natalie, a young woman he met in San Francisco, California, to bring him to know Yeshua.

After the war, Joseph had left Israel to study in the United States at the University of California, San Francisco. In late 1979, he met Natalie as he was heading out of one of his classes. She was wearing a shocking T-shirt that instantly caught his attention. Its large white screen-printed letters proclaimed, "Jews for Jesus." Honestly, he would not have given her the time of day had she not been so stunningly beautiful. Her sweet smile drew a single dimple on her left cheek. There was something wholesome and positive about her that drew him in. She gave him a pamphlet, which he promised to read if she would have coffee with him. They spent every day together after that first date.

She was an American Jew who had grown up in a privileged home, the only daughter of a highly successful surgeon. Her conversion to Christianity—or as she insisted on calling it, her becoming a true Jew, a faithful follower of Messiah—had not caused an ounce of trouble with her family. They were not observant of the Jewish faith.

He, on the other hand, was from a faithful Jewish family who had escaped Eastern Europe just before World War II. At first, Joseph was troubled by Natalie's faith in a man whose name brought to mind endless persecution for their people. They would debate fiercely, neither one willing to give ground, each convinced of the truth of their viewpoint. Finally, one day Joseph taunted her to give him evidence not from her New Testament, which was anathema to him.

"Joseph, you have surely read Isaiah?" Her tone had been

sweetly patient.

"No, but I have heard passages read at synagogue of course." Even though he was irritated, her clear brown eyes staring up at him made him want to smile. She was like a bulldog. Tenacious.

"I would like you to read Isaiah 53 by yourself when you go home." She affectionately put her hand on his. "Pray and honestly ask God to show you the truth. God is faithful, and if you come to Him, humbly wanting to know, He will show you." She had stood up, kissed his cheek, and left the coffee shop where they met daily.

That night he had read, and read, and read. He read not only Isaiah 53—a passage he could not recall ever hearing proclaimed at synagogue but that so clearly was a prophecy of the man Jesus Christ—but he also read the Gospel of Matthew. *A Jewish book,* he'd thought. Then he read Mark, and Luke, and John, all *Jewish* books. Their contents were so thoroughly Jewish that he ended up on his knees that night weeping and pleading with the Lord to help him and forgive him. He gave his life to the Messiah, Jesus . . . Yeshua.

Shortly after, he too began to wear that strange T-shirt that read, "Jews for Jesus." He and Natalie worked for the ministry for many, many years. Eventually, they moved to Washington, DC. God had never blessed them with physical children, but they had numerous children in the Lord. Many people had been brought to faith through the Levys' faithful ministry.

Natalie had gone to be with the Lord almost ten full years ago. Joseph smiled at her image in the picture. Every day that passed, he still felt a sharp stab in his heart as he remembered his wife, his very best friend. Of course he knew he would see her again one day. He did not sorrow as someone who had no hope of that; he simply and profoundly missed her.

He looked at the clock. He had just enough time to shower and change before his meeting with young Father James Martin. Joseph prayed as he started to get ready, softly humming hymns as he talked to God. He knew the Lord had a plan. He prayed the plan would include the salvation of his young friend. Father Martin loved

ONE WILL BE TAKEN

God, Joseph was sure of that, but it was clear the priest had not yet seen the truth that salvation was in Christ alone. Father Martin still had the mistaken idea that he could somehow make himself fit for heaven on his own.

4

WASHINGTON DULLES
INTERNATIONAL AIRPORT

Arturo sat back in the leather chair, satisfied. He wiped his mouth carefully with a linen serviette as he looked across the table at his partner, Stephen. Arturo smiled a bit smugly as he noted the richness of his surroundings. Not many men in the world could afford to travel the way he customarily did. The high-gloss cabinetry in his Gulfstream G550 gleamed. The plush interior designed to his precise specifications testified to his good taste and deep pockets. All of this made his frequent trips from Rome to Washington quite pleasant.

Arturo noted that Stephen had not eaten much of his meal, which had been specially prepared by Arturo's personal chef. "Is something troubling you, Stephen?" Arturo inquired solicitously.

Stephen spoke carefully, "It is about Luca, Arturo." He glanced around to insure their privacy, but the two stewards were busy in the galley. "I am concerned about his educational progress. He seems to be bored by his tutors now; I think he has surpassed their abilities. He needs new challenges."

Arturo felt a twinge of alarm. He had been a bit neglectful of his son in recent weeks due to a lovely young doctor who worked for him. Right now she was waiting eagerly for him in his private cabin. His mind flashed to her curvaceous body and long blonde hair. He had never met a woman like her. She was the first woman he had known who was truly a peer—even if she was twenty years his junior. He'd been spending so much of his time with Judith that he had not seen Luca in more than a week.

"I'm afraid I've been . . . distracted by work," Arturo admitted reluctantly.

Stephen stifled a smile. He knew perfectly well why Arturo had been "distracted." Judith was a coworker in the Master's service. She had, in fact, been one of the first successes Stephen had in gene manipulation years before he met Arturo. Stephen had been able to manipulate her genetic code to produce a lusciously intelligent woman, the product of his own DNA and a donor egg. He had implanted her embryo in the womb of a rich New York socialite, who thought the child was a successful in vitro attempt. At the right time, the Master had brought Judith to Stephen for training.

Arturo had no idea that Stephen's genius was guided by the Master, nor that Stephen's success was a direct result of that influence. Arturo was ignorant of what was truly going on in front of his own eyes.

In ancient times, the Master had been known by many names. The fearful and superstitious called him the Devil. Baal, Dagon, Jupiter, and Shang-ti were other titles he had been given. But now that humankind had evolved to this point, the Angel of Light was pleased to intercede in human history once more to bring about the next phase of evolution. Luca was the firstborn of many brethren. Arturo, a rich and successful infertility specialist, had provided the vehicle to bring about the new world order. He was unaware of the deeper truths of Luca's birth.

If he only knew the truth! Stephen gloated as he looked intently at Arturo's handsome patrician face.

"It is time that Luca return to Italy, the home of his birth. It is time that he begin to fulfill his birthright as a member of the Giamo family." Stephen took a sip of cold gin from a glass sitting in front of him. "I have taken the liberty of engaging Billings Mason as a private instructor for the boy. I'm certain that Luca will find his instruction challenging!"

Arturo was stunned. Even a man of his wealth and influence would not have been able to secure Billings Mason as a private instructor. Years before, at the tender age of sixteen, Billings had taken an exam at a prestigious university in the United States. His results allowed him to go to law school without an undergraduate degree. A few years later, he simultaneously completed a master of science in chemistry and a master of philosophy from Yale. He went on to become an ordained Episcopal priest before entering into his life's passion, serving the poor on the African continent. His incredible success in that endeavor earned him the Nobel Peace Prize in his early thirties. He was world renowned for his intelligence, his social conscience, and his ability to rally many volunteers to his now worldwide ministry to the poor. He was respected by people from every faith—and non-faith. For the first time in human history, it seemed possible that poverty could be effectively eradicated, due primarily to this charismatic man.

"How were you able to do that?" Arturo stammered.

"We are old friends, Arturo. When I spoke to Billings about Luca, I showed him the boy's intelligence tests and examples of his essays, along with what he has achieved in his language studies. Billings recognized that we have in Luca someone who can offer the world hope. Billings believes that with Luca's genius, abilities, and family background, he can become a true world leader. Billings would like the privilege of being part of that process."

Arturo's eyes gleamed with pride. "I am amazed. I know Luca is special. I had thought that he would follow me in my clinical work, carry on the family business, as it were. I had not thought on a larger scale . . . but the Giamo family has served in the Italian government in the past."

Stephen smiled. *Such a small mind, really; he had no scope of Luca's potential.* "Yes, Arturo, and maybe one of the presidency trios?" *As a beginning.*

Arturo had not considered politics for his son before. He nodded his head thoughtfully. "You have been a good friend to Luca, Stephen. Thank you." His thoughts drifted back to Judith. He was sure that she was waiting impatiently for him, as she always was. She loved his attentions.

"You'll excuse me, dear friend. I am quite tired after a long day." Arturo left the table and headed for his cabin in the aft of the aircraft.

Everything is going according to the Master's plan, Stephen thought. *Luca will be groomed by other followers of the Ancient One to take his birthright at the appropriate time.*

Rome, Italy

Teo slumped dejectedly in the antique silk chair. She had come for a mini-getaway at her father's beautiful palazzo in Rome while DC traveled with the general to New Babylon for the State Department. Built in the fifteenth century, the palazzo had been lovingly refurbished and improved over the years by her father and his team of expert interior designers. Situated on the Via delle Coppelle, it was within walking distance of the Pantheon. The lavish home was completely staffed. Teo had anything she desired within minutes. *Everything but what I really want!* she thought to herself. Tears of anger and frustration ran down her face. She curled up and let herself cry, her sobs echoing across the elaborate vaulted ceilings.

DC had been wonderful and supportive about the whole situation. She couldn't have asked for him to have said or done anything different. But unfortunately, he could not fix the problem. Over the last few months, the tension between them regarding their family plans had increased. DC was easygoing, but Teo had always been a type A personality. She was determined and motivated, and she had a hard time taking no for an answer. DC was ready to move on with life, but she was determined to have what she wanted. A baby. DC had suggested adoption, but Teo wanted her own child. Then he had suggested surrogacy, but she wanted to experience pregnancy. How ironic that she could not experience it when she wanted it, after all!

She threw the coffee cup in her hand at the pale yellow

wall across from her. The cup's delicate china roses shattered into hundreds of pieces on the marble floor, and coffee dripped down the wall in little rivulets. She dragged her fingers through her hair in frustration and sat with her head propped in her hands.

She had not talked to Stephen Amona yet. She had known the sixty-something-year SavTec old assistant to her father all of her life, but she did not know him well. She remembered that Stephen was the genius when it came to developing new techniques to aid in infertility treatment. He took the harder cases and had developed the process by which her brother was conceived. That process and its codes were known only to Stephen. Even Arturo did not know all that it entailed.

Teo stood up and tied the white belt about her robe defiantly. Stephen could help her. He could come up with a new technique. So they said her uterus couldn't sustain a pregnancy. But what if Stephen could somehow . . . give her a new one?

A voice deep inside of Teo suggested that this was something DC wouldn't want to be a part of. There could be serious risks involved, and she knew he wouldn't want to put her life in danger. She shrugged the thought off. First she would speak to Stephen and find out the risks, and then she would talk to her husband.

For the first time in a long time, Teo smiled. She felt hopeful as she went into the bathroom for a shower. Her father and Stephen would be arriving in Rome later that evening, so she knew she wouldn't have to wait long to speak to Stephen. Things could finally go her way!

New Babylon, Iraq

DC had to step quickly to keep up with General Stanton. They were being given a tour of the restored city of Babylon. In an effort to encourage lasting peace in the Middle East, the United Nations Educational, Scientific, and Cultural Organization, called UNESCO, had joined together with Iraqi leaders in the early part of the millennium to continue the rebuilding of the city.

Red pebbles crunched beneath DC's and the general's feet as they walked swiftly. *For the life of me, I can't see why anyone would want to build anything in this heat!* DC surreptitiously wiped the sweat from his forehead. The general, of course, was cool, not portraying even a hint that the pounding heat affected him adversely. DC tried to pay attention to their guide's comments about the Ishtar Gate.

Marveling that it had been only seven years since the United States and the United Nations had joined forces to rebuild this ancient wonder into a modern one, DC gazed at the figures of dragons and bulls on the azure-colored bricks. One of eight gates to the city, the Ishtar Gate was the most spectacular. It was literally breathtaking.

DC and the general made their way into the city center. UNESCO's archaeologists had preserved the ancient ruins in unique ways throughout the city. Small brick walls outlined some ruins while other structures created pathways that wound through the remains, enabling visitors to experience the city's rich history. Once a wasteland inhabited only by nomads, New Babylon was a monument not only to the past but also to the brilliant future.

The hanging gardens had been designed by some of the world's most eminent horticulturalists, who utilized methods similar to the "green" or "living" walls developed in Japan, Canada, the United States, and other countries at the beginning of the millennium. DC had seen some of these walls in New York City recently. To his taste, they were sometimes overdone, but Babylon was unlike anywhere else in the world. DC could not get over the sublime beauty of the gardens. Greenery covered many of the buildings, and vines speckled with red and pink blooms cascaded over almost every surface. Fountains spouted sparkling water and created a delightful mist. DC was tempted to sprint to the nearest one and dive in.

With every single technological advance available, along

with the abundant financial resources that flowed in through post-war reconstruction funding and private investors, Babylon was an oasis of beauty, technology, and comfort. *At least inside where it is air-conditioned,* DC mused. The guide's monotonic voice tore into DC's thoughts as he heard the man mention 12/12.

12/12. It had changed the world forever. A series of massive earthquakes had struck throughout the world, triggering tsunamis and floods that had devastated many countries. Over 700,000 people had died in the cataclysmic events. The entire chain of islands that had made up the Maldives had been hit hard by tsunamis. There were literally no survivors from that nation of islands.

The man-made modifications to the Euphrates River, especially over the last century, made the devastation in parts of Turkey, Syria, and Iraq worse than it might naturally have been. Dams broke, causing flooding, destroying even more property and taking more lives. It was tragic chaos for millions of people around the planet.

Due to the encroaching desert and drought, the nations of the world had struggled to bring aid to the affected areas. However, Iraq actually benefitted from the changed topography of the Euphrates River. At the beginning of 2012, the ancient river had been on the verge of drying up in Iraq. Now, it rivaled the strength and size of the mighty Mississippi. Ships could now easily navigate its waters, all the way to New Babylon. After struggling with food security following Saddam Hussein's regime, the Iraqi people now had rich, fertile soil on either side of the river, and that soil brought abundant harvests. In addition, the navigable river and the deep harbor the Iraqi government had dredged made Babylon an even more attractive site for the World Union headquarters.

After 12/12, the impotent United Nations had collapsed. The governing structure of the European Union took leadership in uniting NATO, SEATO, and CSO with the African Union into a truly effective governing body. Up until then, the United States had been the dominant power in the world. But the wars in Iraq and Afghanistan, as well as an unstable economy, had forced the United States to relinquish its role as the world's police. Rapidly gaining power and influence, the leadership of the European Union had effectively appealed to many nations to set aside selfishness for the collective interest of world security. These leaders had initiated reform to global governance and brought security to an extent the world had not yet known, and they had done all this under the auspices of a new governing body called the World Union. Once established, the World Union was to make Babylon its headquarters.

DC was relieved when he and the general headed back to the truck and told him they were going on a tour of ComCenter Babylon. Before 12/12, a communications hub had been built on the spot where the ComCenter now stood, but that facility had been severely damaged in one of the earthquakes. Serious time and money had been poured into the center in the last eight years to create a massive, highly technical world communications headquarters that someone had nicknamed "Babel." Supposedly, DC had been told, in ancient times men had joined together to build a tower named Babel that reached to heaven, but God had confused the human language in order to divide mankind. Apparently the story was in the Bible. DC scoffed inwardly. The modern Babel had capacities ancient man could not have begun to fathom.

The inner geek in DC was excited to see the insides of ComCenter Babylon. Banks of screens covered every wall. There were rooms even the general did not have clearance to enter, guarded by stalwart Marine security officers who were supplied by the US State Department. Security teams from other nations were also here under the authority of the World Union. In one room, they saw intelligence analysts from many nations assembled, each one fluent in at least three languages. English was always the common language used among them. Real-time video streamed from vital points all over the world. From this one vantage point, vast amounts of data were gathered and analyzed; from tracking terrorists' cell phones to predicting weather events, Babel had eyes everywhere.

ONE WILL BE TAKEN

❧

Washington, DC

Father Martin sat on the bench gratefully. He had been so busy lately that he had not had a free moment. So as soon as he found the time, he had called a cab and had the driver drop him off on Garfield Circle. Father Martin had leisurely walked to the Botanic Garden—one of his favorite places in the city. It was a pleasant spring day in Washington, DC, and the fresh air seemed to lift his weary spirit. He had wandered through the garden for hours. Now, he sat and watched the people who passed by him.

People. He loved people. Though, if he were candid, sometimes he did not. Today was one of those days. He'd been feeling stretched too thin lately and simply wanted to be alone to think and pray. In the past three months, his congregation had swelled in size. People came early to Mass to ensure they had a seat, but only on the days when Father Martin presided over the service. This had caused turmoil within the diocese. *Even the clergy is not exempt from the temptations of the rest of humanity,* he sighed. Additional meetings and surprise observations by the leadership of the diocese were making him feel defensive.

To be honest, the increasing number of participants in the church was tempting him to feel prideful. Many of these new congregants wanted to meet with him for spiritual counsel. There were many hurting and lost people, people struggling with addiction or abuse or depression. Lately, he had been in meetings or on the phone so much that he'd had little opportunity to even read his Bible and pray. As a matter of fact, it had been weeks now since he had had any time with God alone. There just weren't enough hours in the day. As Father Martin thought about this, he sighed deeply. He felt conflicted about his lack of time with God.

He ran his hand through his hair and saw the gold wedding

band on his finger glinting in the sun. Not all priests wore one. He did, however, to help him remember his commitment to the Church as his bride. Serving the Church was his calling. Lately, though, he was beginning to feel overwhelmed with the tasks set before him—there were so many people who needed his help! Yet he felt weary and tired himself. Who was he to talk to about his own troubles?

Father Martin closed his eyes. The warm sun shone on his face, and he let his body relax. Every major moral failing his congregants disclosed to him was like a nail driven into his own soul. When they shared with him their brokenness, it broke him too. Some of them he wanted to shake out of their self-absorbed blindness. Many of them did the same wretched things over and over, hurting themselves and their loved ones. He felt like he was making headway with some of them, but the need was still so great.

He opened his eyes and saw a few sparrows pecking the cement near his feet. Memories of his last counseling session intruded into his thoughts as he absently observed the birds. He remembered the Gospel verse that said God knows when a sparrow falls, and humans are of much more worth than sparrows. The sickening images the woman had detailed of the abuse she had suffered at the hands of her own father made him want to retch. He could strangle the man.

The perpetrator was one of the deacons at St. Andrews, a church in northern Virginia. A man of faith committing such heinous abuse—it was absolutely abhorrent. Father Martin prayed God would give him strength and wisdom for what lay ahead. Nathan Penal was a very wealthy and influential man. He had many friends of high standing in the church. *And now one enemy.* The more Father Martin thought about the situation, the more he realized that something needed to be done. It occurred to him he would need an ally, at least for moral support, as he tackled this issue. Joseph Levy had become a good friend, and since he was not a Catholic, he would not be affected by any fallout. Determined, Father Martin stood up and went to find a cab.

5

GEORGETOWN,
WASHINGTON, DC

Teo set the bottle of expensive red wine on the long dining room table. DC would be home soon. As she turned to go fetch dinner from the kitchen, she caught a glimpse of her reflection in the mirror. Her red dress clung to her slim figure in a way that made her smile. She could not help but be proud of her good looks. She took care of herself, realizing the importance of using every advantage nature had given her.

Stephen had been very encouraging when she met with him. It was indeed possible to transplant a uterus, if she were a viable candidate. Teo had flown back to the United States and had already had the tests run at the fertility clinic before DC even returned from his tour with the general. Now, she just had to wait until Stephen found a suitable donor. She shivered at the thought. *Better to not think about that. Better to not mention that part to DC.*

But what if he asks me outright? She had never lied to DC, at least not about anything major. She was not sure what he would think about Stephen's donor pool. All of the potential donors were young women from rural India. Stephen preferred virgins, so venereal disease would never be an issue. Each girl's family was paid a fortune. In exchange, the parents gave their daughters over to Stephen's team, never to see them again. Teo justified it in her mind by thinking about how well the girls were treated before and after their uteruses were removed. It all sounded fine when Stephen had explained it to her.

I don't think DC will like the idea, but it's my body. I want a baby. Besides, the donor will be set for life. That is a fair exchange. She'll never have to worry about anything. It will work out. It's not like the girls are being forced to do it.

She heard the back door open and smiled. All she really needed to communicate to her husband was that a gifted surgeon could fix their problem. There was no need to pass on details of what the cure actually entailed.

Rome, Italy

The door closed with a soft click. Billings Mason shook his head and grinned from ear to ear. *Finally!* He turned to Stephen Amona. "All that the Lord of Light has promised is coming to pass, Stephen!"

The older scientist smiled in return, wrinkles fanning out from his clear blue eyes.

"The boy is amazing," Billings exclaimed. "His intellect is astounding. He is so . . . beautiful! *Beautiful* is the only word I can think of! He is everything you predicted he would be so many years ago. I can hardly believe I am standing here now to see it all unfold. All the things you told me so long ago are actually happening!"

"Indeed, Billings." Stephen puffed up with pride and antici-pation. "You have become one of the world's most admired men. People of all faiths respect your spirituality and your faithful work on behalf of the world's poor. You will increasingly gain more ap-proval as our good Father adds his gifting to you." Stephen shifted his weight as he looked up at Billings' blue eyes. Billings was much taller than Stephen. "You will pave the way for young Luca to take his rightful place in the world community. Now is the time for those seeds to be planted," Stephen declared.

Stephen walked to the desk, opened a drawer, and took out an envelope. "Inside are tickets to Tanzania. You will fly into Dar es Salaam. There has been an outbreak of a new strain of Ebola in a couple of the villages bordering Uganda. You will be accompanied by your team, of course, but also a reporter from the *Washington Post.*"

"My team will be eager to be of any help," Billings replied.

"They are to be there, but their help will be minimal, Billings."

Billings was taken aback.

"Our Father has decided to give you the gift of healing. You will be able to heal anyone you desire. In this way, his son's advent will be prepared. You will be the Master's prophet." Stephen handed the envelope to Billings.

No achievement, award, or discovery had ever thrilled Billings Mason as much as hearing Stephen's words did. He thought back to the time when his life had been changed forever by meeting Stephen. Billings had been disillusioned with life when they first met. He had sought meaning in philosophy and science, and although he had succeeded in both fields academically, he had not found true significance in either. So he'd pursued meaning in the Christian religion. Spurning the narrow interpretation held by the so-called evangelicals, he had become an Episcopalian priest. But his new pursuit of meaning yielded him little reward, and he became discouraged. He could find no real meaning to life. Then he met Stephen on a spiritual retreat in Mallorca.

Over dinner, Stephen had talked to Billings about the Divine Being. Of course, as a priest, Billings believed in the idea of God. In his thinking, God was in everyone and in all of nature. He dismissed any idea of a personal god or one all-knowing deity who purposefully guided your life. He and Stephen had had a good-natured debate throughout dinner and parted with a handshake. That night, the Father had appeared to Billings for the first time, and Billings had been the Father's faithful follower ever since.

Billings brought his thoughts back to the present and smiled warmly at his mentor. He could feel the elation begin as he sensed the Presence. Slowly it filtered into the room like a cloud, but it was refreshing. It was ecstasy. He began to tremble as the room became brighter and warmer as if it were on fire. A golden-yellow glow was cast on his surroundings, and his body reveled in the glory. Billings fell to his knees in wonder. Stephen joined him, and they both prostrated themselves on the floor before the beauty of the Master.

Arlington, Virginia

". . . and so she came to me. Her father is involved in the ministry to those seeking the sacrament of confirmation, so she is worried that other young women will be drawn in by him."

Joseph noted with concern the dark, heavy circles under Father Martin's eyes as he listened to the young man on the couch across from him. Farther Martin was obviously extremely tired. The cares of ministry were manifold, as demonstrated in the sordid story the priest had just told. He had called a short while before, wondering if he could meet with Joseph to discuss something important. He had arrived at Joseph's small apartment just a few minutes before, words pouring out of his mouth almost immediately.

"Can we pray before we talk anymore, James?" Joseph asked, closing his eyes without really waiting for a response from the younger man. After a good five minutes of imploring the Lord for wisdom and discernment, Joseph looked up at Father Martin.

"I need to do something," Father Martin said. "I cannot in good conscience allow him to continue this abuse! You know the great shame the Church has endured in not dealing properly with this issue in the past."

Nodding his white head in assent, Joseph responded, "Yes, shameful indeed. How long have you known Miss Penal?"

"Oh, she is his stepdaughter. Her name is Grayson, Cynthia Grayson. He adopted her when he and his wife married. Recently, she took back her father's surname. She just started attending Holy Apostles about a month ago." Father Martin took a breath. He was speaking quickly and anxiously. "Because of the abuse, she has not been in church since she left home. She said she tried to tell one of the priests, but he told her to stop speaking evil lies and to repent. I'm not sure if she has told her mother or not."

"So there really is no way to verify her story, is there?" Joseph was concerned. Something in his spirit felt uneasy.

Father Martin stood up, outraged. "What do you mean, Joseph? How was a young woman supposed to have verified something like this? What would she have to do to prove it happened?"

"James, sit down. Why are you responding in anger? This is the sort of thing that your leadership is going to ask you. Isn't it better to hear it from me first?" He smiled encouragingly as Father Martin took his place on the couch again. "Is she willing to make a formal complaint?"

"No. She is engaged to a very close friend of the family. She is afraid that if he knows what happened, he will end their engagement." Father Martin adjusted his position on the stiff couch. He was feeling irritated. "Also, the fallout could destroy many of her friendships because her friends' families are all very close to Mr. Penal and view him as a true man of God. But I have to do something, Joseph. I cannot leave this man in place to abuse others!" Father Martin ran his hand through his hair unconsciously. He would feel tremendous guilt if this man did the same thing again.

"Perhaps you need to discuss that with her. I feel certain there must be ways to keep her identity confidential." Joseph remained calm.

"Maybe I should. But her father will know who is making the allegations. She seems to truly fear him." Father Martin stood up and reached his hand out to Joseph. "Please pray for me, Joseph. I have so many duties and have been so busy lately. There are problems with one of the other priests at Holy Apostles, and I'm being watched because of some complaints he has made about my sermons . . . and now this. I sometimes feel like it's all too much. I can't handle all the weight of the ministry."

Joseph stood up, grasped the younger man's hand, and pulled him into an embrace. "You don't have to handle all this alone, James." Then he prayed for his friend.

Georgetown, Washington, DC

DC stretched beneath the cool white blankets, keeping his eyes closed. He enjoyed the quiet dark of the early morning hours, especially when he could stay in bed and sleep. The private warmth of the cozy bedroom he shared with his wife was heaven. The grandfather clock in the downstairs hall began to chime. He missed the clock he had grown up with; the classic Westminster chimes had measured the many hours he had spent as a child playing without a care in the world. The clock downstairs had been a gift from Arturo. It was handmade and elegant, but the chime was all wrong. Arturo said the discordant tune was some Norman invention or something. DC sighed and pulled the covers over his head. It was only four o'clock in the morning.

Teo slept soundly next to him. He rolled over carefully and put his arm around his wife's petite waist. She had been so excited last night about the possibility of having their baby. He had felt troubled as she shared her conversation with Stephen and his opinion regarding her test results, but between her happy chatter and his jet lag, he had not explored that feeling.

What are the risks? There are risks with any surgery. He hugged his wife a bit tighter. There were things they still had to discuss. He wanted Teo to be happy, but he also wanted her to be well. The thing was, this was such a sensitive topic for his wife, but it didn't much matter to him. DC was happy with just the two of them. Did they really need a baby?

I'll take her to Annapolis today. She loves walking around there. Maybe we can talk over lunch. He would take her to her favorite hamburger joint. He relaxed, holding his wife in his arms, and fell back to sleep.

Rome, Italy

Luca clicked the print button on his laptop. Hearing the printer's whirring, he closed up the computer and set it down next to him. He had just finished his last assignment for his last university course. Billings and his other tutors had moved him along rapidly, yet it was all so *easy*.

He stood up, walked over to the television, and picked up the remote. He flicked on the large screen. As he flipped through the channels, he considered Stephen's admonition to him last night to acquaint himself with Italian politics. Luca was about to join in the game, in a small role at first, but it wouldn't be a small role for long. His abilities, charisma, and the blessings of his true Father would see to that.

Luca sat down again and watched the bright screen, thinking. In the months since he had found out the truth about his birth and his real Father, he had matured in many areas. School had always been easy for him, but now he could pick up new languages in a matter of days and master mathematical and scientific subjects with little effort. According to his doctor, he had experienced his final growth spurt. At six foot two, he was now taller than Arturo. Luca thought despairingly of his "father." He hadn't seen the man in weeks, which was just fine with Luca. *That whore keeps him busy. As long as he stays away from me, I really don't care.*

The time Luca was spending with his real Father made Luca more and more critical of Arturo and his women. When Luca was younger, he had revered the man he thought was his father. He had not seen Arturo's weaknesses at all. In the light of his Father's glory, though, Arturo's weak and base nature had been revealed to Luca.

And the weak nature of women. Luca thought. *They are all corrupt. But with my Father's help, I will help to create a world that is better— where the people are better. Wiser. Stronger. More purposeful.*

Luca was sure that his Father's plan would not fail. Luca would be the Angel of Light's representative here on earth. It was his destiny to usher in the new age of man. Humanity had finally reached the stage in its evolution and technology where it was capable of taking the next great step and accepting the rules of its True God.

Luca knew he could trust Lucifer to reveal his plan to him. The Father had already blessed him with many gifts and would give him all he needed to accomplish his mission. Billings would, and in fact was, preparing the way for Luca's unveiling. Luca smirked at the irony. The Father's plan did mirror the old Christian myths, but that was because they were only a precursor to the true Messiah, Luca Giamo.

Arlington, Virginia

Elena sat in a coffee shop, sipping a foamy latte and reading a book, but with little real interest. It was a rainy spring day in Washington, DC. Because it was Saturday, the few friends she had were busy with their families. She thought a moment about calling Teo, but was afraid that her call would not even be picked up. Elena would rather not try than be ignored. She sighed and turned back to her book.

"Is it that bad?" a voice asked from the table next to her. She looked up to see an attractive man, in his mid-fifties or so, with clear blue eyes gazing at her questioningly. His half-smile made her feel confused.

"I'm sorry?"

"Is the book that bad?"

Elena felt a bit of a thrill in her stomach. "Yes, or maybe it's just the weather. This is the most dismal time of the year for me, just before spring really begins." She smiled timidly. "Would you like to join me?" she heard herself say. Then, "Oh, I'm sorry, you're probably meeting someone." *I'm such an idiot!*

"No, I'm not meeting anyone. I'd like to join you, actually. I've been cooped up in my apartment all week and haven't talked with a living person in days. I'll order my coffee and join you."

He went to the counter and stood in the short queue to order. Elena took her compact out of her purse and looked in the mirror surreptitiously, then quickly put the compact back. In a few minutes, the man returned and sat across from her.

"I'm John Foster," he said as he stretched out his right hand to shake hers. "I have to admit, I've seen you here before, and I've wanted to introduce myself for a while."

Elena smiled. "I'm Elena Giamo." His hand felt warm and sturdy as she shook it. "What do you do that keeps you cooped up?"

John returned her smile. "I'm a reporter for the *Washington Post,* but right now I'm working on a book."

"That's interesting! What are you writing about?" she inquired earnestly, brushing her bangs away from her eyes.

"Well, it's primarily about the culture wars in the United States, how the conservatives have lost them, and the effect on our society now." John spoke clearly, with confidence. "I'm a closet conservative myself."

Elena sipped her drink. "Why a closet conservative?"

"In my business, being a conservative is like being a leper. I would not go very far in my career if I came out," he said with a chuckle. Elena liked the sparkle in his blue eyes.

"But won't everyone find out when your book is published?"

John shook his head. "They will, but hopefully the book will be met with such success that it won't matter! The way things are going in our country, people have to take a stand."

"I agree with you, John. I hope your book is successful."

"What sort of work do you do, Elena?"

"Well, I suppose my work has been to raise my daughter, Teo. Since I 'retired' some years ago, I've just been puttering around. I like to visit museums, go to plays, that sort of thing—to keep out of trouble."

"Does your daughter live in the area?"

"Yes, but she's extremely busy. I hardly get to see her or her husband." Elena tried not to let the complaining tone Teo always accused her of having creep into her remark. *I don't want John to think I'm a bitter old woman.*

"So, do you and your husband live near here?" John said, looking at the ring on Elena's finger.

She sighed. "I'm divorced. I don't know why I keep wearing this silly thing. For a while I hoped that my husband, well, my ex-husband, would decide that his love for me was too important to lose and would come back to me. Then, when he continued his horrid work and married someone else, I wore the ring for what had been. Or what I thought had been."

"I'm sorry that you were hurt. But I'm glad that you aren't married," John confessed with an embarrassed grin. "I've been coming in here for coffee every day for the last few weeks, hoping I'd see you here again. I hope that doesn't sound strange to you.... Would you like to meet somewhere for lunch or dinner, maybe? I would really like to get to know you better."

A strange sensation bubbled in Elena's stomach. She hadn't felt that peculiar thrill in so many years. "I would like that," she stumbled over her words. "I really would." She smiled across the table at him.

6

WASHINGTON, DC

Father Martin sat in front of the bishop's desk, trying to stop himself from exploding in frustration. He had shared with Bishop Ellis his concerns about Nathan Penal, but had not used Cynthia Grayson's name. He could not do that to her—she was still too afraid of the potential fallout. He had tried to convince her that her silence might endanger others, but she remained firm, and Father Martin respected her choice.

"Bishop Ellis, I cannot reveal the identity of the woman, but this *must* be investigated! What if he abuses one of the children in his confirmation classes? What if it comes out that the Church knew and did nothing?"

Bishop Ellis looked over the top of his reading glasses sternly. "Father Martin, I know Nathan very well. I have known him since we were boys together. He is one of the most kind, upright men I know. It's unthinkable that anyone would bring such an accusation against him."

Feeling as if he were talking to a wall, Father Martin stood up and smashed his fist on the desk. "Why won't you just investigate? This is absurd!" There was obvious anger in his voice.

"You would do well to remember who it is you are talking to, Father Martin! Sit down!" The bishop waited for the young priest to take his seat. "I do take that sort of thing seriously. I have personally laicized several priests—on the basis of solid evidence. I know Nathan. I'm telling you that it is not possible. I will not bring such a charge against him without evidence. If this young woman you spoke with is not willing to come forward, my hands are tied."

Father Martin shook his head in anger. "If you had heard her—if you had heard the things she described . . ."

"Unless you have a witness—no, *more* than one witness—I don't want to hear another word about it, Father Martin. And you had better make sure that you don't speak about this with anyone. Do you understand?"

Father Martin stood up. "I understand, Your Excellency."

"Good, then go back to your church and do the work of the Lord. I assure you, son, Nathan Penal is a good man, a good Catholic, and devoted to God. We will not let false accusations tarnish such a good friend of the Church. He has served his bride faithfully throughout his life."

And given a lot of money . . . Father Martin was careful to keep his face from expressing the deep disgust he felt. He bowed, kissed the bishop's ring, and left his office.

The bright sunlight dazed him for a moment when he walked outside. As he made his way to his car feeling defeated, he decided to visit Cynthia Grayson again. He remembered Joseph's concerns, but Joseph had not heard the detailed account, or heard the anguish in the young woman's voice. Someone had to protect her and any other young victims of this monster. God had placed him, Father Martin, as shepherd over this flock. He would not rest until this wrong was made right.

Washington, DC

DC pulled into the parking lot. It was a few blocks from the State Department, but he was grateful to find a spot within walking distance that charged less than twenty dollars a day. He stopped by his favorite coffee shop and bought a drink for himself and some bagels for his coworkers.

He had worked as a diplomatic security agent for a few years as a civilian. When he was a Marine, he'd been assigned as a Marine security guard for the State Department as well. It was a mission he felt was essential, and he liked that he still had the opportunity to work with the Marine Corps. Marines were critical to the multi-layered approach to security that the Bureau of Diplomatic Security used. They ran physical, cyber, and personnel security programs twenty-four hours a day, seven days a week. Douglas Charles Bond liked nothing better than a challenge, and his job provided plenty of challenges. He smiled as he thought about the day ahead.

His smile faded when he entered the office. It was full of tense people; you could see it on their faces. Some were watching the television on the wall intently; others were at their desks typing furiously. He saw the general's secretary on the phone, speaking urgently with sheer panic on her face. As a pit formed in his stomach, he turned to the television and grimaced. The screen showed a broad view of a city that looked like New York. The camera pointed across the river, to an image that should have included the Freedom Tower. Instead, there were thick clouds of billowing black smoke and shooting flames of fire. *Not again,* he thought in despair. As the camera panned, he saw that the destruction was not limited to One World Trade Center. Many buildings were on fire, blown up, and damaged. The city was in chaos.

"What is happening?" he asked the general's other aide, Philip, who was standing next to him.

"Looks like bombs were used. There really is no solid intel right now, DC. It just happened about ten minutes ago."

Another explosion rocked the city as the camera continued to record the destruction. The shocked commentator stood completely still with his hand covering his mouth in horror. The Statue of Liberty stood untouched in front of the destruction, just as it had many years before on 9/11. DC watched in dread as a small commuter plane entered the field of vision on the right. *This cannot be happening, not again!* The tension in the room grew as the plane became visible to all.

"No! No!" screamed the commentator, shaking his head violently, crying.

But the plane did not head toward a building. It headed toward the iconic green beauty that stood in New York Harbor. With a tremendous crash, the plane took down Lady Liberty. The aircraft exploded with a bright and violent flash.

DC looked around the room. There were tears on many faces, including his own. General Stanton opened the door to his office and motioned for his two aides to come in. There was work to do. Grave, grave work. DC went in and closed the door softly behind him, leaving his coffee and the bagels completely untouched on his desk.

Arlington, Virginia

Joseph turned on the television, sitting down in his favorite chair to catch up on the news with his second cup of coffee. Horror met his eyes as he saw the destruction on the screen. Heavy dread filled his heart.

"All we know, Mitch, is that New York City is being hit in many different ways. There have been bombs detonated in dozens of buildings. A suicide bomber blew up a train on the Lexington Avenue Express. The video you're going to see now is a commuter plane that just crashed into the Statue of Liberty."

The somber reporter was replaced with a video of a small plane. Joseph sucked in his breath as the aircraft hit the Statue of Liberty and exploded into flames. A symbol of freedom and safe haven for so many generations was now fallen. Gone forever.

He muted the television and immediately got on his knees to pray, right there in his small living room. His heart was pounding with so many emotions. He wasn't sure what was going on, but he knew the One who did.

Arlington, Virginia

Elena and Teo sat on the couch in Teo's living room watching the news together. Elena had finally convinced Teo to spend a day with her. They had just been about to leave for a special breakfast at the Mayflower when DC had called and asked them not to go anywhere. So far, attacks were taking place in New York City, but Washington, DC was on high alert, he cautioned.

"This is horrible, Mom," Teo said in disbelief at what she was seeing. She had been a girl when 9/11 happened. She remembered being locked in at school, scared and wanting her mother, and Elena remembered her frantic efforts to get her daughter home. It had been a traumatic day for both of them. Once home, they had stayed glued to the television.

"This is even worse, Teo," Elena whispered brokenly. They both tensed up when the Emergency Alert System interrupted the newsman. The system's voice instructed citizens to remain in their homes to allow emergency responders, police, and the National Guard to respond more effectively to the current terror attack. The attacks were now going on all around Washington, DC.

The local reporter who came on-screen was visibly shaken as she described new reports of the bombings in the nation's capital, as well as in New York City. So far, no terrorist organization was claiming responsibility.

Elena and Teo continued to hear bits and pieces of news from the numerous reporters on the television. The president and his family had been evacuated from the White House. Members of Congress were being transported out of the city as well. There had been several suicide bombers on the National Mall. One of them had blown himself up, damaging some cars nearby, but no one else had been hurt.

There were reports, so far unconfirmed, that a Washington, DC, cop who had just gotten off duty and was heading home on the Metro had seen a suspicious man entering the train. The cop had been able to restrain the man with the help of several passengers. That man was now in custody, according to the reports.

Elena asked Teo if she wanted some coffee. It was going to be a long, hellish day.

Arlington, Virginia

Father James Martin turned his television off and closed his eyes. He could not wrap his mind around the devastation. New York was in a shambles, as was Washington, DC. Terrorists had also targeted the Mall of America near Minneapolis. Huge gaping holes, the result of bombs, showed on the façade of the famous mall. No one knew yet how many had died. In Florida, Disney World had been targeted. Not only had there been suicide bombers; men with guns had also boldly walked through the park and picked off their victims with detached relentlessness. Security cameras throughout the park had caught those images.

Father Martin bent over, rested his head on his knees, and breathed deeply. The Children's National Medical Center in Washington, DC, had been bombed, too. The images of the destruction were burned into his mind. Cameras had recorded the grief of the first responders as they removed injured children. He had watched the rescue attempts, praying. Retirement homes and apartment complexes had also been targeted. It seemed to be a deliberate attempt by some terrorist organization to kill and maim as many as humanly possible. It was a coordinated attack throughout the United States. No one had claimed responsibility for it—at least, not yet. This was worse than 9/11, a hundred times worse. The entire country was wrapped in a blanket of dark, dark sorrow. It was estimated that hundreds of thousands were dead.

Father Martin grabbed his keys and headed out of his small apartment. Despite the warning for civilians to remain in their homes, he knew there would be people who needed spiritual care. He would make his way to the hospital. It might take a while, but he needed to do something to help. He knew people relied on spiritual figures during times like this.

Rome, Italy

Arturo slammed down the phone in frustration. Busy. He had no idea if Teo was safe or not. His heart was racing so quickly he could physically feel it bumping inside his chest, and he noticed sweat beginning to form at his temples. He'd never been so worried. He was here in Rome to see Luca receive his degree from the university. It was an important weekend! It was unfortunate Teo could not be with them, as she was attending DC's youngest sister's wedding that same Saturday.

Arturo sat down impatiently in the chair by his desk. He supposed Teo had been glad to have an excuse not to come with them. She and Luca had never been close, and the rift between them had only grown larger in the last year. Arturo loved both of his children and wished that they were fonder of one another. He let out a sigh that only a parent could. He refused to leave the phone, anxious get for a call from his daughter.

Luca sauntered into the room. "Hello, Father," he smiled mischievously, his eyes displaying a curious expression. He sat down in the chair across from Arturo. "What are you doing?"

"I've been trying to call your sister to see if she is all right, but the phone lines are all jammed," Arturo explained. "I'm hoping she will call any minute."

"Yes, I've been watching the news. The United States is taking quite a beating, isn't it? I wonder if it will ever recover. But, since I know you want to know, Teo is fine."

"How do you know, Luca? Has she called you?" Arturo asked anxiously.

"No. She hasn't called. But I do know that she is well. I was able to find that out," Luca said, looking at Arturo with a half smile. Arturo had a million questions.

"What do you mean, Luca? Were you able to get in touch with DC?"

"No, I saw her for myself. She is with her mother. They are both quite well," Luca patiently explained. He was calm and collected, and it irritated Arturo.

"How could you have possibly seen them for yourself? Were you on the video conference with them?" Arturo was bewildered. He had thought to try the service himself but had reasoned that many other callers looking to connect with their loved ones would jam the system.

"No. I have been experimenting with meditation, sort of a takeoff on astral projection. I don't go to the afterlife, but I have found I am able to navigate my spirit." Luca spoke as if this were common knowledge. "I have used this practice to visit all sorts of places lately," Luca said casually.

"You have been leaving your body? Are you serious? Are you joking, Luca?" Arturo stammered even though he was trying to speak as clearly as possible. "I'm really quite worried about Teo. I do not find this pretense amusing." Arturo bristled. His son was brilliant, and becoming even more so, but lying would not be tolerated, especially lying to him.

"I'm very serious, Father," Luca said. "In fact, I saw you at the Plaza Hotel last week. You were staying in the presidential suite with that lovely young woman—Judith, I believe you called her. You two were having quite the fun."

Arturo looked horrified. He wanted to hide his face or walk out of the room. How could Luca know about Judith? He had been in Rome finishing his studies. "I . . . what . . . how do you know about that?" Arturo mumbled, confused and guilty.

Luca leaned forward. "This is what I saw you doing, Father." He bent closer and whispered something into Arturo's ear.

Arturo turned red with rage and embarrassment as Luca chuckled at him. "Don't have a seizure, old man. It's your vice. All of you humans have them." Luca ran his hand through his hair and sank back into his seat. "Yet humanity is at a crossroads. My true Father has decided that the next step in the evolution of man is necessary. The time has come. I am the one who will lead the way to mankind realizing its original destiny."

The anger faded as Arturo listened to his son. Had the young man's incredible mind collapsed?

Luca stood up and clapped Arturo on the back good-naturedly. "I'm not crazy, Arturo. Indeed, I am saner than any human on this earth. You will see shortly. All that is now veiled will be revealed in time—in my Father's perfect time. Next week, I start my political career. I'm running in the next election."

"But you are too young!" Arturo protested.

"Yes, I am, Arturo. But haven't you heard the phrase 'A little child shall lead them?' " Luca laughed as he left the older man in the room, alone and dumbfounded.

7

MARYLAND

Dc looked over at Teo in the passenger seat. Her lips were pressed tightly together in a frown as she read through some briefings on her iPhone. She had agreed to visit his parents, but reluctantly. The fertility clinic had been damaged in one of the Washington bombing and she wanted to oversee its repair. There was significant damage, however, and a long wait was anticipated for the workmen. DC thought it would be best for him and Teo to get away from the carnage and upheaval just to take a quick breather, to relax and collect themselves. They were heading east to St. Michaels, Maryland. His mom and dad were at their home there, safely away from any of the terror attacks. Traffic was heavy as he and Teo headed north.

"Teo?" She looked up from her phone. The spark that usually lit her eyes was gone. Dark shadows were smudged under her eyes,remnants of mascara that she had not taken off the night before. Teo was always meticulous when it came to her appearance. She seemed tired. Weary.

"Listen, Teo, I know things are frightening right now, but we'll be fine. Everything will be okay, I promise." DC stretched out his arm and placed his hand on her headrest. "We'll help rebuild. We'll punish the terrorists behind this. Things will be good again." He slowed to a stop behind the Mercedes in front of him and turned to his wife. "I promise to take care of you, Teo."

Teo sighed and looked out the window to her right. A parallel line of cars was moving slowly next to them. It felt like they were crawling. She could see children in the backseat of the car driving beside them. They were playing on video game consoles, oblivious to the reasons they were traveling away from their homes—if their homes were even still standing.

"DC, I don't see how things will ever be the same. Not only have New York and Washington been attacked, but national icons like the Mall of America and Disney World, too. It's outrageous! DC, they *shot* children!" she cried, her voice breaking as she began to sob. "It's crazy. It's like hell has broken loose and is present here on earth. Where can we be safe? How can we have our own children in this insanity?"

DC put his arm around her shoulder and pulled her over to him in a side embrace, keeping his eyes on the slowly moving traffic ahead. "It's going to be all right, Teo. You'll see. In World War II, the Japanese miscalculated our resolve as a people, and so have the terrorists. They will pay. We will be safe again sometime very soon."

He looked at the GPS. Two hours to his parents' house if they weren't stuck in this parking lot of a traffic jam on Highway 495. Thousands of people were fleeing the city. More than likely, it would be closer to eight hours until they pulled into the driveway of his childhood home, but he was determined to get there to see his parents. His mom would take Teo right under her wing and make her feel better. That was his mom's way. He just had to get there.

Arlington, Virginia

Joseph carried the warm bowl carefully and made his way through the cots arranged in some bit of order in the elementary school gymnasium. He handed the dish, along with a napkin and spoon, to a young woman. She whispered a raspy "thank you" to him, not wanting to disturb the toddler asleep on her lap. Joseph smiled in response and stood up straight, looking over the crowded and humid room.

There had to be almost two hundred people in the gym. Some had cots; others had the floor. It was unnaturally quiet. After all, they had all just gone through an entirely unnatural experience. There was still no final count of the dead and wounded. The last attack on the United States had happened early in the morning in Missouri. A suicide bomber had driven a moving truck loaded with explosives to the center of the Mississippi bridge leading to St. Louis, Missouri and detonated the vehicle. Traffic, thankfully, had been minimal, but the relatively new bridge connected downtown St. Louis with southwestern Illinois. Its destruction would affect many, leaving them stranded from their homes, work, or families.

That seemed to be the thrust of all the attacks, to terrify America and make her realize that even her heartland was vulnerable. The people in the room around Joseph had lost their homes in the attacks on Washington, DC. Apartment complexes, office buildings, and even day care centers had been targeted in the nation's capital. The room was tangibly filled with deep sadness.

"Hello, Joseph." A deep voice from behind him cut through his thoughts. He turned around and saw his friend Rafa. Joseph and Rafa belonged to the same fellowship of believers. Joseph embraced his friend warmly, thankful to see he was safe and unharmed.

"I'm so glad to see you! How are the others?" Their fellowship was small and very close-knit.

"No one was harmed, Joseph, praise the Lord! A couple of the men are here with me. Some of the women are helping in the hospital nursery. It's chaos over there." Rafa's face seemed tired. "The attacks have caused many pregnant women to go into premature labor. The doctors are busy with the wounded, as are many nurses. We have a few doulas in our fellowship, so they went to help." Rafa looked around him. "What can I do here, Joseph?"

"Just look for needs, Rafa. Offer to pray for those who are willing. Pray silently for those who refuse." He knew God could reach people in even the darkest of times. "Some of these people haven't had anything to eat in the last twenty-four hours. Offer them some of the soup from over there." He pointed to a set of tables full of steaming Crockpots and bowls, manned by volunteers holding ladles and anxious to help in some way.

"It's awful, but beautiful at the same time," Rafa said.

"What do you mean?"

"It's amazing to see the unity that can arise when people are hurt and in need. It kind of renews your faith in humanity." Rafa turned and headed to the other side of the gym where a man was retching, all alone.

Joseph bowed his head, praying quietly. There was such a stirring in his spirit, a sense of urgency and unease. Tears rolled unchecked down his cheeks.

Washington, DC

Father James Martin cradled the mug of coffee in his hands, savoring the aroma that rose with the steam. Dozens of attacks had occurred in Washington, DC alone. One of them had targeted the children's hospital. Huge explosions had been detonated simultaneously, fatally injuring many. Father Martin could not bear to even think of it. Hundreds of children had been killed. He had made his way through the city to help in any way he could, asking strangers what he could do for them. He had been at the hospital all night, praying with aid workers, family members, firefighters, police officers, and doctors.

He had given final rites to far too many.

One young mother stood out in his memory. He had seen her sitting in a hallway, cradling her toddler tenderly. The child had suffered some sort of head trauma and was obviously dead. Father Martin had started toward her to offer comfort, but stopped as he got closer. She was praying, eyes closed, rocking her child back and forth.

"You give and You take away. I bless Your name, Lord. Jesus, You are the One who holds this world in Your hands. You are the author of life. I was Laura's mother for a few short years. I thank You for each moment I had with her. I know she is with You. I know I will see her face to face, Lord." Tears rolled down her cheeks as she had started to sing some sort of praise song. Even as a man of faith, it astounded Father Martin that she could pray such a prayer in a time like this.

He had turned away. He had not expected to hear God being praised amid such devastation. Others had been calling for God's help and had wanted Father Martin to pray for them. But seeing that woman praising God . . . something about that moment had stung his heart, and somehow it did not feel like sorrow.

I'm tired, he thought, *and in shock.* He drained his coffee.

The morning light revealed the destruction around him. The hazy sun highlighted blood spatter on the concrete and tangled piles of metal and debris. Small bodies lay in neat rows, covered with white sheets like horrible tally marks made by the terrorists. For what purpose? To gain paradise and a thousand virgins? He hoped they were rotting in hell. He got up and went back inside to see what help he could offer.

Arlington, Virginia

Elena and John sat in the small French café. John had stopped by her townhouse to check on her the day after the attacks and offered to take her out for some coffee. As she sat shivering—though it was not cold inside—she looked intently at the walls covered in black chalkboards. Some were decorated with drawings, others with witty sayings. One by the door seemed to be some sort of diatribe about Haiti and the lack of care the rest of the world gave to it. Piles of brochures sat on the shelf below the message. The world was full of tragedy. She shuddered.

"It's awful, John. I don't even want to think about it. How is anyone ever going to feel safe again?"

"I know. But Americans always come through difficulties. We'll work through this one as well."

"What does that mean but another war somewhere else in the Middle East? Why do they hate us so much?" Elena didn't know a whole lot about the politics behind the wars, but she felt like her viewpoint was valid.

"I think there are multiple reasons. One of them is envy. We're the biggest world power, a rich nation. Secondly, I think it has to do with the policies the United States has had over the decades since World War II. We've intervened in conflicts in many other nations, with good intentions, but unintended consequences." John paused to take a bite of his crepe. "Finally, and maybe most importantly, we have supported and backed Israel."

Elena played with the croissant on her plate, tearing it into small pieces. She didn't really know what to say at this point. "Thanks for inviting me out. I would have been afraid to leave my apartment on my own. I think I should go to church and see if there is anything I can do to help. What are your plans for the day?"

"I thought I'd head over to the school down the street and donate blood. The Red Cross has a station set up there. How about you go with me, and I'll go to church with you afterward?" John asked.

They both knew they needed to stay busy to survive the sadness and tension. Elena wiped her mouth with her napkin and nodded, saying, "Let's go."

ONE WILL BE TAKEN

St. Michaels, Maryland

DC turned his car into the driveway of his childhood home. The long lane wound gently to the two-story waterfront home that was painted white with blue shutters. All of the lights inside were on, welcoming the tired couple. The sun was just setting over the Chesapeake, and a warm glow made the entire property gleam. His parents were probably on the back porch, sitting by the pool and admiring the view. It was their habit to watch the sun rise and set every day together. They had done it ever since he could remember.

"Teo, we're here," DC said, shaking her shoulder gently. She had fallen asleep before they reached the Bay Bridge. Traffic had been horrendous and the drive tedious. He was glad she had been able to sleep.

They both grabbed a bag and walked to the front door. It wasn't locked, so they went in. The view was spectacular. DC's mother, Abigail, had designed the floor plan to take advantage of the waterfront. Almost every room in the house had a view. The downstairs was made up of one large great room that ran along the back of the house. Folding glass doors could be opened and slid into pockets on either side of the room, creating a space that was both indoor and outdoor. It was the ultimate space for entertaining.

DC and Teo headed to the back patio to greet his mom and dad. Both of his parents smiled and stood up when they saw their son and daughter-in-law. They all wrapped each other in warm embraces—silent signals that they were thrilled to be alive and together. Family was the glue they needed to hold themselves together right now. Abigail announced that dinner was waiting and soon had them settled at the table. DC tapped Teo's arm under the table as a reminder that his dad and mom bowed their heads to pray before each meal. Teo quietly put her fork down and bowed her head, too.

After a few silent moments, DC's father, David, asked him if there had been a lot of traffic getting home. They chitchatted about inconsequential things throughout the meal. Teo was very quiet, and her eyes were downcast. Abigail tried to draw her out, but without much success.

Teo finished and thanked her mother-in-law for a delicious meal. "Would you mind if I just went to bed? I'm so tired, I just want to lie down."

"That's no problem; I have your room all ready, dear," Abigail reassured her.

Teo said good night and went upstairs to the cozy room she and DC usually shared when they visited his parents.

"She is really stressed by all the attacks," DC admitted. "She's having a really hard time."

"Well, there's good reason for all of us to feel that way," David said as he got up and put both of his strong hands on DC's shoulders. "Do you want to go out with me while I scrub down the grill?"

"Sure, Dad."

Abigail began to clear the table while the men went outside. David grabbed his wire brush and set to work, scraping the remaining charred fat off the grill.

"What's your opinion about who is responsible for these attacks, DC?"

"I don't have any more idea than you do, Dad. So far, none of the usual terrorist groups has made a claim. With the amount of devastation, you'd think we'd have one or two, but it's all quiet."

"Could it be some new organization?"

"It could, but to pull this off required a lot of coordination and money. You'd think that one of the agencies would have some sort of intel—not that I'm cleared to know. Maybe there's a new alliance." DC shook his head and dipped his toes in the cool water of the pool as his father continued to work on the grill. "At least they seem to have stopped, for now."

"Thousands are dead and even more thousands are wounded. This is going to have a devastating effect on our country, DC. My only hope now is that the churches won't just be full a few weeks after this, like they were on 9/11, but that many people would also question their eternal destiny and turn to the Lord."

DC didn't know what to say, so he said nothing. His parents had become committed Christians when he was seventeen. He had seen a big change in both of them, but it didn't really affect DC personally. They tried to encourage him to go to church with them, but he had never gone. His younger brothers and sisters were all professing Christians, too, but no one ever pressured him. Everyone in DC's family talked to him about their faith often, but he realized they did so only out of their love for him. While it made him uneasy, he listened politely and expressed appreciation for their care. The conversations always ended with DC saying something like "I'll think about it."

Standing there with his father, about to repeat that same phrase, DC realized he never really thought about what they said. He would take the books and CDs they gave him, but he never read more than a few pages, never listened to any of the sermons. Somehow after all the destruction of the day, the thought made him feel a bit guilty. They loved him and wanted him to know more about something very important to them.

"Dad, would you mind explaining more about that to me?" He grabbed a beer from the small refrigerator nearby and sat down at the patio table. Trying not to look surprised, David sat down with his son and began to talk.

Over the Atlantic Ocean

The large jet hummed and vibrated. Stephen looked out of the window at the rising sun as strings of scattered clouds passed by. He was on his way to New York, where he would meet with Billings Mason. Billings had just completed his mission in Florida, and they had plans that could only be accomplished in person.

Stephen opened the morning paper and smirked. So much destruction! Billings Mason was now heading up the entire Red Cross organization. His ability to heal the Ebola outbreak had stunned the world, bringing him greater fame and admiration. Video clips were appearing on almost every continent, hailing his success. It was a bit irritating that so many wanted to give "God" the credit for the healings, but Billings was careful to redirect that thinking in any interview he gave, instead positing that any human being might be capable of such things. He intimated that he had recently made a great spiritual discovery, but was not yet ready to reveal it. It had been such a personally incredible experience that he just could not talk about it yet. In every interview, tears of joy brimmed in the man's eyes as he spoke.

Luca had done well with his plan to emasculate the United States, a necessary move in order for the power to shift from West to East and for Luca to take his rightful place. He had found many willing to follow him, even to death. It was not surprising, really, for not only could Luca transport his spirit at will, he also could appear to others. He had used this ability to influence key people—pilots, ordinance officers, and others—to carry out his plan of attack on the United States.

Such destruction would be a severe blow to the US economy. Significant economic damage was already evident, yet Stephen anticipated it would take more to affect the power distribution. He wasn't worried, though, nor was he disturbed by the number of fatalities. Sometimes sacrifices had to be made when major changes occurred in a society—even more so when those changes were remaking not just one society, but the whole world.

8

WASHINGTON, DC

"Why, hello Father! Do you mind if I join you?"

Father James Martin lifted his head from its resting place on his hand and rubbed his eyes, smiling as he recognized Cynthia Grayson standing next to him with a tray.

"No, please sit with me. This place is crowded." He gestured to the rest of the hospital cafeteria. Every table was filled and people were even sitting against the walls, trays in their laps.

Cynthia sat down, took her food from her tray, and tucked the tray neatly under his, looking at him with a fresh smile. "I just got here. How about you, Father?"

"No, I've been here for a couple of days now. First I went to the children's hospital."

Cynthia's smile disappeared. "I'd heard a lot of the wounded were brought here. I came to see how I could help."

Father Martin just sat silently. He was so tired. What was there to say, anyway? How could he describe the trauma of what he had seen?

Cynthia put her hand over his and patted it gently. "I know what you're going through, Father Martin. I was on Kauai when the tsunami hit. I'd decided to sleep in late. My friends all went to the beach early." Her voice broke as she spoke. "I went searching for them. I saw so many dead people. It was so unreal, but so horribly real at the same time."

Father Martin looked across the table at her. Cynthia, too,

had experienced so much trauma. He thought of Nathan Penal and marveled at how courageous this woman was. He put his other hand over hers and gave a squeeze before letting go and picking up his coffee, smiling at her in sympathy and understanding.

Arlington, Virginia

Joseph was lying on his couch, too weary to move more than to turn on the news. He sat up abruptly when he saw who was on the news—Billings Mason. The stirring in Joseph's gut began right away. Joseph had no doubt Billings was an apostate "minister" of his own gospel, but the older man's suspicions about what else Billings might be were being confirmed by the miracles he was performing and his references to a great spiritual discovery of immense power. Joseph watched the man on the screen, his heart beating faster at what he heard.

"After much prayer, my team and I felt directed to go to Orlando. We had to choose one place, you know. I wish I could do more, but I could only be in one place at a time. So many children were targeted in Orlando, so much innocent blood." Billings looked almost holy in his white button-down shirt, the collar opened casually at his neck. Although still a relatively young man, he had a definite aura of authority about him, tinged with just the right amount of humility.

The reporter responded with intense enthusiasm, "Sir, I have no words to express how amazing this is. Let's just let the video tell this incredible, miraculous story."

Joseph watched with increasing interest as the video montage showed Billings and his team walking through the Walt Disney World Resort. Apparently they had arrived just as the emergency crews had begun to help the victims of the terrorist attacks widened by the number of people still lying on the ground. The camera panned over to Billings as he stood looking at the bodies of an entire family. The mother and father had obviously tried in vain.to shelter their little boy and girl. Billings bent over the parents and placed a hand on each. He closed his eyes and lifted his face up, his mouth moving in prayer.

Then the unthinkable, the unimaginable happened. The father came back to life! Then the mother. Before the parents could take in what was happening, Billings had moved on to their two children. He prayed, and they too began to stir and come to life before the camera and the eyes of the watching world.

The video went on for a few more minutes, following Billings as he prayed over the dead and brought them back to life. Tears rolled down the news reporter's cheeks as he stuttered into the camera, "What you are seeing right now is a miracle. Billings Mason, the director of the Red Cross, a humanitarian of renown, restoring life to those massacred at Disney World!"

Speaking directly to Billings, the reporter said, "Mr. Mason, we are speechless. How is this possible?"

Billings took a deep breath. "I'm not sure I know myself. I wish I could resuscitate everyone, but I am only a man, a vessel. As I have said before, I have made a few significant spiritual discoveries. This is only one of them." He turned to face the camera, his eyes filled with tears and joy. "I have the privilege to be the heralding voice. The one to tell men and women everywhere that soon you will see, and be seen. You will know, as you are known. Love is stronger than hatred. Love conquers all, even death."

Joseph took a deep breath and turned off the television. He had known things were moving. Prophecies were being fulfilled and had been for a while. Still, he was stunned by how good the other side looked. If he did not know better, he himself would be taken in by the man he had just seen on the television, who appeared to be so sincere and good and righteous. But Billings Mason was a man, Joseph knew, who served the kingdom of darkness, not the kingdom of light.

Joseph got on his knees to do battle in the heavenly realm. It was only a matter of time before the true battle lines were revealed to the world more clearly.

Arlington, Virginia

Elena sat in bed sipping her morning coffee, uncertain how to process all the destruction that had occurred over the last few days. She was afraid to turn on the television and see even more reports pouring in about other shootings and attacks in public places. Even grocery stores seemed to be targets, and she glanced gratefully in the direction of her own well-stocked panty. At least she wouldn't have to go out for provisions for a while. People were going crazy. There were riots in all of the major cities, Washington, DC, included.

She sighed as she reflected on the intensity of the last week. John, concerned for her safety, had been staying in the guest room of her small townhouse in Arlington since the first day after the attacks. At first she was worried about what people would think, but John had been more than respectful of her, and with things spiraling out of control so quickly, she appreciated his company.

Picking up her Bible, she opened it and started praying for Teo, glad that DC had been able to get them both to St. Michaels. They had to be safer there than in the city. Quickly, Elena thanked God for her daughter's safety and asked for His continued protection. She tried to read, but her mind was too troubled to do so.

With trepidation, she turned on the small television in her bedroom, flipped through the channels, and tried to absorb the reports from all over the United States. It seemed like every one of the fifty states had suffered some sort of attack or riot. It was like evil was being unleashed. She watched the muted screen and thought back to a conversation with a friend during high school. The memory lingered.

ONE WILL BE TAKEN

They had gone one evening to see a frightening movie about doomsday. Elena still recalled the image of a woman dressed in scarlet, drinking blood; the sight had deeply disturbed Elena. Her friend, Johanna, had not been so disturbed; in fact, she had seemed excited. After the movie, they had gone to a local diner and talked for hours. Johanna seemed to know a lot about prophecies in the Bible and what they said about the end of the world. It was interesting, in theory. The Church didn't hold to those teachings, so Elena had dismissed the whole topic. After all, God was good. He would not destroy His children. He would not allow such devastation.

But it was all coming back to her now. As she sat thinking, Elena looked at the book on her lap. She began to wonder if there was something to the things her friend had said so long ago. She looked up at the images on the screen. Was the world ending?

Rome, Italy

Arturo sat at his desk, tapping the letter opener in his right hand against his left, then placing the instrument carefully on his desk. He ran his hand against the desk's smooth black surface and admired its beauty. This was one of his favorite rooms in his villa in Rome. The black walnut shelves contrasted with the red walls, which provided a perfect foil for the priceless works of art hanging on them. Many of these pieces of art had belonged to past generations of his wealthy family. He turned his chair around to enjoy the stunning view of the fountain in the charming courtyard just outside his office.

He had a lot to think about. Teo was safe, but there was no way he could observe that for himself. The continued attacks and civil unrest in the United States had made traveling there very difficult. Now volcanic ash from Iceland was again hampering travel in Europe as well. At least he had been able to get through to her by phone. She was safely away from the city. Apparently, his clinic had been destroyed in one of the bombings. That thought caused his blood pressure to rise. Insurance would handle the cost of rebuilding, but there were costs insurance did not cover. The embryos they had stored there were worth hundreds of thousands of dollars. If he wanted to retain his highly skilled employees, he would have to continue paying their salaries for months without any money coming in from the clinic.

Then there was the problem of Luca. Arturo had been so concerned about Luca's mental state that he had called Stephen in for a meeting about it. The conversation had reassured Arturo a bit, but Luca had moved out of the villa yesterday. The boy had been calm but steadfast in his refusal to stay. He was eighteen years old. He had an apartment of his own in the city. He had gone on a bit about "being about his father's business." Arturo had no idea what Luca was talking about. Was his brilliant mind overloaded? He had completed such a heavy course load, work that would have taken others years to complete. That stress must account for the strangeness Arturo was seeing in his son.

Still, Arturo had no way to keep Luca from going. He was certainly well provided for. Years ago, at Stephen's urging, Arturo had put millions of dollars into a Swiss account for each of his children. Doing so, Stephen had advised, would be a sure way to keep some of his immense fortune safe for each of them, just in case. Now that Luca had reached the age of eighteen, the money was legally his.

Picking up the red telephone on his desk, Arturo quickly dialed Stephen's cell phone. There must be something he could do to keep an eye on his young son. The boy thought he was an adult, but Arturo knew better. Luca still needed guidance. If he would not listen to his father, then his father would find someone else to step in. Luca had grown close to Stephen in the past year. That relationship might be a solution.

ONE WILL BE TAKEN

St. Michaels, Maryland

Teo was crying. DC hated that, but there was nothing for it. "Babe, I have to go. You'll be safe here with my mom and dad."

"I don't want to stay here, DC. Let me go back to the city and stay with my mom," Teo implored.

"No, Teo. There are roadblocks set up now on every road into the city. They've called in the National Guard; there are curfews because of the riots. You're better off here in St. Michaels. I've been called back in to work."

Teo wiped her eyes. "What's your new duty assignment?"

DC took a breath. He knew Teo was going to be even more upset when she found out, but he could not keep it a secret. "I've been assigned to the new US embassy in Jerusalem."

Teo was stunned. "In what role?"

"I'll be providing security for the ambassador."

9

JERUSALEM – 2021

DC put his keys down on the counter in the kitchen and walked up the stairs to the bedroom. Teo would not be home for a while. He ran his hand along the carved wooden balustrade, admiring the beautiful home in Abu Tor that had been a "gift" from Teo's father. As much as DC wanted to live on his own salary, Teo's enthusiasm for the house swayed him. *Once again,* he sighed.

Moving to Jerusalem had been stressful for both of them, although Arturo's gift had made it less so from Teo's point of view. Plus, she had been able to transfer her position in her father's company to their new Jerusalem headquarters. Of all the Middle Eastern states, Arturo felt he had the most freedom in Israel. It certainly helped that the nation had for many years covered unlimited IVF treatment until a woman reached forty-five years old. Providing those procedures in itself was good income. His other treatments were even more profitable. He had assured DC that the peace of mind Arturo would gain from having Teo in Jerusalem with her husband and closer to her father in Rome would be well worth the home's $4 million price tag. After all, his daughter's safety and well-being were concerned.

DC shook his head negatively. He always gave in to his wife and her father, mostly because he did not like to deal with conflict of any kind with his wife. He loved her. If something made her happy, then it was fine with him, even if it meant accepting expensive gifts from her father.

Stepping out onto the patio, DC gazed at the Temple Mount.

ONE WILL BE TAKEN

The view was incredible, part of the price tag on the house. There was something about the Temple area. The first time he had visited it, the age of the place had overwhelmed him. In the past, he and Teo had toured much of Europe and, being from the New World, had marveled at the history in many of the old cities, especially Rome. The Temple area had a similar ancient feel, but there was something else. As he watched the men praying there, he thought of the generations of Jewish people that had wandered through the world. Tears sprung unexpectedly to his eyes as he remembered the Holocaust and all this people had suffered. They persevered. How amazing that after so many centuries they had gained a homeland again.

DC smiled as he thought about the tenacity of the Israelis. After decades of diplomacy, the Israeli government had finally convinced the United States to implement a law the US Congress had passed in the mid-1990s that called for the United States to move its embassy from Tel Aviv to Jerusalem. The new embassy had opened in 2016. The fact that vast oil reserves had been discovered in Israel helped facilitate the American government's decision. Now there was a US embassy in Jerusalem and friendly oil prices fueled American tanks.

He heard the chime of the security alarm. Teo was home. Walking back into the house, DC went downstairs to greet her in the kitchen, where she stood in front of the opened refrigerator. Smiling at him, she pulled two beers from inside the door and gave him one, along with a kiss full of sweet promise.

"I had a very good day today," she exclaimed.

"I'm glad to hear that. What made it so good?" He took a swig from the bottle. The cold liquid was refreshing. It had been a long, difficult day for him.

"Stephen has found a match! I can have the surgery in a month or so, after the drugs have had a chance to take effect." Teo sat at the counter opposite of DC and grinned from ear to ear.

DC took a stool beside his wife and set his beer down with a clunk. "Teo, I know you want to have children, but this is still a very dangerous surgery. I don't want to put your life at risk."

"DC, we've talked about this. The risk is not so high now. The Swedes completed the first successful transplants in 2012, and the success rates have only gotten better over time. Stephen has found an extremely effective way to insure a 90 percent success rate on uterus transplants." Teo spoke carefully. She knew that if DC discovered where the womb donations came from, he would absolutely forbid her to continue. He did not often assert his opinions, but she knew that when he felt something was wrong morally, he would not be moved.

"Babe, I need to know more about this. I want to talk to Stephen myself first. I want to see and talk to other women who've had this procedure. I want to see the data. I love you and I need to make sure this really is safe." DC pulled her off of her stool and close to him, nuzzling her neck.

Teo wrapped her arms around his neck. "I'll set up an appointment with Stephen. You'll see—it's absolutely going to work for us." As she kissed her husband, she listed the warnings she would give Stephen. DC could not know where the donor wombs originated. She would have a baby. Soon.

Rome, Italy

Billings Mason reclined on the bronze suede oversized couch in the living room of the penthouse. A smaller couch sat to his right, and on the shelves built into the wall behind it were stacks of ancient books and artifacts. He perused Luca's collection with curiosity. The boy was not quite twenty years old, yet in interests and knowledge, he far surpassed anyone Billings had ever met. The young man even surpassed Billings. *As is fitting for the savior of mankind!*

Luca had asked to meet with Billings and Stephen Amona. According to the man who had let Billings into the penthouse, both the boy and Stephen would be arriving soon. Over the past year, Billings had been quite busy laying the groundwork for the revelation of the coming One. They had more to do before the time was right. Luca had begun by entering Roman politics in a minor role, securing a seat in the Chamber of Deputies. It was only one out of six hundred plus seats, but it was a beginning. *The beginning,* Billings thought, *of his rise to power.*

Billings rose, strode to the koa wood staircase across from him, and walked up the rich wooden stairs. At the top landing, he pushed a button on his right, and the ceiling opened. He continued up the stairs to the roof terrace. Although he himself was a very wealthy man and had traveled the world over, he found the terrace view of St. Peter's Basilica impressive. Stephen had remarked to him that it too was central to Luca's plans. Its role was the main issue they were going to discuss tonight.

"Ah, Billings, I told Stephen we would find you up here," Luca interjected cheerfully. Billings turned to see the young man approach him with arms held open. Luca and Billings embraced, and Luca welcomed his mentor with a kiss on each cheek. Stephen clapped him on the back.

"Stephen and I have spent the past few days discussing our strategy, Billings. Your role, as you know, is to be the one preparing the way. The world must be prepared for my revelation. You are the central figure of that plan. The Father has given you the gift of healing, and even of raising the dead."

Billings nodded his head humbly. "For that I am very grateful."

"As is right and fitting, Billings." Luca smiled, the dimples on either side of his face lighting up his countenance with goodwill. "Now it is time to take the next step in our plans to pull the world back from the brink of destruction and set it on the next level of evolutionary development and security. Peace, Billings. The world needs peace. Real and honest peace. Then we can bring about prosperity and real hope for every human being."

Joy filled Billings' heart. Here at last was the hope he had longed for. The truth he had sought stood before him. Luca was so good, so capable. Surely, at last, mankind had found its savior. "Just tell me what you would have me do, Luca."

Luca turned to look at St. Peter's, glowing in the distance. "I want you to become a Catholic priest, Billings. You will enter the priesthood, humbly declaring your faith in the true Church."

Billings looked confused.

Luca continued, "You will be granted, instead, the title of Cardinal, due to your obvious gifts and work on behalf of humanity. After dealing with a horrible tragedy in the center of the United States that will occur shortly after you take up the cloth, the pope himself will appoint you as a cardinal."

"I will do as you wish, Luca. But why go this route? It's surely unnecessary."

"The structure of the Catholic Church fits well with my designs for the world's future. Think about it, Billings. This church is in every nation of the world. It has a great deal of influence in world opinion, even for those who don't truly believe. There is also a lot of wealth there, Billings. Besides, I hate that mewling savior of theirs. So think of this as a benevolent takeover—at least at first. You will use your influence to weaken the authority of this pope and anyone who supports him. We will consolidate our power in the next few years, until we are ready for our next move."

"What's that?" Billings inquired.

Stephen answered this time. "Why, Billings, you are going to be the next pope!" Stephen and Luca laughed at the astonished expression on Billings' face.

ONE WILL BE TAKEN

Arlington, Virginia

Cynthia Grayson sat nervously in the waiting room next to Father Martin. She had been meeting with the Diocese of Arlington's victim assistance coordinator, Wendy Finch, for months. Father Martin had insisted on the meetings, and as their friendship had grown, she felt more confident going this route. Now they were waiting to give testimony to the bishop. Father Martin rubbed the back of his neck as he recalled how angry Bishop Ellis had been when the young priest had insisted that Cynthia's accusations be given a hearing. He had reminded the bishop of the diocese's commitment to investigate credible allegations. Bishop Ellis had to recuse himself because of his friendship with Nathan Penal, so Bishop Ellis's assistant, Bishop Atay, was in charge of the case.

The door to the conference room opened and Nathan Penal emerged. Father Martin had never seen him before, but realized who the man was by Cynthia's reaction. His looks were not in keeping with what Father Martin knew of his character. Nathan looked more the part of a kindly old saint than a child molester. Father Martin was surprised to see the man walk across the room toward them.

Cynthia squirmed uneasily in her chair as her father looked down at her.

"Cynthia, I don't understand why you are doing this," he said. He moved to take the empty chair to her left, but Father Martin stood up and placed a hand on his shoulder.

"I think you had better go. Cynthia has nothing to say to you, but she does have a lot to tell the bishop."

Tears filled Nathan's bright blue eyes. "I have never harmed a hair on her head, Father. Since the day my wife and I married, I have loved Cynthia and cared for her."

Father Martin tried to pull the older man gently away. "I think you should go, sir."

The older man resisted. "Father, I am telling you that you are wrong. You don't know what you are dealing with here. I'm trying to spare us all."

"Spare me, okay?" Father Martin snapped, having had quite enough. "Please leave now."

Nathan patted Father Martin's hand. "You can let go, Father. Her mother and I had to years ago. Bishop Ellis knows the whole sad story. I wish you had listened to his counsel." He turned to Cynthia again, sighed, and left.

Father Martin turned to Cynthia. "I am sorry you had to go through that. They were supposed to make sure that your interviews did not overlap."

Cynthia stood up. "You know, Father, I think I'd better go now. I can't do this right now."

Father Martin put an arm around her shoulder sympathetically. "I know this is hard. Your father is a wealthy and powerful man, but the Church is here for you, Cynthia. And we have to go through with the interview. You don't want other young girls to suffer what you did, do you?"

Tears rolled down Cynthia's face. She started hyperventilating. "I have to go . . ." She ran out of the waiting room.

Father James was about to follow her when the door to the conference room opened. Bishop Atay stepped out of the doorway with a serious look on his face. "Father Martin, you are wanted now."

Lyons, Colorado

She stretched her legs and rolled over, letting the cool air from the open window blow softly on her face. Snuggling in deeper under the flannel sheets and feather comforter, Elena looked out at the dark sky. *It must be cloudy outside,* she thought, as the filtered light just made the outlines of the trees visible. She loved this time of year. It was cool, and the bright colors of the trees had always seemed to her an exuberant last expression of life before winter set in.

Turning over, she looked at the profile of her husband. Husband. She could never have imagined the past year, not in her wildest dreams. After the attacks, she and John had tried to help where they could, growing closer to each other in the process. She smiled. She smiled a lot now, Teo had told her that at the wedding. Three months of married life with John, and she was more content than ever before in her life.

The alarm went off on John's side of the bed. He grunted and slapped at it, turning it off. Elena knew it would go off three or four more times before John actually woke up. Maybe after a while she would find it irritating, but right now it was endearing.

They were in Colorado for John's interview on the local news station this morning, all a part of his book tour. The conservative, pro-American tone of the book, published after the attacks, appealed to the beleaguered citizenry. John was in great demand as a speaker.

Elena got up and went to the kitchen of the small cabin in which they were staying as guests of one of John's friends. She and John were grateful for the offer of the cabin since John was promoting his book himself. He had been successful so far, but it was a long and somewhat costly enterprise. Whenever they could stay with friends on the tour, they had taken the opportunity. It was exciting to see his book climb on *The New York Times* best-seller list. He had been approached by a major publishing house interested in bringing it out in mass He remembered the Gospel verse that said God knows when a sparrow falls, and humans are of much more worth than sparrows. market paperback, but John had refused them, going instead with a smaller publisher. It was a good choice. A few months after that, the larger publishing company declared bankruptcy.

Elena took her coffee and sat down in the small living room. The view was spectacular, even though the sky was cloudy. The backyard was now visible, and Elena marveled at its peacefulness. In spite of the horrors and difficulties of the past year, life still went on. There were still beautiful things in the world. There was still love.

Arlington, Virginia

Joseph placed a cup of coffee on the table next to Father Martin. His young friend was greatly disturbed—and unusually quiet. Joseph sat on the chair next to the priest and drank his coffee quietly, waiting.

Father Martin looked at him and then launched. "I went against the bishop's order. I had to, Joseph! This young woman has been so misused by her adoptive father. After the attacks, I just couldn't stand to see more evil go unpunished." He picked up his coffee and took a sip. "She was at the children's hospital, Joseph, after the attacks. She worked tirelessly. Day after day she showed up and helped, quietly and humbly. She came to every Mass, taking the Blessed Sacrament daily. What a heart for God she has!"

Father Martin shook his head in frustration, while Joseph felt a heavy uneasiness grow in his spirit.

"After a few months, I talked with Cynthia about it again, and she agreed to pursue an allegation with the diocese. The victim coordinator interviewed her and also believed she was credible. But then Cynthia ran from the interview with the bishop after her father came in and spoke to her. She won't return any phone calls from the diocese, so on the testimony of the other witnesses, the case has been closed."

"James, I have to say it is most likely for the best," Joseph said softly.

"Bishop Ellis warned me that he felt I had defied his authority. Now I'm being censored! For the time being, I am not to serve Mass. This monster that abused his daughter gets to continue working with children in the church, Joseph! And I am not allowed . . ." Father Martin sputtered.

"Did they say anything else to you, James? About the other testimony?"

"No, because the Penals claim to still love their daughter and want to protect her from herself. Can you believe the gall?"

Joseph was concerned. "James, you might do well for yourself to talk to Mr. Penal and see what he has to say. There may be aspects to this situation you are unaware of, things you don't know and need to know to make a wise decision."

As Father Martin went on to explain why that would not be a good idea, Joseph became certain that his young friend was emotionally entangled with this young woman. He started to interject but changed his mind. The younger man was obviously in no mood to be crossed. Joseph began to pray silently as Father Martin raged on against Nathan Penal and the bishop.

10

BOULDER,
COLORADO

Elena sat in the small café on the University of Colorado campus, sipping a cup of coffee. John had squeezed in a radio interview on campus to promote his book. In the meantime, she was enjoying a lovely piece of pie, a cup of strong coffee, and people watching.

A group of six girls sat right next to her, engrossed in what sounded like six conversations at once. Elena tried not to look like she was listening to them. She wondered if Teo had ever been so flighty and fresh mouthed as these girls seemed to be. Apparently, they were rating every male in their view. She heard one of the girls giggle as a tall, handsome man approached them.

He looked older than the average college student, Elena thought, with much more confidence than most young men. Jamaican, perhaps? She eyed his dreadlocks. She did not usually like that style, but decided his looked almost regal. His hair was tied up neatly at the base of his neck. He had a well-trimmed beard and mustache, and as he got to the table full of girls, he revealed a beautiful smile.

"Ladies, it's a pleasure to see young women enjoying themselves, even if it is at the expense of the young men." The girls all laughed at being caught in their game, but Elena noticed the dark-haired girl across from her biting her lip. The man, definitely a Jamaican by his accent, also noticed the girl. As he pulled over a chair and sat down next to the young woman, Elena heard him say, "I perceive you are one of the beautiful people."

A few of the girls left the table to get their drinks refilled. Elena tried to listen over their chatter. She was intrigued by this man's pickup line. It was a bit odd.

"What do you mean?" the dark-haired girl asked.

"Tell me," the Jamaican quietly asked, "what is the central truth of Christianity?"

The girl looked confused. "Um, that we are to love our neighbor, and the Golden Rule, do to others."

A huge smile crossed the man's face as he leaned closer to the girl and patted in a fatherly sort of way the hand she had on the table. "Isn't it that Jesus Christ died for your sins and rose again from the dead?"

He gave her hand another pat, got up, and left the café. Elena was puzzled by the exchange. She looked over the rim of her mug at the girl. All sorts of emotions seemed to be going on: shame, confusion, and conviction. *What an odd thing to witness!* Elena thought. Finally, the girl got up, picked up her books, and left.

Elena sat thinking about the man and what he had said. She had not been to church much since she got married. With the continued sporadic violence after the attacks, and the newness of her married life, there always seemed to be some reason not to go. Father Martin was not serving Mass very often now, and she did not like the other priest at all—a pompous windbag who loved the sound of his own voice too much. But still, for some reason, the Jamaican's words pricked at something in her. She would have to talk to John about it.

Jerusalem, Israel

The television above the bar was muted, which was just as well for DC. He had come with a few of his new friends from the embassy, wanting a chance to get to know them better. The guys routinely went out for a beer at the end of the week, but they were very careful to change their destinations. Jerusalem was fairly safe, but these were strange times. That was the topic of the night's conversation. Unusual rumors ran throughout the city, stories of a man who looked like an old-time prophet, beard and all. In some stories, he healed. In others, he protected someone from a robbery or attack. There were no videos or photos, yet the whole city was talking about him. Even the Americans at the embassy were hearing stories from a few expats living in Israel who had come to the embassy for help with visas or other difficulties.

"It was the oddest damn thing," Dave said, shaking his head and taking a sip of his beer. Dave was one of DC's favorite new friends, a huge young man nearly six and a half feet tall with an obvious affinity for weight lifting and tattoos. Despite his size, he was quick. DC had seen him in action one day when a man approached the embassy gates while DC had been checking on the entrances. He had noticed the man approaching and thought there was something off about him. Before DC could act on his suspicions, Dave had the man flat on the ground, his arms pinned behind his back. On the ground next to him, a 9mm. DC smiled at the memory and turned his attention back to his friend.

"This man wanted to see the ambassador to get his son's paperwork expedited. I was hoping to talk to Marie, so I was sitting and waiting for her coffee break. The man started telling me this crazy story, kept praising God every other sentence."

"What happened?" one of the other men asked.

"He'd been in a hurry to get to work at the Ministry of Education and Culture and was driving through the Me'a She'arim area. A little girl ran into the street. He couldn't stop his car in time, and he hit her. He got out, of course, and ran to the front of his car. The girl was bloody, white froth drooling from her mouth. Her mother ran screaming into the street; it was a nightmare. There were some Israeli Defense Force officers on the street, who assisted and called for an ambulance. The little girl started convulsing, and no one knew what to do. Just then, this guy everyone in Jerusalem has been talking about showed up out of nowhere.

"He knelt down beside the girl and touched her shoulder. Immediately, the convulsions stopped. He lifted his right hand up in prayer and called out in Hebrew for God to heal her—get this—in Yeshua's name!"

DC was startled. "Was the guy who was telling you this story Orthodox?"

Dave nodded. "Yeah, I've been here long enough to be startled to hear that name from an Orthodox Jew. The fact that he would even say the name of God was wild."

One of the other men, Mark, urged Dave to finish his story.

"Well," he said, "the girl stopped convulsing. She turned her head, looked at the man who had prayed, smiled, and stood up. As her mother hugged her, crying, the little girl said that she had seen the Messiah, Yeshua, but that he had sent her back to her mommy."

"Then this guy went over to the Orthodox man who'd hit the girl with his car; Aric was his name. He couldn't believe what was happening. Then the miracle-worker guy goes on to tell Aric about himself, talking to Aric about Aric, that he'd divorced three women and neglected the children God had blessed him with. That he'd been selfish and ambitious. That he needed to repent and return to God. And that only through Yeshua could he find forgiveness and life."

"Did he do it?" Mark inquired eagerly. All eyes were fastened on Dave, waiting for the rest of the story.

"Yes, he did it! Who wouldn't, after an experience like that? He prayed with the man, but when he opened his eyes, the man was gone."

DC had heard rumors about this "prophet" in the last few weeks. Weird. "Did the man tell Aric his name?"

"No," Dave answered, "and the first thing Aric said he did after that was to immediately contact his children. Only his youngest son was willing to talk to him. That's why he was at the embassy, to get his paperwork done as quickly as possible. He was afraid his son might change his mind."

Mark smiled. "I've heard a lot of similar stories. In some, this guy heals the sick. In others, he knocks on doors, comes into the home, preaches to people, and they turn to faith in Jesus—Yeshua. The Orthodox rabbis are in an uproar. No one can find out where this guy lives; he just seems to appear and disappear."

"My mom is a Christian. She's really big on the whole 'end times' stuff," DC said. "I told her about the rumors. She said some guy is supposed to go through Israel, restoring the Jewish family or something like that. This has got to be some sort of hysterical mass delusion. Things are getting hot and heavy with Russia allying itself with Libya, Iran, and Turkey. You can feel the tension wherever you go in Jerusalem."

"We're on heightened alert," Mark answered, "but I think there's something real going on. There are too many people having the same experience."

The waitress stopped at their table, cleared off the empty bottles, and after asking if they wanted more, went to get them refills. They started discussing the threat of the Russia-Iran alliance and how they planned to protect their families if missiles started falling on Jerusalem.

Arlington, Virginia

Father James Martin sat uncomfortably in front of Bishop Ellis, who had just informed him that Bishop Atay declared the charges against Nathan Penal officially dropped.

"As for you, Father Martin," the bishop continued, "I am very displeased at your involvement in this witch hunt." The older man's face became stern as he discerned the young priest's bristling attitude. "There are things you do not know about this young woman.

You would have done well to listen to my counsel."

"Sir, if you would only speak to Cynthia yourself, you would see what a fine, upstanding young woman she is. She has the purest faith I have ever witnessed—in spite of all of the evil done to her by her own father!" Father Martin thought of Cynthia's actions throughout the past year: serving others in need, worshipping daily—even after the Church had failed her in regard to her wealthy father.

Bishop Ellis drew a deep breath. "Father Martin, I am under obligation to Nathan and his dear wife not to reveal what may harm Cynthia. I can only say, with the utmost concern for you, that you must heed my warning. She is not what she appears. I have known Nathan since we were boys. He is a true believer in Jesus Christ and loves Him wholeheartedly, as does his wife, Marie. I wish I were free to tell you more, but I am not. You must trust me in this matter.

"It is not good for you to continue to see Cynthia Grayson. I will talk with her about moving to another parish. It is obvious to me that there is too much concern on your part for this young woman."

Father Martin's stomach churned with anger as the bishop spoke. "Are you accusing me, Bishop Ellis, of breaking my vows?" His hands clenched the arms of his chair.

Bishop Ellis looked kindly across his desk at the younger priest. "No, Father Martin, my greater experience as a priest, a bishop, and a man leads me to this decision. Sin wraps itself in beautiful garments, and the enemy is too good at knowing our particular vulnerabilities."

"I have not stepped over any boundaries!" Father Martin exclaimed.

"Not even in your thoughts?" the older man inquired quietly. "Even so, Father Martin, you are a man and she is a very attractive young woman. It is wise to distance yourself. I'm sending you on a month's retreat."

Father Martin started to protest that his congregation needed him, but Bishop Ellis raised his hand. "Stop, Father Martin. We all need to renew and rest ourselves from time to time. You have been busy serving the community and the church this past year. But I wonder if you have been too busy? Have you spent time searching the Word of God and seeking after the Lord each day, or are you too busy serving to do so? How can you serve Him if your spirit is empty?"

"Bishop Ellis, this is unfair! I have obligations to fulfill there," Father Martin insisted.

"I think you will find, Father Martin, that the world will continue going on, even without your help! You will do as you are ordered. Please see my assistant. He will give you the itinerary."

Father Martin stood up. "Bishop Ellis, please!"

"That is all, Father Martin," said Bishop Ellis, smiling sadly, "and I would prefer it if you did not see Miss Grayson again, or even contact her."

New York City, New York

Billings Mason sat in the makeup chair. The green room of this news outlet was just like all the others he had been in. He smiled at the young woman applying his makeup, commenting jovially about making sure he looked natural. She assured him she would make sure he did not look made up.

"Umm, I was wondering, Mr. Mason, or Reverend, if you would see my little brother after the show? He had an accident when he was little," the makeup girl faltered.

In the past year, Billings had received many requests to heal family members, even to raise the dead. The video of the resurrections in Florida had been played over and over on various networks and on the Internet. His office was flooded daily with phone calls and letters imploring him to help. It was sometimes exhausting. He looked up and saw the tears running down the girl's face. Without thinking, he reached up and brushed one away. As he touched her face, knowledge came flooding into his mind. This was happening more and more lately, too.

"You were supposed to watch him while your mother went to the grocery store," he began. She sobbed and shook her head. "But you were on the phone with a friend."

"I didn't see him leave the room. He got into some medicine my dad had left on the bathroom counter. By the time I got there, he'd eaten all the pills."

Billings stood up and put an arm around the girl. "I understand. You brought him here today with you, hoping I would help."

She nodded. "He's in the staff break room. If you would see him after the show, I would be so grateful, sir."

"No need to wait, Maya. It is Maya, yes?" He smiled as she nodded. "Let's go and see your brother now."

Billings' heart filled with compassion as they entered the room. A boy of about twelve years old sat in a wheelchair. He was wearing shorts and a T-shirt. A large bib was tied around his neck to catch the drool that ran down the side of his mouth. His body was stiffened; his arms and legs were stick thin. It was obvious he could not walk. Billings doubted the boy could do anything for himself. An older woman sat next to him, patting his hand. She started when she saw Billings enter.

"Maya! He came!"

"Yes, Mama, he did!" Maya went over and hugged her mother. "Reverend, this is my brother, Jake."

Billings walked over and stood in front of the boy. The blue eyes that moved back and forth were oblivious to the older man's presence. Billings patted the boy's shoulder and looked at the two women standing behind him.

"I am not always able to heal every person. The gift I have been given is to aid mankind, but also to point the way to the One who is coming. There is one much greater than me, and this gift of healing is from Him."

"You mean God, sir?" the older woman asked. "Jesus?"

102

Billings shuddered and forced himself to speak softly. "No, that one was a god, but not the True God. You must understand, that we are all, in reality, gods."

The woman looked confused and uncomfortable. Billings reached out and took her hand in his. "You are Jake's mother, Susan. I understand the last ten years have been difficult. Your husband left you alone to care for the children. You turned to what you thought was God in your grief, but what you sought you could not find, could you?"

"No, there were times when I thought I had found God and found peace, but then something would happen and I would become unsure. What are you saying, Reverend?" She looked at him searchingly.

"Susan, we have greater strength and power than we know. We have all been given this power, this gift, but we have to discover it, or rediscover it. Soon the whole world will know the truth and be set free. Set free from the tyranny of sickness and death. This is the truth I have discovered—rather—which discovered me."

He turned to the boy and put one hand on his head. The other hand he raised above his head. "I ask that this boy be healed. Let your true power be seen in him!"

Billings noticed that more people had entered the room and that some were recording videos with their phones. *Good.* He kept his expression serious as the young boy began to moan. The child started to tremble and his limbs shook. Billings continued to pray in another tongue, one he had learned in the past year, a spiritual language.

Jake slumped forward in his chair.

"Jake, get out of the chair now. You no longer need it," Billings commanded.

There were shouts and cries in the room as the boy sat up and then rose from his wheelchair. His blue eyes were clear, and his face was flush with vitality. Unbelievably, his arms and legs had filled out as well. He walked, a bit stiffly, over to his mother.

"Mama!" he cried, dimples appearing on each side of the huge smile on his face. "I love you, Mama!" They embraced, crying with joy. Maya wrapped her arms around both of them. The room erupted with applause.

After a few minutes, the boy turned to Billings. "You healed me." He threw his arms around Billings and gave him a huge hug, which Billings returned, ruffling the boy's hair affectionately. Billings knew the video would be all over the Internet and news by evening.

Arlington, Virginia

The candles in the wrought iron candelabra flickered brightly. Each night, Mary lit them for the evening. Joseph finished his meal by their light and then pushed back his plate.

"Mary, that was the best meal I've had in months. Thank you for going to such trouble for me."

The red-headed woman smiled across the table. "I'll go and start the coffee. I'm glad you liked it, Joseph. Rafa, why don't you and Joseph go to the living room? I'll just clear up here and bring the coffee in when it's ready."

Rafa took his glass from the table and led the way to the living room. Joseph sat down in his favorite chair. He had been friends with the Cohens for years. Ever since Natalie had gone to be with the Lord, the Cohens had insisted Joseph share Sabbath dinner with them. Joseph was grateful for the fellowship of his good friends, and Mary was a fantastic cook.

"So, what do you think of all that is going on in our world now, my friend?" he asked Rafa. Never had Joseph met a man who had such a wide grasp of Scripture. Rafa had studied to be a rabbi before coming to know Yeshua. He had whole passages of the Old and New Testament committed to memory. He was a well-respected teacher in their community and, until the attacks last year, had traveled all over the world teaching.

"Well, things do seem to be lining up for war, don't they, Joseph?" Rafa answered. "What do you think of this Billings Mason?"

Joseph shook his head and made a sour face. "Rafa, you and I both know where his power comes from! Isn't he packaged well too? Now he's gone and become a Catholic priest, have you heard? Why on earth would he do that?"

Rafa snorted. "I'm sure that nothing on earth gave him that idea! Think about it, Joseph. There is already talk of making him a bishop because of the miracles he's doing. Once Islam is discredited—and it will be—and once the real Church, those who truly believe in Jesus Christ, are taken up before the Great Tribulation, every society on earth will be in shambles."

"How do you mean?"

"Once all that happens, there will be no institution for mankind to rely upon. Islam will have lost its power. All true believers in Jesus Christ will be gone. All the smaller denominations will have folks left, of course, but they are too small, too insignificant. Losing large numbers of members will make them ineffectual. Only the Catholic Church will be left, a worldwide organization. It is so large; losing its believers will not cripple it. All its true believers will be gone, leaving unsaved men to steward its vast treasures. Whoever the Antichrist is, Joseph, he's going to need a lot of money."

"Do you think this Billings person is the Antichrist?" Although Joseph knew it was a possibility, saying it out loud made him feel sick.

Mary entered the room and took a seat on the couch next to her husband. "I don't know if he is, but he scares me. He looks so good, so fatherly in a rugged, manly sort of way. Yet everything he says is deceptive."

"I am curious as to why you think Islam will be discredited, Rafa."

"They are about to go toe-to-toe with God's chosen people, Joseph. All of these nations massing troops on Israel's border—

doesn't that strike a chord in your memory? They are all from Ezekiel's prophecy. Things are about to get very supernatural here on earth!"

"With Billings Mason, I'd say they already are!" exclaimed Mary. "I am concerned about the possibility of war though, Rafa. With the president we have and all of the disasters America has faced, I don't know if Israel will have anyone to support it against these aggressors."

Joseph thought about that. Things did seem to be lining up with Ezekiel's prophecy. According to that, no nation would end up doing anything more than protesting. In the world's eyes, Israel would stand alone, but the world had forgotten God in the equation.

Jerusalem, Israel

Arturo paced the floor in front of Teo's desk. He had been desperately trying to convince her to leave Jerusalem. *She is as stubborn as her mother,* he thought.

"Father, I am fine. DC wouldn't let me stay here if he thought we were really at risk."

"Teo, I am privy to information that DC does not have. In the next month, this will not be a safe place for you. How can I convince you? Please just come back to Rome with me for a while. Go and visit your mother. You and DC take a holiday—maybe take a tour of New Babylon. I've heard it is spectacular. Just get out of Jerusalem."

"Father, you don't understand. Israel has the most progressive and effective treatments for infertility. Stephen has already set up my surgery. It's all ready to go in the next few weeks, once the hormone levels are right."

Arturo stifled a curse. He knew his daughter well enough to know that this issue was one from which she would not back off, no matter what the cost to herself—or others. He understood her stub-

106

bornness to some extent. It was that desire for a child, a son, that had propelled his research, culminating in Luca's birth.

He also knew the president of Russia personally, having aided his wife in finally giving birth to the son Karl Voga had desired. Arturo was a frequent guest of the Vogas. In fact, Rema was now eight months into her second pregnancy. That is how he had come to know the Russian president's plans, because Rema had insisted on Arturo presiding over the scheduled delivery of the couple's second son.

Arturo could see the passion building in Muslim nations against the Jewish nation—even in Europe and America. Really, Israel's doom had been sealed in the last few years upon discovery of huge oil and natural gas reserves. This tiny nation was now the seat of great wealth. That was the real reason behind Russia's design. Oil. More oil than any other nation had ever seen. That and a port in the Mediterranean Sea made it inevitable that Israel would face war.

"Teo, please. Come to Rome with me. We can arrange the surgery there. Luca is there too. You haven't seen him in a while. . . ." Arturo spoke persuasively. "Just do this for me, Teo, for your father's peace of mind."

Teo stared at her father. She knew the situation in the Middle East was always tense, but her father seemed genuinely upset. The surgery was set, but she supposed it really would not matter if it were done in Jerusalem or in Rome, as her father wanted. But DC could not just come and go with his job. *Surely,* she thought, *if it is as bad as he is saying, the United States would be sending families home.*

"Father, I'll talk to DC about it tonight, okay? That's all I can promise right now. Can we get back to the projections for the next quarter? For some reason, business is booming. Seriously, we are pulling in profit above anything we imagined!"

Arturo sat down and listened as Teo talked about the business. He was pleased that his daughter was such an asset, and even more pleased as he listened that his personal assets were increasing.

Now he just had to find some way to get Teo out of Jerusalem. As she talked, he seemed to recall something Stephen had mentioned in passing about her surgery. What was it? Something that hovered at the edge of his memory. He smiled at the photo on Teo's desk of him and DC—her two favorite men she had said as she snapped the photo—just days before her and DC's wedding.

It was about DC, Arturo recalled. *Teo hasn't told DC that the surgery was only possible because of the young Indian girl.* The older man looked at his beautiful daughter. She would be furious if he were the one who told DC, but he could find some innocuous way for DC to discover that the "cure" for Teo was the uterus of a thirteen-year-old girl whose parents were being paid a modest amount by Western standards. Arturo might be able to use the ensuing emotional debate that was likely to occur between DC and Teo to pry her away from Jerusalem.

11

ALEXANDRIA,
VIRGINIA

Father Martin pulled up in front of the tan and white house in the Del Ray area of Alexandria. He had never been to Cynthia's home before and he was surprised by how large it was. It had to be worth about a half million. He supposed her parents must have bought it for her. He sat in the car for a moment, thinking. Bishop Ellis had been adamant that Father Martin not see Cynthia before he left. He was sure the bishop would have a really hard time if he knew the young priest was at her home. But he could not just disappear for a month—especially after the fiasco with her father—without saying good-bye.

He got out of the car and walked up the sidewalk lined with small landscape lights all the way to the front step of the inviting porch. Several large baskets filled with mums of different hues provided a beautiful foil for the wreath of autumn leaves, cattails, and green apples that hung on the white door, welcoming visitors. Father Martin knocked. He could hear someone moving inside.

The door opened a crack, and then wider. Cynthia stood there, eyes questioning, then welcoming. "Wow, Father Martin! I didn't expect to see you here. Would you like to come in?"

She opened the door and stepped back to allow him in. Closing it behind him, she asked if she could take his jacket.

"Let's go in the living room. Would you like some coffee or water, Father?"

Father Martin shook his head. "No, I can really only stay for a moment, Cynthia. I just wanted to make sure you were all right after the other day."

She sighed, pushing her red hair back away from her face. "Why don't you sit down here, Father?" She joined him on the soft, sky-blue couch, tucking her feet up underneath her and turning her body toward him. "I was freaked out by the whole thing. My engagement is off now. My fiancé was tired of all the drama, and I think afraid of offending my dad. You know our families are lifelong friends and all, but it's okay. Actually, I think it's for the best, you know?"

Father Martin smiled encouragingly at her.

"The past year, working at the hospital with you, Father, well, it's made me feel a lot better. I just have never felt safe with anyone else the way I do with you." Tears welled up in her green eyes.

Something strange and unfamiliar rose up inside of him as Cynthia spoke, something powerfully moving. A voice somewhere inside tried to warn him to leave, but he assured the warning voice that he had it all under control.

"Well, I'm glad to hear that. But it makes what I have to say a bit harder, Cynthia. I have to go away for a while, on a retreat. I'll be gone for about a month. I just didn't want to go without letting you know and saying good-bye." His voice became apologetic as he noticed tears well up again in her eyes.

He tried to stand, but as he did, Cynthia leaned forward and kissed him on the cheek. "I'll miss you, James," she said, whispering his name. He turned his face toward hers. The scent of spicy citrus and the feel of her warm breath was all he could register. He did not think as his lips tasted hers, first gently, then with more insistence.

When Cynthia stood up and pulled his hand, he followed her to the back of the house to her bedroom. She kissed him again as they stood by the bed, and the last bit of his defenses fell.

Arlington, Virginia

Elena sat quietly listening to the women in the group talking about the Bible passage they had just read. John's book tour was finished, and they were finally back home, where Margaret had welcomed them by bringing them dinner. John asked her to stay and join them. The chili and the conversation were wonderful. When Margaret had asked Elena if she wanted to join her at the study the next day, John insisted Elena go. He had an article he wanted to work on.

Elena was trying to pay attention to the Bible study, but she was worried. She had not heard from Teo or DC in a few weeks. It was difficult with the time difference, but the political situation was really heating up. In fact, the topic of John's article had to do with the president's weak response to the difficulties facing Israel.

The study was over before she knew it. She chatted with a few of the other women before joining Margaret.

"Are you okay, Elena? You seem distracted today."

"I just was thinking about Teo and DC. They're in Jerusalem right now. I saw on the news this morning that Iran and Russia have both moved ships into the Mediterranean. John told me of reports that troops are massing at the northern borders with Syria and Lebanon."

Margaret grimaced. "Have you talked with them?"

"No, I can't get anything other than voice mail. The time difference doesn't help. I don't want to wake them in the middle of the night. . . . Surely the embassy would send dependents home if there was a real risk, wouldn't they? There are always things like this going on in the Middle East."

"You're right, Elena. I'm sure it will end like it always does, with Israel bombing some military target or other and the other countries backing off."

Elena smiled. "I'm sure that's right. Why don't we go and get some lunch?"

Jerusalem, Israel

DC got to the clinic just minutes before the appointment. He was supposed to have met Teo fifteen minutes ago but traffic had been overwhelming. With the threat at the northern border and in the Mediterranean, a lot of folks were leaving Jerusalem.

He navigated his way to the office of Dr. Alfasi, the surgeon to whom Stephen had referred Teo at her father's insistence. Dr. Alfasi had performed more uterine transplants than any other surgeon, and he wanted to meet with both of Teo and DC to walk through the procedure scheduled for Teo the following week. The nurse nodded at DC. "They are waiting for you inside, Mr. Giamo."

"My wife is Giamo. I'm DC Bond—no relation to James!" The nurse looked puzzled and DC stifled a sigh. Some things just did not translate between cultures. It used to bother him that Teo had not taken his last name, but as with many things, he found having a sense of humor about it helped.

Dr. Alfasi stood up as DC entered the office. Teo sat on a chair to the right. After shaking the doctor's hand, DC took the other chair.

"Good, Mr. Bond. It is wonderful to finally meet you. Teo has told me so much about you," the doctor smiled. "Now we can begin. Teo, you have been taking the daily injections?"

She nodded.

"Wonderful. Before you leave, we'll get a blood sample and check your hormone levels. I am also going to give you some prescriptions to fill before the surgery. You will be in the hospital for about a week. After that, we want you to stay nearby the hospital for the first three months. Rejection should not be a problem since we have tested the young girl and made sure you are a compatible match."

DC saw Teo shake her head almost imperceptibly out of the corner of his eye. "What do you mean, 'young girl,' doctor?" DC asked. He could feel his blood pressure start to rise.

"Why, the orphan girl from India. She's been here for the last two weeks, also undergoing testing. We wanted to make sure she was completely healthy and, um, intact, as it were. Everything looks good."

DC was incredulous. "What do you mean?" He turned to his wife. "What is this, Teo? You told me that the organs come from organ donors or women who volunteer."

Teo stammered, "Um, DC, I know that your parents feel very strongly about this issue, and I know how you worry about me, so I just thought that it was better if you didn't know all of the exact details."

Dr. Alfasi tried to reassure DC. "Mr. Bond, I assure you, your wife has been very generous toward the girl. In addition to our customary fees, she's given the girl $30,000. That will enable Pryia to go back to India and start a good life there."

"How old is this girl, Dr. Alfasi?" DC asked quietly.

"Oh, of course she's not yet menstruating. We've found that to be a key factor in insuring fertility once the transplant is complete. Since she's an orphan, we are not quite sure. I'd say she is ten or eleven years old."

DC could not believe that the man in front of him could speak so matter-of-factly about harvesting organs from a child. An orphan. He glared at Teo. "How could you possibly think that this is all right, Teo?"

He did not wait to hear her response. He got up and left.

ONE WILL BE TAKEN

Jerusalem, Israel

Arturo tried to calm his daughter. She had come to his hotel suite at the American Colony, hysterical. It had taken him almost fifteen minutes to get her to the point where she could communicate what had happened. Apparently, Dr. Alfasi had come through quite well, following through on the suggestions Arturo made a few weeks ago.

"Here, dear, take this," he said, handing her a glass with some whiskey in it. "It will help."

She took a sip and stifled a sob.

"Father, he wouldn't even listen to me! He just left the office. He won't answer his cell. I waited hours, and he didn't come home. I am so afraid now. . . . What should I do?"

Arturo had made plans already. "I think that you should go home, in a taxi. You're much too distraught to drive. Then tomorrow, when you and DC talk, you need to apologize. Teo, what were you thinking, lying to him like that?"

"I thought that he wouldn't let me go through with it, Father. I just want a child so badly," she said, starting to cry again.

"I know you do, Teo. Believe me, of all people, I understand what you are going through. You know what I did to get Luca. I am going to help you." He sat in the chair across from his daughter.

"You go home, talk to DC, and then pack."

Teo wiped her eyes with a tissue from the box next to her.

"Pack? Why? I'm not going to leave DC, Father!"

Arturo smiled. "No, but you are going to go to Rome with me for a while until the political situation here cools off."

Teo made a face. "Father, I told you that I'm not worried. It's nothing. I'm sure that it's perfectly safe here."

"Nevertheless, you will come with me anyway. Indulge a father's fears for his daughter, Teo. I also have made arrangements that I am certain will entice you to leave with me tomorrow."

"What could that possibly be, Father?" she asked.

"I've arranged for you to see Billings Mason. He'll be in Rome this week. I believe he is being made a cardinal in the Catholic Church."

Teo sat upright on the sofa. "Can he . . . is he actually able to heal me?"

"I believe so. I don't understand what is going on, but Stephen told me that everything we have heard about Billings is very real. When you and I talked the other day and I realized you wouldn't leave Jerusalem, I had him get in touch with Billings." He moved next to her and put an arm around her shoulder, drawing her into an embrace. "I am not above bribery to keep you safe, Teo. And just think, DC couldn't possibly object to you being healed without surgery or an organ donated by this girl."

Teo turned and put both arms around her father's neck, sobbing now for joy.

12

UNION STATION
WASHINGTON, DC

Father Martin leaned his head against the impact-resistant window. His train would not leave for twenty minutes or so, and he had the cabin to himself. Thankfully, it would take twenty-four hours to get to Chicago. He really needed to think—and pray. Praying just did not seem like an option, though. God had to be even more disgusted with him than he was with himself. *Why . . . why did I let it happen?*

He thought of all that Cynthia had endured and how he was the one person she could trust. He had violated that trust. It didn't matter that she had said she wanted him; he was a priest, her priest. When she had fallen asleep, he left. *Like a thief.* He just could not face her. He could not face anyone now.

After he finished packing his suitcase for the retreat, he had thought about calling Joseph. He realized now, too late, that this was just what Joseph had been trying to warn him about—what Bishop Ellis, too, had been trying to warn him about. He thought of all of those times in the confessional when he had heard sordid stories from his parishioners. Giving them penance and relieving their guilt with a few prayers had seemed sufficient from his vantage point at the time. There was no way such formulaic rituals could cleanse him. His guilt was too great.

The morning sun gleamed on the gold ring on his left hand. Father Martin looked at it in despair. Intellectually, he knew the Church's teaching that there was forgiveness if one was repentant.

He twisted the ring. He thought about the vows he had made on the day of his ordination. Now he had sinned against God and against the Church.

Something about that thought jarred him. The Church. He looked at the ring on his finger again. Who exactly had he committed his life to? Was it to God? He wasn't sure. It was good he was going on this retreat, but if anyone knew what he had done, he would lose it all.

Did he love Cynthia? He did not know. *If I loved her, I wouldn't have . . .* He sighed. It was one thing when priests fell in love and left the priesthood for honorable marriage, but to sin in this way . . . He realized at that moment that he had thought himself closer to God than others because of his collar, because of his commitment to celibacy. He had sacrificed a normal life to serve God. Or had he? Was it really God he was serving? Truthfully, he had not thought about God in quite a while. Now God had turned His back on him. That was only just.

Pounding his head softly on the window as the train began to move, Father Martin realized he was lost. He had failed God. He had failed his church. He had failed Cynthia. He did not know where to turn.

Jerusalem, Israel

Checking to make sure DC was asleep, Teo got out of bed silently. When she had returned home, she found DC sitting in the dark on the bed in their room. She sat at the foot of the bed, cross-legged.

"I'm sorry," she whispered. "I never wanted this to come between us. I thought it would bring us together." She began to weep softly.

DC was stone faced, although his insides were churning. "Teo, how could you? This is not who you are. How could you rob the promise of life from a young child to feed your own desires? You are relegating her to the same torment of childlessness you have endured. Look at what you've become."

Teo thought quickly. Should she push her case? She thought better of it and decided to back off for the moment. "I said I was sorry. I'll give the whole idea up. I promise." She did not think it was prudent to mention her meeting with Billings Mason right now. Part of DC's anger was over her obsession with getting pregnant.

DC softened and reached out for his wife's hand, pulling her into his embrace. "I'm sorry, too. We can make it through this together." They sat in silence for a few minutes as their thoughts, and then their conversation, turned to the future.

"My father is worried about the forces gathering on Israel's northern border. He wants me to go to Rome." To her surprise, DC agreed.

"There is a lot going on here, Teo. I have to say, I would have thought that the embassy would have sent families home by this point. The president is pushing Israel to not strike preemptively. But I don't think Israel is going to sit by while more troops are staged on her northern border. It's bound to get ugly, but the ambassador is staying. I'd feel a whole lot better if you were with your father in Rome. I really would."

"But DC, Israel has been in this same position before. Surely it won't come to actual war?"

"This is different. Israel now has oil, lots of it. Before they found that oil reserve, Israel was only a target for the Muslim world. Now Russia has set its sights on that oil—and on a foothold in the Middle East. Whatever political reasons Russia gives, the reason those troops are being staged in the north is to take over this nation and gain those oil reserves and the port cities. None of the Western nations are speaking out against this mobilization, and that's making the Russian confederation bolder. I think it's just a matter of time before they attack."

Teo left DC's arms and went out to the balcony to think as

119

he flipped on the television to watch more news. She was a business woman and a wife. She wanted to be a mother. She looked at the beautiful homes that surrounded her and remembered the agony of the terror attacks in the United States. The country was still devastated. Earthquakes, floods, and other natural disasters seemed to be increasing throughout the world. Would that sort of thing happen here, bombs falling, people dying? She started to feel the panic again. Was there any safety in the world anymore? Money and position used to ensure that, but these days even affluence provided only an illusion of safety.

Mom would pray. But if there is a God, He must not care—or He must not be strong enough to bring peace and safety to the world of men.

She went inside and did what she always did when the panic began. She took a pill and went to sleep. She would feel better in the morning.

Rome, Italy

Luca opened the door and let the young woman out with a smile. He closed it softly behind her and went to his living room. Grabbing his glass and the bottle from the coffee table, he went up the stairs to the roof terrace, where he settled comfortably into one of the chairs, sipping his wine. *St. Peter's is an impressive sight,* he thought.

He was quite excited, and his visit with the beautiful model had only added to his mood. Troops were massed on the northern border of Israel, troops that were going to invade. He snickered to himself as he contemplated the Jewish defense. There was not one nation, not one world leader, who would do more than faintly protest. This was his plan. It was really rather like a good game of chess. He wondered idly what the pontiff across the road might say.

That one is a problem. An actual believer. Luca could not

stand believers, although he had not met many of them in Europe. He hated them because they were closed off to him. It rankled Luca that he was not able to enter any mind he wanted; some minds were stronger than others, especially among Christians. He had tried the pontiff, but there was no access.

Ah well, my time will come. It is coming, in fact. He smirked as he finished his wine and gazed at the city below him. The man across the street would be gone. Someone else would take his place. That someone was Luca's prophet. Soon, Luca would have the entire world at his feet. He would rule it all. There would be a new order but, as with all revolutions, it would need to be born out of blood and pain. Luca smiled in anticipation as he refilled his glass. His kingdom would be an everlasting kingdom. Not *all* of those ancient prophecies had to come to pass. He could insure it. He had no doubt.

Raising his glass in a toast, he whispered, "Just as you said, Father. There is a way around what has been foretold. Your plan is working. Nothing can thwart it."

Arlington, Virginia

Joseph awoke with a start. Something was wrong; he felt it in his spirit. In his younger, less experienced days, he would have ignored it and tried to go back to sleep. Instead, he got up and started to pray. The phone rang.

"Hello," he said quietly.

"This is Rafa. I just got a call from the pastor. People are gathering at church. He's had about twenty calls in the last half hour. The phone tree has been activated to call all of the members to join at church for prayer."

"I'll be there, Rafa. Has something happened? Is there something on the news?"

"Mary looked online. There doesn't seem to be, but many of us have the urgent sense to pray, so Pastor Moshe thought it best if we pray together. I'll meet you there, Joseph."

Joseph hung up and went to get dressed.

Jerusalem, Israel

DC scrambled to pull on his shirt as he ran downstairs and into the garage. He was thankful that Teo was with her father in Rome. An alert had just come through for the emergency response team to get to the embassy.

Racing his car through the dark streets of Jerusalem, DC reviewed what he knew from the briefing he had attended earlier in the day. Russia, Iran, Libya, and some other nations had amassed thousands of troops and tanks on Israel's northern border after mobilizing for the past week. The ambassador had been up for the last twenty hours trying to intercede with Washington, but with no success. The US president refused to do more than object to Russia's president and the supreme leader of Iran.

DC supposed the alert meant troop movement. Briefly he wondered why there were no sirens warning citizens, but how and to where could they escape? Israel was the only safe place for the Jews. The ambassador understood that. DC didn't know why it was such a hard concept for America's president.

As he pulled up to the embassy, DC noted the guards at the gates had been doubled. Everything was locked down. He showed his ID to the guards, who waved him in. He made his way to the guard barracks, arriving just moments before his supervisor, Philip Grey, came in. All of the Marine guards stood at attention and saluted.

"Please sit down, gentlemen," Philip directed, nodding to the staff sergeant, who began passing out small packets. "This will only take a few minutes. About an hour ago, Alliance forces crossed the border into Israel's mountains. Troops from Russia, Sudan, Turkey, and Libya have joined with the Iranians. They have tanks, fighter jets . . . you name it. Israel has been strangely reluctant to attack. I'm not privy to the ambassador's interactions with the Israeli prime minister, but I can only surmise that they are reluctant because of pressure from the United States.

"Consequently, we may be facing an invasion of Jerusalem. Our mission is to defend the embassy. You each have your assignments. Note them and get into position. That is all." He turned abruptly and left the room.

DC got his men together, and they took their places by the front gate. The sun was just beginning to rise. Lights in the city twinkled on the hills in front of him, still visible in the receding darkness.

He heard the jets before he saw them. Then, in a flash, they were gone—vaporized. A flaming meteor passed right above them.

"Damn, sir! Did you see that?" one of his men exclaimed.

DC did not have a chance to respond. He heard a huge explosion, then noticed the gates moving strangely. He fell to the ground as the earth began to shake violently and roll. He turned and looked out the gate. Jerusalem itself seemed to rise and fall right before his eyes. Behind him, he heard the cracking of timber followed by screams. He whipped his head to the left in time to see a huge hole appearing all around the American embassy, and he watched in horror as the entire complex collapsed into the hole's center. Flames shot up from various places in the fallen building. He turned back as the lights of Jerusalem flickered out. Then the hail began.

Rome, Italy

It was dark in the room when Teo woke suddenly. Something was wrong. She heard the crash of breaking glass in the bathroom. She sat up, startled, and froze as she listened. Nothing. Getting out of bed carefully, she tiptoed to the bathroom door, switched on the light, and looked in. A shelf next to the claw-foot bathtub had fallen from the wall. The beautiful glass perfume bottles her father had given her throughout her childhood lay smashed on the tile floor.

She started into the room but a knock on the door behind her caused her to turn around. Opening the door, she found the maid, Alameda, looking pale.

"Are you all right, Miss?" Alameda asked.

"Yes, why? Has something happened?"

"There's been an earthquake. Your father, he asked me to have you join him downstairs."

Teo grabbed the green silk robe from her bed, pulled it on, and followed Alameda to the living room. Arturo was already up and dressed, sipping some coffee. "Teo, I think you are going to want to see this," he said, gesturing to the television on the wall. She nodded yes to Alameda's offer of coffee and continued staring at the screen.

Her father had a split screen showing four separate stations. The ticker along the bottom of each screen projected numbers of dead for different parts of the world, along with warnings of landslides and localized flooding.

"What has happened?" Her mouth felt dry and her stomach cramped.

"There has been some sort of tectonic shift, authorities think. We're seeing reports of astonishing incidents, in Russia mostly. Earthquakes, hail—Moscow is almost completely destroyed." Arturo stood up and put an arm around his daughter. He led her to the couch and asked her to sit down.

"Teo, reports of an earthquake are also coming in from Jerusalem. No one is sure of the magnitude," he said gently.

They both turned to watch the television. Arturo picked up the remote and chose one of the stations.

"All we have is amateur video," the moderator explained, "but here you can see this building collapse. It weaves like a drunkard and literally falls. Similar reports are coming in from other parts of the world. Multiple tsunami warnings have gone out because of all the earthquakes occurring in a number of nations. We are looking at an event unprecedented in history." The moderator appeared visibly shaken as he read from his teleprompter.

"This just in," he said in a heightened tone, "the armies that had been massing on the northern border of Israel have been decimated. We are not sure what has occurred at this point. Apparently, in the middle of the night, they crossed Israeli borders. Our sources in Jerusalem say that the Israeli government did not, I repeat, did not have a chance to respond to the incursion because of the large earthquake that rocked the city. Reports from a few survivors have been called in to various news outlets. We have raw video feed from a few of these survivors, which we will bring to you as soon as possible."

Arturo flipped the station to the BBC feed. Teo was astounded to see video feed of Jerusalem, near the Wailing Wall, but something was very wrong with the scene.

"The Dome of the Rock is gone," said Arturo. As the camera panned the area, Teo could see the devastation. Arturo turned up the sound.

"This is perhaps the most significant destruction in Israel," the reporter said. "Eyewitnesses say that a meteor of some sort, streaming with fire, hit the Dome of the Rock just before the earthquake began. If you look carefully, you can still see fire in the ruins. The significance of this incredible situation is yet to be seen."

Teo stood up. "I'm calling DC right now." She ran back up to her room and got her cell phone. She dialed with trembling fingers, breathing rapidly. Panic was about to overwhelm her. She could not get a call through. Teo hit redial over and over for the next ten minutes. Throwing the phone on the bed and fearing the worst, she began to hyperventilate.

ONE WILL BE TAKEN

Arlington, Virginia

John leaned over and kissed his wife, setting the mug of coffee carefully on the nightstand. "Good morning, love."

Elena smiled sleepily and stretched. He went into the bathroom and started the shower running. She could just hear the sound of his electric toothbrush over the water.

She got up and took her mug with her into the kitchen, where a small alcove served as an office of sorts for her. Turning on her computer, she sat down and sipped the strong brew while the hard drive booted up. John had insisted on getting her a new computer shortly after they were married. She did not think her old one was so bad until she had started using the new laptop. It was so much easier to use—quicker, too!

She clicked on the newsfeeds tab as usual, and quickly put her mug down in disbelief as the horrifying news unfolded before her. Israel had been attacked in the middle of the night. One of the headlines read, "An Act of God?" She clicked on it and started reading the account of the allied armies' invasion of Israel in the dark of night, just before dawn. It was a tale of utter confusion. As soon as the ground troops entered the mountains, they had encountered problems. Artillery and other ordnance detonated spontaneously, killing and injuring many. Some soldiers fired on their own troops in the midst of the ensuing chaos. Jets sent to drop bombs on the Jewish nation had crashed or blown up without reason. Not one of them had a chance to deliver their payloads. The strange thing, the report went on, was that the government of Israel, in a shambles due to the massive earthquake, claimed *it had been unable to coordinate its defense.*

"What?" Elena jumped up and ran back into the bedroom,

calling for John, who came out of the bathroom dripping wet, a towel wrapped hastily around his waist.

"What is it, Elena?"

She told him quickly about the attack on Israel and the earthquake. She started crying as she wondered if Teo and DC were all right. John pulled her down next to him on the bed and grabbed the phone, rapidly dialing DC's cell phone number. The call would not go through. John put the phone down.

"Listen, Elena. The lines are not working. I'm sure it's because of the earthquake and the invasion. No doubt thousands—hundreds of thousands—of anxious people are all trying to get through. We can't panic. I'm sure Teo and DC are fine."

The phone rang. John answered quickly, and Elena sighed with relief as he said, "Teo!" He handed the phone to her.

"Teo! Are you all right?"

Elena could hear sobbing on the other end. "Teo, it's okay. Honey, where are you right now?"

Teo sobbed and tried to speak, but it was obvious she was terrified. Elena could hear the deep tones of a man's voice asking for the phone.

"Elena."

She could not help it; her heart stopped as she heard Arturo's voice.

"Arturo," she said, hardly able to speak. Confusing emotions cascaded through her, clouding her thinking even more.

"Teo is beside herself. I have the doctor coming to give her something. She is safe here with me in Rome, but we don't know anything about DC. The American embassy was destroyed in the earthquake; I was able to find that out from my contacts. There are a few survivors, but as you may expect, the IDF search and rescue units are extremely busy right now. I will let you know what I find out. Rest assured, I will do whatever is necessary for Teo."

"But . . ." The phone clicked off before she could say anything more. Whatever emotions had been choking her a moment before at the sound of her ex-husband's voice fled at the flaming anger that overtook her now. She slammed the phone down and turned to John. "Teo's 'safe' for now with Arturo. She's hysterical, and he won't let me talk to her. He's *handling* it!"

John put a hand on her shoulder. "What about DC?"

"Arturo doesn't know. Oh, John, our embassy was destroyed! What if DC was there?" She choked back a panicked sob, and her husband pulled her onto his lap and wrapped his arms around her.

Jerusalem, Israel

DC woke up in pain. Something had hit the back of his head, and he sat up and touched the spot carefully. He could feel a big lump. He looked around him at the destruction clearly illuminated in the morning light. He must have been out for about an hour, judging from the position of the sun.

No one else was in sight. Odd. Surely his men would not have just left him there by himself. He could hear gunfire not too far away. He looked and saw smoke coming from the Temple Mount area. Standing, he surveyed the scene. The embassy had been completely destroyed. He walked over to the cavity that was still smoldering and peered into the dark hole. Surely no one could have survived in there. Picking up a discarded M4 on the ground next to his right foot, he started toward the gate. Amazingly, the fence around the perimeter of the embassy was intact and the gate was open. He walked out.

Devastation surrounded him. He could hear sirens, but not the sound of people anywhere near him. Again he heard gunfire, and he started toward the sound, in the direction of the Temple Mount. He remembered the meteor; it had been headed in that direction. He began walking that way.

He finally saw people, all covered in blood or dust or both

and looking shell-shocked. He noticed a few bodies, obviously dead, some crushed by all sorts of debris. A baby dressed in pink and white lay on the ground; he went over to check on her. A bent stroller on its side rested beside her. He could see the feet of a woman under a pile of bricks and glass nearby, probably the mother. He wondered if she had tried to push her child to safety. He got down on his right knee and touched the baby's throat to feel for a pulse. None. He could see no obvious signs of trauma. The child looked like she was merely sleeping. DC picked up the stroller, set it straight, and gently placed the baby in it, covering her with the embroidered blanket he found in the small basket underneath the stroller.

He was surprised at his own sense of calm in the face of so much horror, pain, and death. He continued walking. Buildings had collapsed everywhere, no doubt because the older buildings in the city had not been built to withstand earthquakes. DC recalled hearing somewhere that although the Israeli government had initiated a plan to bring the buildings in Jerusalem up to earthquake code, the red tape involved had discouraged any significant renovations. The last major earthquake in Israel had been in 1927, so the possibility had not seemed urgent.

The sound of gunfire was more sporadic now. DC turned a corner and stopped in amazement. Where the Dome of the Rock had stood, its gleaming gold dome splendid in the sun, was another crater. He stepped toward it, careful to stay near a wall or a building. As he drew closer, he saw that the whole Temple Mount area was filled with Orthodox Jews. The site was usually patrolled by Muslim security, the Wakf guards, but they were nowhere in sight. DC saw Israeli soldiers, though. He entered the area cautiously.

It was a surreal scene. Men and women were kneeling and praying. Others were cheering and clapping one another's backs in great joy. An IDF officer walked by, and DC asked him what was going on.

The young man grinned. "The Most High has interceded for His people! The enemies were killed in the north, and here, the Holy

One has rid us of the Dome! Men are already down there, inspecting." Tears ran down his face, and his voice broke. "Already we can see the evidence of the Temple there!" He pointed to the crater, embraced DC, and went on.

DC's head began throbbing harder, so he sat on a rock and just watched. Never had it occurred to him that the prophecies his parents, especially his mother, had so often talked about could possibly happen. Despite the pain in his head, he clearly remembered her saying the Temple would be rebuilt. But the Dome had stood in the way—until now. He watched, overwhelmed, while people celebrated around him. Thoughts raced through his mind as he tried to recall things his mother had said over the years. What was this supposed to be the beginning of? Was it Armageddon?

A rush of nausea hit him just then, with a force. He bent over to retch and then passed out in his own vomit.

Amtrak Station, Dodge City, Kansas

Father Martin read the magazine with amazement. Of course, he knew there were battles going on in Israel, some upheaval, but he'd had no idea of the extent of it. After all, the retreat center had been built and situated where it was for the sole purpose of helping people get away from it all. There was no Internet, no television, and no radio. All guests were required to surrender their cell phones when they entered St. Paul's Monastery in Kansas. He had no idea of the scope of what had gone on while he had been on retreat for the last month.

Set on the Midwest prairie, the monastery was completely isolated. Father Martin had enjoyed the time alone. He did not have to talk with anyone, and he had not. He had tried to read his Bible and pray, but most of the time, he had left in the morning with a small lunch in his rucksack and stayed out until dusk. He walked and thought. He was still no closer to any resolution, but he did feel rested.

He turned to the articles again instead of thinking about Cynthia and the confrontation that awaited him in Washington, DC. Pondering the news of the attempted invasion, Father Martin thought back to his youth when the United States had been at war with "terror." He and his brothers had loved watching videos on YouTube from Afghanistan and Iraq. The group of brothers had been especially exultant when a camera caught a terrorist suicide bomber blowing himself up too early. It seemed just. Their uncle had been killed by an extremist who thought he would get himself a thousand virgins for his trouble. Father Martin's brother called it "war porn." The young priest shook his head at the thought.

He picked up the newspaper he'd bought at the newsstand just before getting on the train. Thousands were dead in the Israeli mountains, with no accounting for the total defeat of the invading armies other than an act of God. One witness, a soldier, described the horror of trying to find his brother who was in another unit: "I made my way through the carnage. The few survivors I saw along the way told me to flee. As I got closer, I saw evidence that some sort of bombs had been detonated. Then I saw the bodies—the flesh had melted off them. There was no way to tell who was who. I turned and ran."

The report went on to detail that the devastation had been incredible and swift. Believing that the Israelis had fired nuclear weapons, the Russian president retaliated, authorizing use of nuclear missiles. However, the missiles had detonated prematurely despite accurate targeting and redundant fail-safe mechanisms, killing even more of the allied forces.

The front page declared it would be months before all the bodies in the Israeli mountains could be properly buried. Several mass graves were being prepared, some very deep, complete with containers able to be sealed airtight. Right beside the feature article was another discussing the Temple Mount area, now completely under Israeli control. Since the meteor had destroyed the Dome of the Rock, various groups that had been looking to rebuild the Temple had taken over the area. IDF troops now backed up these groups and stood guard. There were some Islamic protestors, but they were few and far between in Jerusalem. And many Jews who had been nominal in their faith were returning to the faith of their fathers.

The article's author surmised it would be only a matter of months before the building of the Third Temple would be completely underway. Father Martin marveled at the thought. At the moment, the article went on, archaeologists were combing the site, exploring and finding the religious relics that had been exposed. It was amazing! Groups that had, for decades, prepared for the rebuilding of the Temple were coming out of the woodwork. That quickly, everything was set for the Temple to be rebuilt and furnished.

Father Martin set down the paper and stared out at the changing landscape. So much in the world was changing so fast. Violence, war, floods, earthquakes, terrorism. He wondered if God had really come to Israel's defense. He knew many who would believe it. He was not sure. God had not come through for him, though he had served God faithfully. Sure, he had made a mistake with Cynthia, but no matter how he cried or prayed, God had not answered him.

He picked up his cell phone and thought about calling Cynthia. He put it down again. Soon enough. He would have to deal with it all soon enough.

Washington, DC

The coffee shop was empty except for Joseph. He rubbed his face and yawned. The last month had been exhausting. His church group had been organizing a blood drive for the past three weeks, and he had put together a recruitment team to solicit donors. Blood supplies were at a critical level throughout the world. Relief drives everywhere were gathering resources to help beleaguered areas that had been struck with devastating earthquakes and other disasters. Moscow in particular had been hit hard.

As spring approached, the Russian nation was suffering from intense flooding. Disease had broken out as well. Each of the nations involved in the attack on Israel had been beset by natural disasters, one after another. Some media sources speculated that the few survivors of the attack on Israel had surely been exposed to the biological weapons detonated in the isolated Israeli mountains, and these survivors had brought diseases back to Russia and the other allied nations. A strange shaking disease was running rampant among children from the nations that had attacked Israel. Once the neurological symptoms began manifesting themselves, the children rapidly deteriorated, becoming catatonic and then dying. Health-care providers and hospitals were overwhelmed by the devastation and disease.

It seemed to Joseph that every day brought news of another flood, earthquake, or tsunami. The United States also had to deal with such things, though not at such a profound level as the allied nations.

Bless those who bless you! Joseph thought wryly. In the months after the allied invasion, God's promise to Israel had once again proved true. That invasion, prophesied by Ezekiel centuries ago, had caused many people around the globe to come to faith in Jesus Christ. The Muslim dominance in Islamic nations had lessened significantly and Joseph marveled at how the many secret believers in those nations had begun to boldly proclaim the gospel message. A true revival was spreading all through the Middle East, except in Israel. Some there had converted to Yeshua, but the numbers were scant compared to surrounding nations. Although many Israelites had seen the Dome of the Rock destroyed by the meteor and considered the destruction of the armies to be an act of God, the Jewish nation had not turned to Jesus as Messiah. The synagogues, however, were full each week.

Joseph sighed. He knew what was coming and it gave him

no satisfaction. It made him pray all the more fervently, though. The door chime rang as the door was pushed open. Joseph looked up to see Father Martin coming in, a rueful smile on his face, probably because he was late.

Joseph stood up and gave the younger man a bear hug. "It's been so long since I've seen you, James! My goodness, have you been fasting the whole time you were gone on your retreat?" Joseph pulled back from his friend and looked at him with concern.

"Oh . . . well . . . lots of walking. I didn't have much of an appetite for the food, but that wasn't the point of going." Father Martin took a seat.

Joseph had ordered a pot of tea, and there was a small arrangement of fruit and pastries. The older man smiled at his friend and poured him a cup of tea.

"You look a bit worn yourself, Joseph." Father Martin took a sip carefully and put the cup on the saucer with deliberation.

"Ah, well, with the disasters, there has been a lot of need for volunteers."

"I was astounded when I left the monastery and saw the news for the first time. It's like the whole world is unraveling—wars, disasters of all kinds. Almost every day since I've been back, there have been some major catastrophes. And the stuff in Israel! The Dome destroyed, the Temple being rebuilt . . . it's almost as if we are living in the days of Noah—floods and all." The young priest chuckled nervously. "Not that it's really funny."

"No, it really is not funny. So, tell me, James, how are things going for you?"

"Since I've been back, I just don't seem able to do more than go through the motions," Father Martin admitted. He ran his hand through his hair distractedly. "Maybe I just need to buckle down and work harder. You know, prove I can be a team player."

"What does that mean, James?" inquired Joseph softly. He still had that nagging feeling that there was something very wrong. He had an idea what it was, but he could not be sure.

Father Martin shook his head to clear it. "You know, I'm just in one of those desert places people talk about. Listen, I know I was late and all, and I'm really sorry, but I have an appointment to get to. We'll have to get together again soon." He looked at Joseph but could not quite meet his eye.

"You know, if you have a problem, you can talk to me, James."

"Oh sure . . . it's just everyday kinds of things. Just keep me in your prayers," the young man said lightly.

"What's your appointment about? Are you sick?" Joseph pressed.

"Oh no, I have an appointment with Miss Grayson. I haven't seen her since my retreat. I just want to see how she's doing with everything," Father Martin said, a bit too brightly. "I'll give you a call next week, Joseph. You take care!" He stood up, shook his friend's hand, and rushed out the door.

Joseph stared after him and shook his head slowly. There really was nothing new under the sun. Resting his head between his hands, Joseph started praying silently for the young priest.

Rome, Italy

Teo got up from the hospital chair and stretched. DC was still unconscious after being found on the Temple Mount. Apparently, he had made his way there before collapsing and falling into a coma. Arturo had seen to DC's medical transport to Rome to insure he received the best care possible. The doctors called it an epidural hematoma. All they could do now was wait.

She walked over to the small table by the window and softly touched the flowers on it, white lilies in a vase from her half brother, Luca. She opened her purse and unzipped the side pocket. Taking out a tin of mints, she pulled up the bit of waxed paper from the bottom and took out one of the pills hidden underneath. She popped the pill into her mouth and swallowed with a sip of water from the bottle in her hand. She was almost out.

Looking at DC made her want to cry. No one could tell her what to expect because no one knew. She turned at the sound of a soft knock. The door opened, and one of DC's doctors came in. He smiled and quietly greeted her.

"Hello, Mrs. Bond. How are you this morning?" he inquired kindly, taking one of her hands in his.

"There is no change, Dr. Bruni." She thought quickly. "With all that has been going on, I forgot to bring my prescription with me from home. I am almost out of my medicine. I don't have a doctor here, and I was wondering if you could recommend someone?" She let a tear roll down her cheek unchecked.

"Oh, my dear, I am certain I can be of help. What is it you need? I can write you a script right now and have one of the nurses fill it for you at the pharmacy," he said, peering sympathetically at her over the top of his glasses.

"I just, well, I suffer from an anxiety disorder. After the terror attacks, it started up again. My doctor put me on benzodiazepines. They've really helped."

He looked concerned. "I see. How long have you taken these medications, Mrs. Bond? Those attacks were almost a year ago now, and these medications are meant to be used for short periods of time only."

Teo rushed to assure him, saying, "Oh, I haven't taken them the whole time, Dr. Bruni, just when the attacks happened and in the last few days since DC was hurt." She wondered if he could tell she was lying. She looked him straight in the eyes and smiled, tremulously. He patted her hand again and pulled a pad from his pocket.

ONE WILL BE TAKEN

Rome, Italy

Arturo stepped out of the shower and onto the plush, white mat. As he dried himself, he thought of the morning he had just spent with Judith. It had been far too long since he had been able to see her. Since Teo was at the hospital, he had taken the opportunity to surprise Judith at her hotel early in the morning. They had watched the sunrise after a rapturous time together.

Slipping into the robe that hung on the door, he noted the hotel logo with satisfaction. The exorbitant rates were well worth it for Judith's comfort—and his. He thought, not for the first time, how pleasant a wife she might make. There was some trite saying about a fourth time—or was it a third?

He walked over to the mirror and combed his thick, white hair. He was still quite attractive, he thought. Not what he had been in his prime, but still attractive. He thought of his other three wives in comparison with Judith.

Elena was quite the most beautiful, he had to admit. Even now, well over fifty, she was stunning. Her long auburn hair complemented her olive green eyes nicely. He had been quite enamored at first, but after their honeymoon, he had lost interest. She was not as adventurous as he would have liked, but there were other women to meet those needs. Her foolish insistence on her religion had spoiled the relationship.

He considered Sylvia. Dark-eyed Sylvia wasn't exactly beautiful, but she had seemed the perfect mother for his new son. She was devout, without her devotion truly affecting her behavior or thinking. She looked like a Madonna, innocence mixed with deep wisdom, but that was a façade. He could feel his blood pressure rising as he thought of the number of men with whom she had betrayed him.

He'd found that out only after discovering her with her latest conquest in his own bed. He had hired a private investigator and ended up with enough evidence to insure that Sylvia would not have any chance to see Luca, the son she claimed to have loved as if he were her own.

The short marriage to Cassandra he discounted—truly a lapse in good judgment.

Maybe marriage was not such a good idea, he thought glumly. Just then, he heard Judith call him from the next room. He opened the door and went eagerly back to the bedroom.

Rome, Italy

Stephen sat at the back of the busy restaurant and watched as Luca made his way to the table. The young man's extreme good looks were enough to guarantee most of the women's attention, and some of the men. Satisfaction permeated Stephen's mood, and he picked up his wine, sipping the expensive vintage appreciatively. Luca stopped here and there, shaking hands with those he knew from his government work and being introduced to others. Luca Romano Giamo was a rising star in Italy. His family pedigree accounted for some of his popularity, but his ready wit, good looks, and accessible charisma were propelling him forward with remarkable speed.

Stephen stood respectfully as his young master neared their table. "Luca, it is so good to see you."

Luca shook the older man's hand with a strong grip and smiled winningly. "Stephen, please, let's sit."

A waitress came over immediately to insure the young man had everything he needed, including a menu. She left hurriedly with his order for lemon water.

Luca looked after her shapely figure with a grin, then back at Stephen. "So, I am assuming all is going according to our plan? Billings has been meeting with World Union leaders in preparation for the opening ceremony of New Babylon?"

"Yes," Stephen confirmed, pausing to wipe his mouth with the linen napkin, then clearing his throat. "As you know, all of the recent disasters have affected the completion date for the city and the opening ceremony. But now everything is ready to inaugurate the city and open World Union headquarters. Billings has already garnered a seat on the disaster relief committee. Each nation has its appointed ambassadors, ready to take residence in New Babylon."

"With the rise in natural disasters, the increase in famines, and the civil unrest, how difficult do you think the next transition will be?" Luca inquired.

"Well, the United States is on the verge of collapse. Their debt was already substantial at the turn of the millennium, and now with all of the terror attacks, earthquakes, floods, tornadoes—not to mention all the years of war in the Middle East—they have very little interest in maintaining their dominant role in world affairs. The battles along the southern borders are spreading; their armed forces are very thin. President Jacobi is one of our own. His choice for World Union ambassador is going to be of great help to us.

"China is sending its own ambassador, as are many of the Asian nations. Most of the EU countries will want to send their own ambassadors. Australia and Canada are sending ambassadors as well. We will start off with many representatives, but in the next few years, I believe we will be able to organize the World Union into a truly cohesive government."

Luca nodded his head in agreement. "And I was asked just this morning by our president to be Italy's ambassador in New Babylon."

Stephen beamed. "So, our plans are on track, Luca!"

"Did you ever doubt it?" the young man inquired of his mentor. "He even thought it was his own idea!" Luca lifted his wine glass in a toast.

13

ARLINGTON,
VIRGINIA

Father Martin sat on his bed in the darkness and stared blankly at the clock in front of him. He had tried to sleep, but it was useless. He did not bother trying to pray, for the same reason. He thought back over the past week.

He had gone to see Cynthia, intending to somehow make amends. She was not at home. He tried calling her cell, over and over, but got no answer. He did not leave a message. What he needed to say could not be left in a voice mail.

Finally, tonight, he had gone to her house again. There was a car in the narrow driveway. He had gone to the door and knocked softly. Cynthia came to the door wrapped in a robe, loosely. He started to speak, but a man joined her. It was obvious what the priest had interrupted. He apologized quickly and left.

He did not know what to think. By breaking his vows, had he caused her to turn to promiscuity? Or had she turned to this other man when he had run away to the monastery? His cell had logged numerous calls from her while he was at St. Paul's.

Getting up, he went to the small kitchen and started making coffee. While it brewed, he cleaned the dishes in the sink. He decided he would try again. Cynthia deserved some answers from him and, to be honest, he had some questions of his own.

Rome, Italy

John helped Elena out of the taxi. They had taken the cab straight from the airport to the hospital. It had taken quite a few days to get a flight to Rome from Washington, DC and Elena was frantic with worry. John paid the driver and rushed in with Elena to the building.

Elena found the help desk and asked in fluent Italian for DC's room number. She thanked the woman and led John to a bank of elevators on their right.

"John, I'm worried. DC's parents weren't able to get tickets out. I feel guilty not giving them ours, but Teo sounded so strange." Tears filled Elena's eyes.

"We're here now, Elena. We'll see what is going on and help her," he assured his distraught wife.

The elevator doors opened silently, and the couple followed the signs on the wall to DC's room. The door was closed. Elena opened it carefully and peeked in. DC was in the bed and Teo was asleep in a chair right beside it. Elena and John entered the room quietly. John put their bags to the side.

"Teo," Elena said softly as she shook her daughter's shoulder gently. "We're here."

Teo woke up and blinked her eyes groggily. "Mom? I wasn't expecting you to come."

The young woman stood up, hugged her mother, and began to cry. "I'm so worried. No one can tell me anything, Mom! I've been here with DC for a week, and he hasn't even moved."

Elena turned to look at her son-in-law. His face was pale and drawn. She noted the IV and feeding tubes. At least he was not on a ventilator.

"They don't know when or even if he will wake up," Teo said, still tearful. "They don't know if there is any permanent damage. I'm at my wit's end. The world is going to hell in a hand basket. These earthquakes and meteors, and . . ." She stopped and began sobbing, then hugged her mother. "I can't face all of this without DC, Mom. I can't."

John watched the scene uncomfortably. He moved over to the bed as Elena whispered to Teo and comforted her. He noted that DC was exhibiting some rapid eye movement but decided not to get anyone's hope up. *It may just be something normal for a coma*, he thought.

The door opening interrupted his thoughts. He turned to see a very distinguished gentleman enter the room, along with a younger man that John recognized from photos as Luca, Teo's half brother. John saw his wife stiffen.

"Oh Stephen, I'm so glad you came!" Teo exclaimed as she gave the older man a hug and then moved to her younger brother. "Thank you for the flowers, Luca." She turned to indicate her mother and John. "I'm sure you remember my mother—and this is her husband, John Foster."

John shook hands with Stephen, wondering who he was, and then rotated to shake Luca's hand. John watched Luca with interest as the young man turned his charismatic charm on Elena. Luca began to speak to her in pure Castilian Spanish, a language she had learned at a young age spending summers with her cousins in Madrid. John could not understand much of what Luca was saying, but he spoke in soothing tones—something about being very sorry. A nurse came bustling into the room, and Luca switched effortlessly into Italian. John noticed the middle-aged woman blush as she smiled at Luca and then left the room quickly.

"I asked her to make sure my dear friend, Billings Mason, is shown up here right away," Luca said, looking at John with something akin to amusement in his eyes. He put his right hand on Teo's shoulder. "Teo, I've asked Billings to come here and heal DC. When Father told me the doctors had no insight into treatment, I knew that I had to call in a few favors for my brother-in-law."

John was amazed. Everyone in the world knew who Billings Mason was, but that he was on his way here as a personal favor to Teo's brother was incredible.

"Oh Luca, how can I thank you?" Teo cried. "With all of the devastation in Russia and the Middle East, I had not even hoped to ask! I know how busy he has been with his relief teams in the worst areas." She threw her arms around her brother. John thought Luca seemed stiff in the embrace, awkward in a way that seemed out of place in the self-assured young man. Maybe it was just the broken family dynamics.

The nurse came back into the room just then, escorting Billings Mason, a new cardinal in the Catholic Church. John had read about his appointment in a magazine just that morning on the airplane. From everything else John knew about the man, he was well on his way to sainthood. Not that John believed any of that sainthood stuff, but no one could argue with the fact that there was something otherworldly about the man. No one in the history of the world could do the things Billings had.

Luca greeted his friend warmly and introduced him to Teo, John, and then Elena. John was a bit taken aback when his wife took Billings' hand and kissed his ring, murmuring, "Your Eminence." He noted Billings was wearing the brown hooded habit of the Franciscan order, along with a red skullcap. John was sure Elena would know the name for it. He didn't mind his wife's Catholic faith but as a staunch American, he was uncomfortable with the royal treatment.

Billings Mason moved to the bed where DC still lay unconscious. The cardinal put his hands upon the patient and began to pray in a language with with which John was unfamiliar. He was startled when DC began to stir, then opened his eyes. Without any hesitation, as if he had only been asleep for a short nap, DC sat up and grinned at everyone in the crowded hospital room. "What's going on here?"

Laughter and expressions of delight greeted him. John stepped back to make room for the others. He moved against the far wall and watched the scene with the detachment of a reporter, taking mental notes. Something amazing was happening here. He observed the rapture on Elena's face and saw her kneel in front of Billings while Teo moved quickly to embrace her husband. She sat down on the bed next to him, and DC put his left arm around her.

"The last thing I remember is being on the Temple Mount," DC said, "and my head felt like it was about to explode on me."

"How are you feeling now?" Billings asked gently.

"Amazing. I feel incredible. Where am I?"

"In Rome," Teo said. "DC, Father organized your transfer here. You were found on the Temple Mount and taken to a hospital in Jerusalem."

John watched, smiling, as Billings put a hand on Teo's shoulder.

"And you, Teo. Luca told me that you have a desire to be healed as well."

"Oh, yes. I would," Teo said softly.

Billings bowed his head to pray, and the others in the room joined him—except Luca, John noted. The young man's head was uplifted, his face radiant with joy, his lips moving silently. John felt he was seeing something holy in that expression of faith, and he bowed his own head, embarrassed, as if he had been eavesdropping as Billings Mason began to pray for the healing of Teo's womb.

Appalachian Trail, Maryland

Joseph walked along the Appalachian Trail a bit behind the rest of his group. They had begun the hike near Weverton, Maryland, just before sunrise. With flashlights and lanterns in hand, they followed the trail to the cliffs overlooking the Potomac River. Almost two-thirds of the congregation had made it to the service. Some had gone back to one of the buses and returned to Arlington. The other bus was waiting in Harpers Ferry for those who wanted to hike down and enjoy the spectacular views and a sunrise service, complete with heartfelt worship, a good sermon, and Communion.

Smiling, Joseph recalled how his wife, Natalie, had once said that taking Communion put her in mind of the unity that believing Christians had with one another as well as with their Savior. She was always so intent and eager when she spoke about spiritual things. She would have loved to walk here along the trail on this autumn day. This was her favorite time of year.

As he looked at the bright yellows, burnt oranges, and brilliant reds of the foliage around him Joseph heard that quiet voice inside him speak, and he stopped walking. He sat on a large rock and listened. Joy filled his heart even as tears streamed down his face. He had been burdened for weeks over the "miracles" Billings Mason had been working. He seemed like such a good, caring man—a truly godly man. But every time Joseph saw or read about him, his stomach began to churn. Joseph had been praying for the Lord to show him if Billings was legitimate or false.

Many unbelievers made much of Jesus's words to "judge not," pulling the phrase completely out of context. Many Christians did as well. Those words were really about discernment with humility. Believers were commanded to examine the "fruit." Billings' miracles were surely good, but he never gave the glory of what he did to God. That's what first struck Joseph as off. Billings' transfer into the Catholic Church and his quick rise within its ecclesiastical power also concerned Joseph. He could see the signs of the times and knew that the Antichrist was about to come onto the world stage.

As Joseph sat and prayed, he felt the Lord confirm to him that Billings was not a believer, but a wolf in sheep's clothing. The mystery of lawlessness was indeed at work, but Joseph was reminded that Jesus had overcome the world, so not to fear. Joseph thanked the Lord, rejoicing in His presence. He sat there for a long time, praying, before he got up and continued his hike.

He thought about the devastation the world had undergone

in the past year. Not one nation was exempt from disaster. Terror attacks and one natural disaster after another had plagued the United States. Many of the troops overseas had been recalled because they were needed at home to help defend the southern border with Mexico. That nation was completely unraveling under the pressure of disasters and economic upheaval. Churches had seen a huge influx of new members, but unlike after 9/11, those new members had remained—perhaps due to the continued difficulties.

Joseph kept a sharp eye on the path ahead; it was steep and a bit rocky until it leveled out on the towpath along the river.

The United States was now becoming insular in its world role. *Really,* Joseph thought, *it is only to be expected.* The nation's problems had only increased after the Russian-led invasion of Israel. The US president, although not openly hostile to Israel (only because of the number of Christian constituents he would lose), would not do anything other than protest the invasion. He claimed America needed her warriors at home to take care of the homeland.

Finding the towpath ahead, Joseph quickened his pace to catch up with the rest of the group. They were all going to meet for frozen custard in town. He thought about Israel and the invasion. The destruction of the Dome of the Rock had led the way for the Temple to be rebuilt. Israel was even more secure after the destruction of the Russian and allied armies than it had been before, the surrounding nations cowed by the decisive victory and the apparent favor of God. It was obvious to many, both in Israel and in the rest of the world, that the Ezekiel prophesies had been fulfilled and, as a result, many in the world had come to faith in the Messiah.

There were many new believers in his congregation. Joseph thought that the number of faithful attendees had doubled. He and Rafa were leading classes for new believers. Both classes were full of people eager to learn more about Jesus Christ and their new faith. In all of his life, Joseph had never seen such a movement of faith. News agencies had dubbed it the Fourth Great Awakening and it was not confined to the United States; many nations of the world were seeing revival, especially those that had previously been Muslim.

As he entered the town, Joseph considered how the conversions to Christianity would alter some of the customs in those nations, particularly for women. Things were changing already. Women in Saudi Arabia could now drive cars and walk the streets without covering their faces. There were still many Muslims, of course, but they were being won over by the love of the new believers in their communities. There were also many stories of Jesus appearing to people in dreams and visions. It was like something out of the book of Acts in the New Testament.

Joseph wondered, as he looked around at the quaint town full of people, how much longer the Lord would wait. He prayed silently, *Come Lord, come quickly*. Ahead, he saw the bus parked across the street from the ice cream shop. He sped up, hoping to get an ice cream and a bottle of water for the trip back.

14

ALEXANDRIA,
VIRGINIA

Father Martin pulled his car to a stop across the street from Cynthia's house. She was on the front porch with a watering can. The sunlight gleamed on her red hair as she tucked it back behind her ear. She did that often, Father Martin recalled.

Conflicting thoughts raced through his mind. What right did he have to speak to her now? And what about the man who had been there the night before? He knew he did not have a reason to be jealous, but he was. Very. And how did that affect his role as priest? He hit his fist against the steering wheel and the horn blew. Glancing over, he saw Cynthia look up, and their eyes met. She put down the watering can and made her way across the street, her eyes locked on his the entire time.

Embarrassed, Father Martin got out of his car and closed the door. He looked down into her green eyes.

"You left before I could say anything to you the other night, James," she said quietly.

"It was obvious I was interrupting something," he replied, a hint of sarcasm in his voice. Right or wrong, he was still a man.

Cynthia smiled up at him crookedly. "Really? Like what?"

"You know exactly what. I'm not here to play games."

"Then why are you here, James?"

"I want an explanation," he said. Her face hardened with anger, so he quickly finished with, "and to explain." She looked a bit less tense.

"What explanation?"

"I had to leave, Cynthia. I broke my vows. What we did was so wrong."

"Was it? What exactly was wrong about it?" She took one of his hands in hers. "I missed you so much."

"Not for long, it seems," he said bitterly.

"James, that was my foster brother! If you had stayed, I would have introduced you to him. I had just jumped out of the shower. He was here for business and wanted to take me to dinner. I've had a very stressful few weeks—as you would have known if you had returned any of my calls."

Father Martin could feel his face redden with shame. "Cynthia, I have sinned against you over and over. First, in taking advantage of you. I had to leave on the retreat—it was ordered by my bishop. It gave me time to think. Now I see that I've hurt you more by not calling you to tell you and by misjudging you the other night. How can you even stand to talk with me? I've betrayed all of my vows. . . ."

Cynthia looked at their intertwined hands. "We fit together so well. I've done some research. Did you know that the priesthood was not always celibate? In fact, there's a movement now to return the Church to previous practices more in line with tradition." She smiled softly at him.

"Why would you do that, Cynthia?" Father Martin asked, puzzled.

"Because I'm pregnant with your baby. I know you've gone through a lot. I know you have vows you made—and broke. I've been telling myself for the past four weeks that it's because you love me that you broke those vows. Am I right?" She pressed her body closer to him.

Overwhelmed, he pulled her tight and kissed her softly, then with greater urgency and passion. Pulling back from the kiss, he looked intently into her eyes. "I think you are. I do love you, Cynthia. I'm willing to leave the priesthood and marry you and take care of our child. I've fought against it, but I can't stand to think of life without you." He kissed her again, intently.

"Come into the house with me, James," she breathed. "I want to show you how much I've missed you."

St. Michaels, Maryland

DC cast his rod into the water again. His father sat next to him on the small fishing boat they had used ever since DC was a young boy. David reached over and gave DC a squeeze on the shoulder. "You don't know how relieved your mom and I are, son."

"I guess now that Teo has been healed, I'll have a chance to find out for myself, Dad," said DC, grinning at his father. "I guess having kids is all about being worried and then relieved, huh?"

"Sometimes, DC, it feels that way," David chuckled. Then he pursed his lips together. "Look, DC, I am not complaining at all about your healing, or Teo's. But I am concerned. I think you know enough about what the Bible has to say about the end times to know why."

Annoyance at his father's words flickered across DC's face. The young man had expected his father to express this viewpoint, but still it was irritating. "Dad, listen. I was there. Billings Mason is not some scary antichrist out to rule the world. He's a guy who's really in touch with God. Only someone who is close to God could do the stuff he did. And if you could only have seen and felt what we did in the room when he healed me and Teo!"

"I didn't say he was the Antichrist, DC," his father began.

"I'm sure Mom has him pegged as some villain in the book of Revelation or Daniel, or whatever. Dad, listen. I don't get all of that stuff—the Apocalypse, the end of the world, and all. But I know good people when I see them. Billings is good. Even Teo's mom is a big fan now." DC slid her opinion in to add weight to his assurances.

151

"DC, do you know that the Bible says the Antichrist will look so good that even believers would be deceived if God didn't make it impossible? This guy does not give credit to Jesus Christ or even to God for what he does."

"Dad, I doubt the pope would have made him a cardinal if that were the case. I'm sure they've examined his faith carefully! You know even Mom thinks the new pope is a real believer, a true man of God who is trying to bring reformation to the faith."

"That, I cannot explain, DC. I don't know how all that works. Your mother and I are very concerned, though. And almost losing you makes us concerned even more about your relationship with God."

DC smiled. "Dad, actually I have one now. I see that God has given us life. He wants us to enjoy it to the fullest measure. In fact, Billings told me that God has begun a new work in mankind. Billings has been chosen to help inaugurate this new dispensation of grace, the final evolution of man. All that mankind has known until now, all of the holy books and religions were tutors, really. They were lights leading us to the truth. What you and Mom and others have known about God is just the tip of the iceberg. You have followed well the truth you knew, and you will be rewarded for it with more truth."

Casting his line again, DC missed the concerned expression on his father's face.

Washington, DC

Elena finished praying at the altar with tears of joy streaming down her cheeks. Four months after her healing at the hospital, Teo was pregnant. She had called early in the morning to tell her mother the good news. Elena was so grateful for the mended relationship, which was another thing healed at the hospital that day. Miracles. Miracles were happening again in the world. Surely that made the tragedies more bearable. God was still at work. Billings Mason was proof of that! Such a godly man . . .

Stepping outside into the bright sunlight, Elena searched for John, her right hand shading her eyes from the glare. It was hot, very hot for April. She hoped the electricity was working today. Since the last intense thunderstorms had hit the East Coast, many people were without power and had been for over a week. *Those poor men from the electric company are constantly busy with repairs,* she thought. It seemed like every day brought a new dilemma, not only in the United States but throughout the world. Cardinal Mason had called them "birth pangs" on an interview with the BBC last month.

A red convertible pulled up in front of her. John grinned at her. "Hey, pretty lady, would you like a lift?"

She smiled and got into the car. "John, wouldn't you like to put the top up and turn on the air?"

He sighed. "No, I think it makes it that much worse when we get home, Elena. Sorry to say, there is still no electricity. How was church?"

"It was good, John. Father Martin wasn't there but the priest who took his place gave a good homily. I wish you could have come with me," Elena said as she swept her hair up into a net she kept in the door pocket. The breeze at least cooled her off a bit.

"I know, but the meeting was important. I have good news, Elena! News to celebrate, really."

"What is it? Did you get an offer for another book?"

"No, even better. I've been offered a job at the *New Babylon Post* as a reporter. I'll have my own byline. What do you think? It will mean moving, of course."

Elena turned and stared at her husband. "You will not believe this, John, but Teo told me this morning that DC is being assigned to New Babylon. I was happy to hear about the baby, but so sad they would be half a world away. And now—God is answering all my prayers!" She leaned over and hugged him, laughing with delight.

ONE WILL BE TAKEN

New Babylon, Iraq

The guide pointed to the inscription on the gold-colored bricks and read the interpretation in English for the select crowd standing patiently in the heat around him. "In the era of President Hussein, all Babylon was constructed in three stages. From Nebuchadnezzar to Saddam Hussein, Babylon is rising again."

Arturo took a crisp linen handkerchief from his pocket and dabbed the sweat on his face as he listened to the guide describe the history of New Babylon's restoration. He looked at the port in the distance. Large cargo ships berthed next to cruise liners. Babylon was open not only for World Union governing officials and ambassadors but also for tourists and businesspeople. He and Judith had traveled in opulent style on the *Crystal Amethyst,* one of the newest vessels in the exclusive Wortherford fleet. His assistant had booked one of the lavish penthouse suites for them. They had enjoyed their accommodations and the excellent service of their private butler and chef, but had decided it would be pleasant to stay in New Babylon at the newest Four Seasons hotel, The Amytis, for all of the dedication ceremonies they would be attending through the week.

Both he and Judith had been impressed when their limousine had pulled up to the exquisite hotel. Judith remarked it was like the hanging gardens of the École Polytechnique in Paris, but on a much larger and lush scale. There was an almost otherworldly balance of greenery and flowers, parting here and there to reveal seemingly ancient marble slabs carved in styles reminiscent of the most antiquated buildings in Rome. He and Judith had been treated to a fine luncheon in their suite before embarking on the VIP tour of the city. The tour was quite interesting, but hot, and Arturo looked forward to getting back into their air-conditioned bus.

The guide continued down the street. "As you may know,

the Americans used Babylon as the headquarters for the First Marine Expeditionary Force after Saddam's defeat in the war. They have remained, courtesy of the US State Department, as protectors for this historic site. There was need for many years to guard the archaeologists and workforce personnel from those who did not share the vision of UNESCO, which was then, of course, under the authority of the UN. After the collapse of that organization and the rise of the more effective World Union body, UNESCO continued under the WU. It and the World Monuments Fund have supplied experts to oversee the rebuilding of New Babylon. You will note that although New Babylon retains its historicity, it is furnished with all of the pleasant attributes modern technology can deliver.

"Much like the beefeaters at the Tower of London, US Marines have continued their role as guardians for New Babylon, along with representative elite soldiers from many nations. As you know, it is World Union's goal to create true unity in diversity. As families and friends of World Union ambassadors, you realize more than many, I am certain, the great hope that lies in their hands. It is the hope of the nations involved to create a governing body that can effectively deal with the new problems the world faces in view of the increasingly difficult times we have endured."

The group followed the guide as he spoke, climbing the steps of the coliseum that had been rebuilt by Saddam Hussein's labor force. "Part of New Babylon was reconstructed under the direction of Saddam. You will see his name inscribed on many of the bricks. The majority of the rebuilding of New Babylon, including the new walls and infrastructure, was accomplished by UNESCO and the WMF. Officials were able to convince the German government to return the Iraqi artifacts it had absconded with during World War II. The Louvre and British Museum graciously returned all of their artifacts as well.

"The Ishtar Gate you saw earlier is a replica. All original artifacts are kept securely in the Museum of Man. At tonight's dinner, you will have time to view many of these artifacts. The curators have assigned each of you a private tour, where a docent will answer any questions you have."

Judith squeezed Arturo's hand and smiled seductively at him. "I think I need a nice long shower when we get back to our suite, Arturo."

The guide droned on as Arturo thought of all he and Judith could do in the expansive bathroom at the hotel.

New Babylon, Iraq

Luca walked around the outside of Italy's villa in New Babylon with the designing architect. Each nation had been given two acres of land on which to build a residence for its ambassador; the allotments were parceled out neatly along the wide avenue. The embassy offices were housed in the massive complex of the World Union headquarters. Ambassador Row was to the east of the Street of Processions. The Italian president himself had selected Giorgio Bianchi to build a villa that fittingly represented the Italian people.

The white villa was spectacular. At the front of the structure, each room on the upper floors opened onto a balcony, while those on the lower floor opened onto an extended, enclosed patio. The stark whiteness of the traditional building stood in contrast to the spectacular trees and gardens. Giorgio's partner and husband, Marcus Russo, had designed the gardens. Citrus trees heavy with lemons, oranges, and grapefruit scented the air. Mature palms, groves of chicos, bougainvillea, clusters of camellias, and other flowers had been brought in. Built-in sprinklers ensured the lush green of the grass and vegetation. The effect of it all gave the residence a true feel of Italy.

"You've outdone yourselves, gentlemen!" Luca exclaimed. His blue eyes glowed with pleasure as he smiled at the men. "The fountain in the front of the villa is a work of art. Italy has been very well represented in your work."

ONE WILL BE TAKEN

"Thank you, Mr. Ambassador," beamed Giorgio. "It is our hope that you find the inside of the residence as gratifying. I designed your suite at the top of the villa. Shall we go up and work our way down?"

Luca followed the architect through the arched front door and up the staircase.

"There is an elevator, of course, sir, but I was told by Mr. Amona that you prefer to take stairs," Giorgio giggled. The handsome young ambassador made him feel a bit giddy.

The central staircase led to the second floor. They walked through a wide, spacious hall right in front of them to another staircase. The white balustrades crisply framed the blackened stairway. Luca liked the contrast. With a flourish, Giorgio flung the double doors open to reveal an exquisite suite.

The room was furnished in a stunningly simple manner, a perfect foil for the spectacular view outside of the sliding glass wall leading onto the covered patio. Luca had asked that the master bedroom suite face the rear of the property, knowing that at this level, he would have an unobstructed view of Nin Makh's Temple, a place of ancient power.

Walking toward the balcony, Luca let his thoughts run to the ancient stories of gods and goddesses worshipped by the Babylonians. Centuries of men and women had worshipped their gods in this city. They had even tried to build an edifice that reached to heaven itself, coating its façade with tar so the Almighty could not destroy it with a flood. Instead, He had confused the language of men, or so the tale went.

Giorgio and Marcus chatted quietly with one another in the bedroom, leaving Luca alone with his thoughts. He couldn't see the well inside Nin Makh's Temple, but he knew it was there. Legend had it that God had suspended two angels in it, just out of reach of the water, in punishment for failing to cleanse Babylon. In his nightly commune with his true Father, Luca was learning the truth behind many of those legends.

The truth was that there was an intense battle going on in the universe between beings superior to man. Luca's Father was on one side of the conflict; "God" was on the other. His Father had once been a true follower of this God, but had come to see the truth—that God only wanted power for himself. To do that, he had withheld power and knowledge from others. Luca's Father had led a rebellion and won. There were still skirmishes, but the ancient king was now able to exert his authority over the world of men. He had chosen this auspicious time to create and reveal his son, Luca.

Luca could feel the ancient spiritual power here in Babylon. The city was one of his Father's earliest victories. There were strong spirits here still bound by the enemy. Some were in the Euphrates River itself; others would be reached soon through the well in Nin Makh's Temple. His true Father had assured Luca that the enemy who restrained them was weakening. Indeed, Luca could sense that himself. He looked forward to their final victory and to claiming his rightful place over the world of men.

"You have truly made this one of the most beautiful residences here in Babylon. Italy's villa outshines all of the other ambassadors' residences!" Luca turned from his thoughts to thank the two men. "I am truly impressed." He shook the hands of both men. "I hope to see you at tonight's dedication."

15

LONDON,
ENGLAND

The BBC reporter put on her reading glasses, perusing the notes she had on her guest, Cardinal Billings Mason. He was promoting his new book, *What God Wants You to Know*. From the research notes in front of her, Kate Havenstone could see he hardly needed to promote it. In the first week, it hit number one on *The New York Times* best-seller list, and after six weeks it had not moved from that spot.

She took off her glasses to allow a last powdering of her face and took a sip of her lukewarm coffee through a straw. The flurry of excitement that filled the room announced Billings' entrance on the set. Smiling, he took the seat next to her and shook her hand.

Kate could not help but smile in return. Billings Mason exuded goodwill and cheer. Dressed in the plain black of a parish priest and sporting a new goatee, he resembled a younger and fitter Father Christmas.

"It is such an honor to meet you, Cardinal Mason! I'm quite excited to begin our interview," she gushed.

Billings smiled modestly and patted her hand. "I am so pleased to be here, Kate. You are one of the most respected reporters in the UK, if not the world. I so appreciated your coverage of the attacks on the United States. It was definitely worthy of the Pulitzer you received."

"We go live in five minutes," Kate told him. "Would you like something other than the water here?"

"No, thank you, I'm quite fine." They chatted for the few minutes leading up to the show's pre-taped introduction.

Kate turned toward the camera's red light. "Good evening! Tonight I have the distinct privilege of interviewing Cardinal Mason about his new book, *What God Wants You to Know*. She turned toward Billings Mason and smiled. "Welcome, sir."

"Thank you, Kate. It's an honor for me to be here to talk about my book."

"I have to admit I found the book so amazing that I've already read it twice! It's so profound, Cardinal, that I had to read it slowly in order to digest the remarkable things you reveal in it."

"I'm thankful to be the vessel through which the truth is being revealed to mankind. We need truth in these dark times, don't we, Kate? To give us hope? Better times are coming. What we are experiencing now are just birth pangs. Mankind began as one people. We were separated because of evil, and now God wants us to know we are in that birthing process of being reunited," Billings explained.

"It interested me to see how all religions are really segments of the truth. After the conflict in Israel and the destruction of the Dome of the Rock, many people turned to Christianity, including millions throughout the Middle East. I believe the Catholic Church itself saw a big increase in membership. How does the exclusivity of Christian doctrine allow for this new teaching of yours?" Kate tapped on her copy of Billings' book for emphasis. She had a reputation for being hard but fair as a reporter, and despite all the good she knew about Billings, she still had questions.

"Yes, well, that exclusivity you mention is actually a misrepresentation of the Christian religion. People who are dogmatic about the Bible have given the Christian religion a bad reputation. I think Gandhi said it best: 'I like your Christ. I do not like your Christians. Your Christians are so unlike your Christ.'

"Christianity is not the whole truth, but it is part of the truth, Kate. I have had the blessing of revelations from the True God. He has shown me how all of these parts will come together as a whole. Mankind was divided long ago, not of our own doing. In our separate states, we could only have parts of the truth. Now that we are coming together in true unity—politically and economically—we can be united spiritually as well. Think about it, Kate—a world with no more crusades or terrorist bombings or crimes committed in the name of any god, but unity in the one True God! Technology has enabled this unification process to begin. Distance and language, Kate, no longer separate us. We are seeing a new, common culture emerge." Billings leaned toward Kate in earnestness.

"Well, Cardinal, you have certainly been given some pretty significant gifts. You have healed many people of cancer and profound injuries, and you have even raised the dead as we saw in Florida and in Africa. Your book contains some prophetic statements as well. Would you care to share any with our viewers?"

"Actually, this morning as I was praying, I received another prophetic word, Kate," he said, turning to the camera. "I would like each of you to be at peace as I share this revelation with you. We will come through a new birth together. All will be well. This week, as you know, New Babylon has welcomed all of the World Union ambassadors. On Friday, they begin their mission to unite the nations of this world. This is a wondrous thing, a huge step for mankind in regaining our unity. As we draw closer to that unification, birth pangs will increase in frequency and strength. The pain is necessary for our 'delivery,' if you will. In the next week, we will experience a blackout caused by volcanic eruptions. Thick clouds of volcanic ash will keep us in darkness for a while, a short while. Prepare your homes. Buy the food and items you need. Preparation is the key." Billings faced the camera. "Think of this as the darkness before the dawn of a new age, an age of peace and prosperity the world has never known."

"Where will this happen, Cardinal Mason? In Europe, as it did in the early years of the millennium?" Kate inquired.

"No, my dear, not just in Europe. The whole world will be affected," he replied with certainty.

ONE WILL BE TAKEN

"How can you be sure of this? Volcanic eruptions are difficult for scientists to predict," Kate protested.

"The True God has revealed it to me, to validate His truth and demonstrate His power. This world has long been in darkness. We will be in darkness for a short time, and then the light will shine. We have been in darkness, but the new age of light is coming soon." Billings spoke with simple certainty.

Kate Havenstone looked troubled and serious. Her favorite cameraman, Christopher, recognized the expression. *Now he's in for it,* Christopher thought.

"Excuse me, Cardinal Mason. You have become a Catholic cardinal. The things you have written and are saying are in stark opposition to Pope Clement's teachings and attempts for revival within the Catholic tradition. Why accept the designation and duties of a cardinal if you are in opposition to the leadership of the Catholic Church?"

Billings Mason stifled a smile and for an instant looked smug. That expression changed quickly to rueful humility as he spoke. "Ah, but my dear, the true leader of every church and denomination is the True God. I am sure you remember Fatima?"

Kate looked confused. "Fatima? What does that have to do with my question?"

"My dear, the third secret of Fatima—what the Catholic Church has kept secret all of these years. That apostasy would come, that the pope himself would fall victim to false teachings and errors and stop teaching the true Catholic religion. This is true of Pope Clement, with his focus on the Bible and the gospel message. It is not his fault though, my dear. There is misunderstanding and deception in many arenas of faith. The coming worldwide blackout is meant to show mankind that we do not see, in truth, but we are like men and women walking in the dark. We think we know what we see, but the truth is revealed in the light. The true light is coming into the world. Hope is about to be fulfilled. The desire of the nations for peace and prosperity is about to be revealed."

Kate sighed heavily, confused. "Well, with that our time is up, Cardinal Mason. Thank you for coming and sharing your insights with us." She turned to the camera. "We'll return after the break."

Washington, DC

Bishop Ellis sat quietly. Father Martin wished he would say something.

"Bishop Ellis, I know you're surprised that I want to leave the priesthood. I—"

"Actually, Father Martin, I'm not surprised," Bishop Ellis interrupted. "I am concerned, though," he said slowly and thoughtfully, "because you are not being entirely honest with me. I'm not sure you are being honest with yourself either."

Father Martin could feel his face flush with heat. He intended to keep Cynthia's pregnancy quiet—and the circumstances that led to it. "I'm not sure what you mean, Bishop Ellis. I've been struggling with this decision for a while now."

The older man sighed. "Father Martin, I've seen a lot in my years of service to the Lord. I've seen many scandals and all-too-common sins involving the clergy. I've seen a change in you in the last year. You've gone from having passion for serving in the church, to rebellious anger, and now to indifference. In my experience, that is often the result of dabbling in something, some sin perhaps."

Father Martin felt pinned in place by the compassionate gaze of Bishop Ellis's clear blue eyes. He swallowed. "I am going to get married, Bishop Ellis. I'm in love." He could feel the heat spread through his entire body.

The bishop nodded. "Well, there is no sin in that, Father Martin. I hope that you know that. Who is it that you intend to marry?"

"Cynthia Grayson, sir," he sighed.

Bishop Ellis looked surprised. "I don't know what to say,

James," the bishop said, addressing the young priest informally and personally. "I've known Cynthia since her parents adopted her years ago. You know that her father and I are friends. He told me last night that she is pregnant, but she wouldn't tell him who the father is. She said it was complicated."

"Bishop Ellis, I never intended to . . ." Father Martin said, then stopped, spreading his hands out in front of him. "It just happened."

"James—"

"No, listen, Bishop Ellis. I know I've sinned. I tried to pray and resist this. I tried to repent and consecrate myself. Over and over I prayed and fasted and took part in Mass, but it was useless. There was no joy or meaning in it anymore. When I saw Cynthia again and found out about the baby, there seemed to be some good in the whole thing."

"James, there's a difference between faith and form. This is what I've been trying to make you see in our conversations together over the past year. You have faith in the form, not in the Savior. When you became the most popular priest at Holy Apostles, it wasn't that the other men were jealous of you. They were concerned that you knew the right answers without knowing the right questions."

"What do you mean? I believe in the Savior!" Father Martin exclaimed indignantly. "Whom do you think I've been serving all these years?"

"Your ego, perhaps? You are intelligent and well-spoken. You have natural charisma, James. Belief is not just intellectual assent. God did not let you down, son. You have been relying on your performance to make you right with God. Since you sinned, no penance has seemed enough for you to feel better about what you have done. Am I right?"

Father Martin nodded. "I prayed and prayed. It just didn't work. I couldn't stop thinking about her, and when I see her—it's just useless. I can't be a priest anymore. Please don't try to convince me."

"I'm not trying to convince you of that, James. I agree; you should not be a priest. My concern is for your soul. I am also concerned about your relationship with Cynthia. She is not at all suitable for you."

Father Martin exploded in anger, shouting, "I knew you would start on her! Cynthia is a fine woman. I took advantage of my position as her priest, but the love we have is very real. I am going to marry her, and there is nothing you can say to change that!" He got up and left, slamming the door behind him.

Bishop Paul Ellis shook his head. *If only he would listen! I've known that wretched girl for too long to be fooled by her ways. James has no idea what she really is.* He could only pray for his young friend.

New Babylon, Iraq

DC grinned at Teo across the table. She was stuffing the last bit of a cheeseburger into her mouth. She swallowed and grinned back at him. "That was so good!"

"Let's hope you keep it down, sweetie! I've never seen you eat like that. I'm amazed!"

Teo kicked him playfully under the table. "Hey, it takes a lot to grow a baby. I just can't get over how often I want to eat. It's nice after three months of 'morning sickness' that lasted all day!"

"Are you looking forward to the dedication ceremony tomorrow night?" DC took a sip of his beer. It was wonderful after being out in the heat.

"I am. My father is very excited and proud. Luca is the youngest ambassador by far—and the most handsome! Did I tell you that Mom and John are also going to be there? John's covering the event for the *New Babylon Post.* Mom is a bit nervous about my father being there." Teo nodded to their waiter as he passed their table.

"Yes, ma'am? Would you care for more water?" he inquired

solicitously.

"Actually, I would love to see the dessert menu," she said. He nodded and moved off, returning quickly with the menu. "Thanks!"

"Why is your mom nervous? She and your father have been divorced for over twenty years now. She's remarried. I don't get it."

"Hopefully you'll never have to, DC! I think it's really just all built up in her mind because she hasn't seen him face-to-face in years. Even though she left him, I think she feels he betrayed her, and that left her very wounded."

DC took his wife's hand and played with her fingers. "You know, Teo, you and your mom have come a long way. I'm proud of you. You've really made an effort since that day at the hospital."

"I feel as though Cardinal Mason did more than heal my body, DC. I was desperate in so many ways before then. I think I had lost hope—not just in having our own baby, but in life. All of the devastation, from the terror attacks in the United States to the natural disasters everywhere. I didn't feel like there was a safe place to be. When you were injured in the meteor strike, I was so stressed. I couldn't handle the thought of losing you." Tears rolled down her face, even though she was smiling. "That moment when you woke up, just like you had been sleeping, was one of the best moments of my entire life. Then, when he healed me as well—I cannot explain the joy I felt . . . the love.

"When we were watching the news last night and Cardinal Mason was talking about the coming problems, I wasn't afraid like I had been. I mean, it's frightening to think there will be more problems, volcanic ash, and more 'birth pangs,' but the hope that we have, DC! We are at the dawn of a new era in history. Our child will be able to live in a much better world. We have so much to be grateful for, don't we?"

Nodding, DC agreed with his wife. "I'm thankful for you, Teo, and our life together. Living here in New Babylon is going to be wonderful. Hot, but wonderful."

ONE WILL BE TAKEN

Arlington, Virginia

Joseph put down the phone. He had been trying to get a hold of Father Martin for the last week. Still no answer, and he was not returning Joseph's phone calls. Joseph had a feeling something was not good with his young friend.

Pulling on his shoes, he headed out the door of his apartment. The heat outside hit him. This was usually a beautiful time of year in the DC area. Cherry, pear, and apple trees in bloom, and the daffodils, tulips, and other spring flowers made the DC metro area a lovely destination for tourists. The heat was affecting everything and everyone negatively. Rolling electrical blackouts were also causing trouble for many people.

It's only going to get more difficult, Joseph thought with a heavy heart. *Lord, I know it's going to get worse, and then when You return, it will be wonderful. I just pray for all of those who will have to live through it all.*

As he entered the coffee shop, he spotted his pastor sitting at a small table in the back. Walking over, Joseph put a hand on his shoulder. "Hi Pastor Kogen, it is good to see you. Do you mind if I join you?"

Moshe Kogen stood up and gave his friend a hug. "Joseph! Sure, have a seat. I had no power at home this morning and I needed my coffee and air-conditioning!"

Joseph sat down and thanked the waitress for the coffee she put in front of him.

"Would you like a muffin this morning, Joseph? Lemon with poppy seeds, baked fresh this morning," she said.

"Sounds wonderful, Suzanne. Thank you."

"So, did you see the interview last night with Cardinal Mason?" Pastor Kogen asked.

"He's quite a deceiver, isn't he? What do you make of his comments about Fatima?"

Moshe wiped his mouth with the paper napkin and put it back on his lap. "He certainly fits the description of a wolf in sheep's clothing, doesn't he? I've been thinking about that, Joseph. I think he is laying the groundwork to discredit the pope.

"Pope Clement has done a lot to restore the Catholic Church to its original adherence to scriptural authority rather than to man-made traditions. He had a rough time of it until the destruction of the Temple. Many are turning to the Word of God. The devil hates that, and you and I both know that this new cardinal does not serve Jesus Christ."

"But what good will it do him to discredit Pope Clement? And could he really succeed in that? Clement hasn't performed miracles but there is no denying he is a godly man," Joseph said.

"It would serve him in taking over the Church," Moshe replied. "Think about it, Joseph. Since the armies attacking Israel were destroyed and the meteor demolished the Dome of the Rock, Islam has become impotent. Millions have turned to Christ in the Middle East and throughout the world, many of them drawn to the beauty of the higher church traditions. The Catholic Church has more members than any other denomination."

"Still, Pastor, I don't recall any time in history when a pope has been removed from his position," Joseph protested.

"I looked into it this morning," Moshe said, gesturing to his laptop on the table. "There is precedence for it."

"Do you think Billings might be the Antichrist, then?"

"No. Remember that Daniel's prophecy indicated the Antichrist would be from the people who destroyed the city and the sanctuary. That was the Romans, so the Antichrist will be of Roman origin—Italian. Billings is an American. He's in a position of religious influence, Joseph. Look at how he's mixing the teachings of Christianity with false doctrines. He's setting the stage, definitely."

Joseph pushed his coffee mug away. "Then you think he is the False Prophet?"

"I do. The time is near, my friend. Most of our time needs to be spent ministering to the body of believers here and sharing the gospel hope with everyone we can."

"Yes, Pastor. My Natalie used to say we need to watch, wait, and look for His coming for us. We don't know the day or hour, but we surely can recognize the season. I've been thinking a lot more of her lately. I'm looking forward to seeing her again," Joseph said, his eyes lit up with a smile.

Moshe Kogen raised his coffee mug in toast. "To the great reunion, Joseph!"

Joseph picked up his own mug for the toast. "Amen!"

16

NEW BABYLON,
IRAQ

John Foster looked around the glittering crowd as people mingled among the ancient artifacts, sipping wine and tasting the hors d'oeuvres carried by young men and women dressed in the costumes of ancient Babylon. Carefully, he carried both glasses of wine over to the large windows facing west. The sun was just setting, and Elena stood gazing at the glorious colors reflected in the man-made lake below.

Handing her a glass, John turned to enjoy the view as well. "The Museum of Man is incredible, isn't it, Elena?"

"I can't get over how this lake has been designed, John. I'm sure I remember an old textbook my father had that had a picture in it just like this."

"That might well be," John explained. "I was speaking to the museum's curator, Javad Parisi, while we waited in line for drinks. He told me the museum was modeled after some sketches done by an archaeologist in the 1800s. The lake and man-made islands on it were also in the sketch."

"It's absolutely beautiful. I love the way the palm trees are silhouetted against the sunset. Do you think we could ride in one of those boats sometime, John?" She pointed to the boats on the lake below, their prows curved like sea monsters. Some had wings rising from the sides, making the figures resemble dragons landing on the water.

John grinned. "I suppose so." He invited Elena outside to the vast patio, which also overlooked the lake.

Elena's turquoise dress billowed in the breeze, emphasizing her slim figure. John wrapped his free arm around his bride. The massive Museum of Man reminded him of a large, white wedding cake, he realized. The base of it was pillared. The top two levels were also pillared, but they decreased in size, each level leading out to separate garden areas. The patio he and Elena were on was full of potted plants—even large trees—and, of course, flowers. Babylon had been famous for its hanging gardens, and the designers of New Babylon had successfully recreated that ancient wonder. Both John and Elena had been amazed at the beauty that bloomed in the desert.

"Have you seen DC and Teo?" John asked.

"Not yet. Of course, they will be at Luca's table with Arturo." Elena's mouth had tightened as she spoke.

John squeezed his wife's waist. "You need to relax about him, Elena. Things are going well with you and Teo. Arturo is her father and nothing can change that fact. He is a part of her life."

Elena looked into her husband's eyes. "I hope you don't think I still have feelings for him, John."

"No, I know how you feel about him, Elena. I understand you are just concerned about his influence on Teo. But she's an adult. I think you are going to have to let her make her own choices."

"I understand that, John. But there is something very dark about Arturo. I just want to make sure Teo doesn't get hurt," she said softly. "He has a way of hurting those he is supposed to love."

"Well, there he is now with DC and Teo," John said, nodding toward the large gallery the trio had just come from. "How about we go and say hello before dinner begins?"

He and Elena walked into the gallery together.

ONE WILL BE TAKEN

New Babylon, Iraq

DC surveyed the platter of sweets on the table with interest and, although he did not usually like sweets, picked up something that resembled baklava. He could not even begin to count how many layers had been hand rolled around the pine nuts and drizzled with honey. Then he noticed Teo smiling at him.

"So I see you're enjoying the local cuisine, DC," she teased in a whisper. "I think you've had five of the ones with the pistachios."

"Hey, you're eating for two and I'm a sympathetic eater," he joked.

Arturo turned and motioned to them. "I think the ceremony is about to begin." Teo and DC were seated with their backs to the stage, so they stood up and turned their chairs around. DC rested his arm around the back of his wife's chair. He could just make out the small curve of her belly where their child was growing. Teo noticed and put her right hand affectionately on her stomach.

A thin gentleman approached the podium and greeted the crowd. "Welcome, ladies and gentlemen, to the first of this week's ceremonies for the inauguration of the first world capital, New Babylon!" Applause erupted throughout the room. Cameras from each of the major media outlets panned the crowd, capturing images of the well-dressed officials, world leaders, and celebrities. Each of the ceremonies was being broadcast throughout the world.

"Tonight we have the distinct pleasure of opening the Museum of Man. I am Javad Parisi, and I have the good fortune to be the curator of this amazing museum. We wish to thank the British Museum, the Pergamon Museum, and the other museums of the world for returning to Babylon the treasures that belong to this ancient place," he said, waiting for the applause to die down. "We are truly grateful to have them housed here where many may view the artifacts in their place of origin.

"I would like to introduce to you a man who truly needs no introduction. For years he has served as a humanitarian as our world has suffered through increases in natural disasters, terror attacks, and war. In the past year especially, he has served mankind in miraculous ways. Ladies and gentlemen, please welcome tonight's speaker, His Eminence, Cardinal Billings Mason!"

Applause again erupted throughout the room as Cardinal Billings Mason rose from his table and moved to the podium. DC could see the cardinal, dressed in his black robes edged in scarlet, stopping along the way to shake a hand or embrace an old friend. Throughout the room, people began to stand, and the applause grew louder as Cardinal Mason climbed the stairs to the stage and stood before the microphone. He nodded acknowledgement with a smile. The video screens discreetly placed to the sides of the stage allowed DC to see Billings' expression. A tear rolled down the cardinal's face as he spoke.

"I am so humbled by your affection! Thank you. Thank you all. Please, sit down everyone." He surreptitiously wiped his eye. "I am honored to be here tonight." He waited a moment while people took their seats.

"As I walked through the museum this evening, I noticed a very special exhibit. I'd seen a reproduction years ago in the United Nations buildings that once stood in New York and was fortunate to see the original in the British Museum after I finished my doctorate. Now I am so pleased to see the Cyrus Cylinder—the first known example of a human bill of rights—in its place of origin, Babylon. "Many do not realize that my own country, the United States, owes a great debt to Cyrus the Great. His biography, the *Cyropaedia of Xenophon,* was an influence in ancient times and in the Renaissance. Thomas Jefferson, the crafter of the Declaration of Independence, was influenced by this book as well. He owned two editions.

"Cyrus was a great ruler who valued humanity and freedom for all and guaranteed religious freedom. He believed that government should be benevolent, and his was. This Persian leader, who conquered the great city we are now in, was one of the greatest the world has ever known, and yet his name is not well known today.

"Mankind has lost much of the knowledge it once had. We have devolved to the point where we have had to make a choice to band together as human beings, or face extinction. Through our indifference, the earth has become polluted, much of our farmland blighted by our own excesses. Terror attacks and localized war have given way to tyranny in many countries. Now natural disasters are increasing exponentially. With the United Nations, we tried to address our problems, but that institution was impotent. Its factious nature led to its demise. This new capital, the new economy that will be established here, the new governing body that will commence here—these are our great hope."

The room thundered with applause.

"Cyrus understood that greatness is achieved through great effort and sacrifice. He established a mighty empire, yet he did not trample upon the individual man's dignity and rights to liberty and justice. His was a rule of true freedom, and I believe that mankind can return to that sort of rule once again, under the governing hand of this, the World Union."

DC felt as if Billings were talking directly to him. As the cardinal faced the camera, his blue eyes glittered with emotion. "I believe the best is yet to be. We are at the dawn of a new age, an age of peace and prosperity. There is great reason to be hopeful. Now freedom—real freedom—will be guaranteed, not just to a few nations, but to all nations."

The room exploded with applause, and DC found himself on his feet with the rest, tears of joy running down his face.

ONE WILL BE TAKEN

Washington, DC

James Martin smiled at his new bride, who looked radiant in her simple white satin gown. His gaze was interrupted by an insistent voice and he shifted his position at the photographer's request. The whole situation was surreal. Cynthia's continued pleading had finally worn him down and now here was, a married man.

He looked across the room at the assembled guests, his eyes narrowing as his glance fell on Nathan Penal at a table talking with one of his other daughters. Cynthia has been anxious to have all her siblings attend her wedding, but they had refused to attend unless their father and mother were also invited. James could not understand how the others could continue to be so blind to their father's character. Cynthia had finally convinced her fiancé that her brothers and sisters' presence was extremely important to her, so in the end, they invited the whole Penal extended family.

There were only about thirty people in the room, all family and friends of Cynthia. He had been too embarrassed to invite anyone he knew in the DC metro area. His parents had been killed in an auto accident when he was in college, and he had no other family to speak of. He had not called Joseph either. *Maybe later.*

"Well, it's time to cut the cake," the photographer announced, marching over to the small table that held two cakes, the bride's and the groom's. She gave instructions and posed the couple again for several shots as they comically fed each other bites of the cake, a small bit of levity in what was otherwise an uncharacteristically somber tone for a wedding.

Cynthia handed the knife to a friend to continue cutting pieces for the guests and led James by the hand to chat with guests as the couple made their way around the room. Cynthia glowed in the soft light. Although it was an afternoon wedding, the blackout had made it necessary to turn on the lights. Ash from the eruption of multiple volcanoes had affected the whole world, obscuring the sunlight for the past three days.

That is probably what is affecting my mood, James thought. He had felt melancholy all day, even through the ceremony.

"I'm going to change into my other dress now, James," Cynthia said, brushing his cheek with her lips. He watched her cross the room with her maid of honor in tow.

"Well, James, I am sorry I have not had an opportunity to speak with you before now." The groom turned and looked down into the sharp black eyes of Cynthia's grandmother.

"I . . ."

"I want you to listen to me, young man. It's apparent to me that you are a fairly decent man who has the grace to be embarrassed at the situation you've fallen into. I say 'fallen into' because you have just exchanged vows with the scheming wretch my daughter and son-in-law had the ill fortune to have as a daughter. From the moment she could speak, it was all lies and half-truths."

James wanted to interrupt, but the look in the eyes of the tiny dynamo in front of him warned him not to try.

"She was raised in a good Christian home. My daughter saw to that. She and Nathan have done nothing but try to help Cynthia. She's a bad seed. A spider—and she's caught you in her web. You may or may not realize it yet, but from your expression during the ceremony, I'll wager it's dawning on you." Her voice softened as she continued, "I want you to know I'm praying for you. We've all been hurt by her. We know."

The elderly woman patted his cheek gently and then walked away. James felt a sick sense of dread in his stomach. He walked over to the bar, got a glass of wine, and sat down to watch the guests mingle and talk as he waited for his bride. He did not hear Cynthia approach.

"Are you ready, love?"

He turned his head and saw she was wearing a daringly low-cut, red satin dress, so short it made him gasp, "Cynthia!"

She grinned crookedly. "I was tempted to sew a big A on the shoulder. Everyone here, except a few of my very good friends, thinks I'm a slut and a whore who stole good Father Martin from God Himself. I just wanted to dress the part for them." Taking his hand, she turned to the room, which had grown quiet. James realized with discomfort that quite a few people had heard Cynthia's words.

"Thank you all for coming to share in our happiness," she went on speaking. "Even though I know not all of you approve, it's like that old saying about the heart wanting what it wants—we fell in love. I know some of you think it's sinful," she said, looking straight at her family, "but God is a God of love. Your ideas are old-fashioned and out of touch. James and I . . ."

James had been studying his shoes, unsure of what to say or do, when Cynthia suddenly stopped speaking. He looked up. Her entire family was gone!

"What happened?" he asked. "Did they all run out?"

Cynthia was pale. The remaining guests were all stunned. James glanced around the room. He had only been looking down for a moment.

"Cynthia? Did they run out?" he repeated.

"No, they disappeared," she whispered. "They were there and now they're gone."

"That's impossible, Cynthia," he began.

"No, we all saw them!" someone next to him cried out. "They were right here and now they're gone."

"My partner was videotaping the reception. He has it on film!" the photographer exclaimed, looking down onto the small screen at the back of a camera.

James walked over to her and took the video camera from her hand. He hit the rewind, then the play button. He could hear Cynthia's shrill tirade again and saw her family clearly on the small screen. To his surprise, when Cynthia said that God was a God of love, joy flitted on each of their faces. Then they were gone.

17

NEW BABYLON,
IRAQ

Luca stepped to the windows overlooking the veranda. If it weren't
for the ash, he would be able to see the full moon. He enjoyed being alone at night. Of course, he was not really ever alone. *I have
you with me,* Father. He sat on the chair by the window as a wave
of shock ran through him like an electrical charge. *Something has
happened! Father, what is it?* He could sense no response. He continued trying for a while before he felt a comforting feeling of power
envelop him.

His cell phone rang. "Yes, Stephen. What is it? Is Billings hurt?
No? Good." He listened with concern. "I will call you later." He sat
quietly for a few minutes.

Swallowing hard, he picked up the television remote and
turned it on. Breaking news banners flashed across the screen; the
reporter sitting behind the desk looked very grim.

"We are receiving reports that there has been a rash of traffic accidents. The strange thing is, this is happening throughout the
world. Other strange rumors are flying around social networking
sites as well. Stay tuned in and we will bring you updates as we receive them."

Luca switched off the television. Billings' limousine had
crashed when the driver, a young priest assigned as the cardinal's
aide, had disappeared. Just vanished. Billings was fine but now there
were many more accidents and strange rumors. Luca decided to
check his contacts through psychic projection. He no longer had

to leave his body to achieve the effects he wanted. As he practiced, it became much easier to make contact, especially if the person he wanted to connect with had a spiritual guardian.

He went through his list of contacts and found nothing helpful until he came to the president of the United States. Of course, President Patrick Wilson had no idea that anyone was engaging his thoughts. He was extremely emotional. He was sitting in the Oval Office, surrounded by many of his advisors and staff. Reports lay on the desk in front of him in large piles. Luca had a hard time hearing what the man speaking to President Wilson was saying, because *It's too late! I am too late!* was running through the president's mind. Panic was a strong emotion that Luca still found difficult to penetrate.

He could see that General Bolling, the US Secretary of State, was standing calmly in front of the president, so Luca directed his thoughts to him. The general's thoughts went along lines that were familiar to Luca, making them easy to navigate. Disdain for the president was foremost in the general's thinking.

Luca pulled himself away from the scene in the Oval Office. *So, thousands of accidents throughout the United States, almost all involving someone disappearing.* There were also reports, and some video, of people disappearing. How can we use this to our advantage?

Picking up the phone next to him, Luca called Stephen and asked him to fly in to New Babylon for a meeting. The World Union would have to address this issue when it met for its first session in two days. They needed to come up with a plausible explanation for the disappearances. This crisis could help them garner more power. It could end up being one more stepping stone to Luca's ultimate goal.

ONE WILL BE TAKEN

New Babylon, Iraq

Teo woke up and looked at the clock. *Two a.m. Ugh!* She reached for DC, but his side of the bed was empty. She got up and walked into the living room, but that too was empty.

"DC?" She looked in the kitchen and then down the short hall to the office. Before she reached the door, she could hear DC crying. Concern filled her as she opened the door. Her husband was kneeling in front of the computer, his head buried in the chair, sobbing.

"Honey, what is going on? Has something happened to your family or one of your friends?" She knelt down beside him and wrapped an arm across his shoulders. It was a while before he could answer her.

"Teo, I was talking to my dad on the computer, telling him all about the party tonight. He was really interested in all of the archaeology and stuff. We were just talking, and he disappeared. Dad was sitting there in his chair, and then he was gone."

Teo didn't know how to respond. "DC, with all the volcanic ash and the solar storms we've been having, I'm sure the Internet connection was just lost. Honey, you are overreacting."

DC sat back on the floor and gestured to the computer screen. "Teo, the connection *isn't* lost. Look!"

Teo looked at the screen of their computer. She could see her father-in-law's den in the background, an empty chair at the forefront.

"DC, honey, there still could be something wrong with the feed."

"Teo," he said, his voice strident, "look on the couch."

She looked back to the screen and saw her in-law's cat, Jingles, licking her paws and grooming her face. "DC, there has to be some explanation. Maybe you actually fell asleep, honey. It's just a dream. You fell asleep talking, and your dad just forgot to turn off the connection when he left the room."

DC shook his head negatively. "Teo, I was not tired at all. I did not fall asleep. I know what I saw and I know what happened."

"What do you think happened, honey?" she asked.

"My mom and dad were both very devout Christians, you know that—"

"DC, what do you mean, 'were'?" Teo interrupted.

"They are not on the earth anymore, Teo. If I'm right, then my brothers and sisters are gone as well."

"They died?" Teo could feel that terrible fear beginning in her stomach. "How would they all just die?"

"They aren't dead, Teo. They are in heaven, with Jesus Christ. He called them, all of them, up to heaven with Him."

"All of who?" Teo asked, feeling more frightened.

"Every true follower, every real Christian in the world. Christians called it the 'Rapture.' Teo, my entire family is gone." DC put his head in his hands. "My dad tried to tell me. He explained it to me again and again. So did my mom and my siblings, but I never took them seriously. I respected them, you know, but I never believed that any of that Bible stuff was true."

Teo felt like she was going to throw up. "My mom, DC. I have to call my mom! She is always praying, always going to church," she cried, her voice growing shrill. She picked up the phone and quickly dialed her mother's number, but there was no answer.

"DC, I want to go to their apartment," Teo insisted, suddenly thankful that her mother had wanted to move into the same complex where Teo and DC lived, in order to help when the baby came. Teo rubbed her stomach, trying to remain calm.

DC got up from the floor and took his wife's hand. He grabbed his keys from the kitchen counter and automatically locked the door behind them. They went to the elevator and pushed the button to go down. The ride in the elevator was quiet. Teo concentrated on breathing and trying to remain calm.

When the door opened, she ran down the hall and pounded on the door to the apartment her mother and John shared. The door opened. John stood there, groggy and confused. "Teo, are you okay?" She sobbed as she pushed past him and saw her mother coming out of the bedroom.

"Mom!" Teo cried, running into her mother's arms.

DC came into the room. He did not know whether he should feel relief or sorrow. He was sure, however, that he was the only one in the room who knew what was going on. Although he never had bought into the whole Jesus, born-again thing, his mother had made sure he knew what the Bible said. She had spoken at length about prophecy and had even dragged him to conferences about the "end times" when he was a teen.

He sat on the couch. Right now, he had to mourn his family.

London, England

The camera zoomed in on Cardinal Billings Mason. His somber tone matched the expression on his face. Kate watched him from behind the camera. Her director had decided that the segment would have more impact if Cardinal Mason just spoke directly to the viewers. She had argued with her director for well over forty minutes, to no avail. She did think Billings was a great man, but as a reporter, she did not think he needed an unchallenged bully pulpit. She listened to his explanation for the disappearances.

"You will all have heard," he continued, "many declare that the Rapture has occurred—that Jesus has come back for the true believers, born-again Christians. This is just not true. I myself am a Christian, as are many of you. It is the way I approach God. Obviously, not all Christians have been taken from the earth. Many of us are still here, as are good people from other faiths.

"I told you some time ago that we are on the brink of a new

183

age. I explained that when the time was right, I would reveal the truths I had discovered when I was given the ability to heal, the reasons behind all of the birth pangs we have experienced in our world.

"There have been rumors over the years of extraterrestrials, Area 51, and so forth. Some nations, like the United States, have actually communicated with beings from another planet. These beings are actually the ones who seeded our world with the first life. They have watched over our planet until we reached the level of evolution and technology where we would not be overwhelmed."

He raised his right hand, as if he were swearing before a courtroom. "I know you may think this sounds like a bad science-fiction movie. But the truth is, we are not alone. We never were. These beings are much like us, although more evolved. They have been watching over mankind since our beginning. With the increase in natural disasters that the earth has been facing, mankind was in danger. The people who disappeared were not taken because they were the only ones who truly believed in God; they were taken in order to populate another planet to ensure mankind's survival.

"I know many areas of the world are weakened by the loss of skilled people, people in key positions. Many of you mourn family members. I myself mourn the loss to this world of our beloved Pope Clement and many of my fellow workers in the Church. But know this, because we have come together as a people of many nations to seek peace and prosperity through one united governing body, because we are trying, truly trying for the first time to beat our swords into ploughshares, the architects of our evolution have decided to come to our aid.

"Now is the time for all of mankind to come together as one—one political body, one economy, one faith. All of our faiths have the same foundation, laid by the ones who established our species here on earth. Due to the fragmentation of our languages over the millennia, the specifics of those faiths changed. Just as our once common language fragmented, so did the truth of our faith. All faith expressions share a common thread of truth. My role here, given by the originators of our world, is to help unite mankind in our common faith. As we leave the darkness of superstition behind and enter into the golden age of peace, we will be blessed.

"The gifts I have been given are evidence from our ancient ancestors that what I say is true. They want us to be comforted. They want us to be encouraged. They want us to be filled with hope and joy for what is to come soon. I am the voice in the wilderness. I speak and serve in order to prepare the way for the One who is to come, the true savior of mankind, the next leap of mankind's evolution. You will have noticed that the ash in the atmosphere dissipated with the evacuation of our loved ones. As a token of great love, the beings that watch over mankind—sometimes seen as angels or spirits of men—will energize and strengthen many of you. Many will be given great abilities: healing, understanding, and insight into great knowledge and wisdom, along with other gifts.

"We mourn for those we will not see until the time we enter eternity, but not as those without hope. Be at peace. The world has overcome, and we earth dwellers will overcome along with her. The labor is almost at an end. The birth is near. Be expectant. Be hopeful. All we have dreamed of is about to take place."

Kate watched as Cardinal Billings Mason raised his hand in blessing and smiled joyously into the camera. His charismatic image, transmitted worldwide, had even the jaded camera crew around her smiling through tears.

Washington, DC – Months Later

Elena sat curled on the couch next to the floor-to-ceiling windows in the rooftop lounge of her favorite hotel. Her wine glass on the table at her elbow was untouched. Outside, the sun was setting. The sky magnificently highlighted the iconic Washington Monument. She stared at it, troubled.

ONE WILL BE TAKEN

The United States had been terribly affected by the disappearances. John had come to do some research, and she had jumped at the chance to go home for a visit. She wanted to see things for herself. She had so many questions. DC had tried to explain, but his words confused and upset her. *I am a Christian! So why didn't God take me?* Those thoughts reverberated chant-like in her mind, as they had since millions of people throughout the world had left the earth in the same moment.

From her comfortable perch near the windows, Elena could not see any changes in the view before her. But they were there. John was tallying the number of accidents and disasters that had occurred because of the disappearances. He had told her story after horrible story from eyewitnesses who had been left behind: friends, spouses, and children.

Businesses were left untended because key people were gone. Houses were empty. Looting was epidemic and beyond the police's ability to contain. The Bible Belt had been especially hard hit. Local economies collapsed almost overnight. The national economy was failing too, with millions of people missing from the workforce. The military had lost hundreds of thousands of personnel, and the president had no choice but to call home the remaining troops abroad so they could help keep peace. Citizens were terrified. Crimes of all sorts had increased to the point where martial law had been instituted.

The once powerful United States government had difficulty keeping its own house in order. At the same time it was losing power, the World Union was gaining it. Since the disappearances, power was shifting from the Western nations and becoming increasingly centered in the Middle East as the World Union brought troubled areas under control. John had told her that there was talk that the WU would be sending in troops to assist the government in Washington and to keep order.

As soon as she could, Elena had gone to her church to speak with Father Martin. He wasn't there. He hadn't disappeared. The priest she'd spoken to said he was apostate. Elena couldn't believe it. Bishop Ellis had disappeared.

She picked up her glass and sipped the wine. Her hand shook as she set it down. Why some priests, or bishops, or cardinals? Why the pope? She'd listened to Billings Mason. Although she respected him and was thankful for all that he'd done, his explanations sounded false and contrived to her.

She lifted her hand and rubbed her temple.

"Headache?"

Elena looked up, startled by the melodious Jamaican accent. Standing in front of her was the same handsome young man she had seen so long ago in Colorado. She remembered that his conversation with a young girl at the table next to her had made her feel oddly uncomfortable.

He sat down on the couch across from her and leaned forward, "Or is it something else, Elena?"

"How do you know my name?" Elena said, feeling her heart beat faster. "I've seen you before."

He smiled kindly. "Yes, you saw me at the university café in Colorado. I was ministering there to my charge, Alyssa Beth."

"Your charge?"

"At the time. Now she is with the Father and the Son, along with the others."

"The others?"

He smiled widely, "Why yes, of course! The Bride! It was a wonder of wonders to observe that holy moment of reunion. All of us watched with exceedingly great joy."

Elena tried to control herself. She understood his words, but the ideas didn't make sense. The man must be a lunatic.

"The Lord has sent me to speak to you now, Elena."

"Why?" she whispered. "Who are you?"

"I am one of God's messengers. I've come to answer your questions, Elena, and show you the truth."

"What truth?"

"Not everyone who says to Him, 'Lord, Lord,' really knows Him."

"But I knew Him! Why am I still here?" she burst out, angry tears spilling from her eyes. "I went to church! I took Communion. I prayed. I even read the Bible! Why is it that only some Christians left? It doesn't make sense. I'm a good person!"

"Are you, Elena?" He touched her shoulder, and she could feel the anger leave and sorrow take its place. She saw herself clearly, her whole life reviewed in just a few moments. It made her gasp. Selfishness and manipulation colored her younger years; her bitter hatred of Arturo colored the rest. She saw outward motions of religious devotion with little to no inner conviction. There were moments in her life when she had been moved by the gospel message—that time in Colorado had been one of them. But those moments had never lasted. The angel man took his hand away, and she looked pleadingly into his deep brown eyes.

"I believed in Jesus, though," she protested weakly. "I don't understand."

"You believed intellectually, but you did not appropriate the truth for yourself."

"What do you mean?"

"You think you are rich and do not require a thing, but you are poor and blind and naked. You are dead in your sins, and you need to be born again. Following the creeds of a religious life saves no man or woman. All must cast themselves on the Savior, trusting in Him alone to save them." His tone was kind as he explained, much as he might speak to a small child. "There is a transfer of government that takes place in that moment, from you ruling your own life to allowing God to rule your life. You never really entrusted yourself to the Savior, Elena. You have remained fully self-directed."

Elena looked him, tears running silently down her cheeks. "I see now. I never did trust Jesus in the way you are saying. What do I need to do?"

ONE WILL BE TAKEN

New Babylon, Iraq

DC closed his laptop and ran his hands through his hair as he rose from the couch and went to the bedroom to check on Teo. She had developed high blood pressure in her third trimester. Her doctor was monitoring her condition, and so was DC. She was asleep. Noticing she had finished her water, he quietly took her water bottle to the kitchen and filled it again, placing it back on the nightstand. He was glad John and Elena had returned from their trip to the United States. He couldn't take any more time off from work. Elena would care for Teo during the day.

Walking back into the living room, he thought about all he had been learning. He had believed immediately after the Rapture. Without any question or argument, he knew the truth and had prayed that very night, giving his life to Jesus Christ. So had Elena.

DC sighed. *If only Teo and John were so easily convinced.* When he was not working at the newspaper, John was constantly examining any bit of information he could gather on the issue. He did not buy Cardinal Billings Mason's ancient extraterrestrial ancestor explanation. Teo, on the other hand, faithfully followed Billings' weekly teachings. She would hear nothing against him. He had made her baby possible, and he could not possibly be wrong.

The trouble is, Lord, I think he is the False Prophet. Even as he thought this, DC felt the certainty of it in his heart. He did not like where his next thoughts went. *If that's the case, then who is the Antichrist? Where the one is, the other cannot be too far away.*

He remembered his mother mentioning that many of the end-times prophecies were in the book of Daniel. He opened his laptop and searched the Internet for the words *Daniel* and *Antichrist*. He clicked on an article titled "The Antichrist's Nationality." Cross-checking his Bible for reference, he read that the Antichrist would supposedly come from the Roman people. Whoever the man was, he would apparently sign some sort of peace treaty with Israel, an event that would start the Great Tribulation detailed in the book of Revelation. *So if this is accurate, I have some time,* he thought. He wanted to be ready, as ready as possible. And he wanted to make sure his family, what remained of it, was as safe as he could make them.

Closing his laptop, DC got on his knees to pray. He needed help, lots of help.

Arlington, Virginia

Snow drifted outside. James could just make out the hedge, covered in snow in the twilight. The fireplace warmed the room, keeping the chill away. He glanced over at the cradle. Five-month-old David Martin slept peacefully.

James felt a disconnect between the cozy scene around him and the state of his heart. A month ago, he had come home from taking David for his checkup to find Cynthia's bags packed by the door. He had supposed her indifference toward the baby was due to postpartum depression. He had encouraged, cajoled, and finally begged her to seek help. She had insisted that nothing was wrong.

What a blind fool I was, he thought.

She had been sitting, waiting for him to arrive home. He was surprised to see her dressed in a white fur of some kind, thrown over an expensive-looking outfit and high-heeled boots that hugged her legs to mid-thigh.

"Finally," she said lightly. "I was getting bored waiting for you. Sit down, James, we need to talk."

He had walked into the living room, the same room he sat in now, and listened in disbelief as she laid it all out. When he had met her, her parents had cut her off financially, hoping that withdrawal of support would turn her around. That was when she came up with the idea of accusing her father of molesting her; she intended to blackmail him with the accusations.

"I had to make them see I would follow through, James. But they wouldn't back down. One day when I was visiting my sister, I overheard my father talking in his office with Bishop Ellis. The bishop was telling my dad about you, how your parents died in a car accident, leaving you a small fortune."

James had felt something very cold wrap itself around his heart as she went on emotionlessly to explain that it was then she had decided to seduce him.

"All of that hospital service, all that ridiculous volunteering— I did that to get your attention." Her eyes glittered as an expression of disgust crossed her face. Then she brightened. "But I don't have to keep that up anymore. With my family gone, it occurred to me that I could have my father's will overturned. I heard back from a lawyer yesterday. My family's money is now mine."

"So you see, I just can't stay here. I'm young and now a very rich woman. This is not the life I want. I don't want to be tied down to a husband and baby."

"You mean *your* son, David? The child you have barely touched since he was born?" James thought of the man he had seen Cynthia with that night so long ago. "Is . . ." he began. Then he stopped and tried to swallow, but his throat was suddenly dry. "Is he mine?"

Cynthia snorted, "Men! Yes, I made sure of that. I didn't want you getting any ideas in your head; I'd lose my leverage. I had genetic testing done. If it had come out that it wasn't yours, I planned to have it aborted and act like it was a miscarriage. By then we would have been safely married. Since it was yours, I figured it would ensure you'd be generous when I divorced you."

James had been stunned. "It? This baby is your flesh and blood, Cynthia, your child. Don't you care about him?"

Smiling coolly, she had simply said, "No, not really. Listen,

James, you'll be a great dad and mom. I only stayed because I wanted to make sure that you understood. I know you've been blaming depression for everything, and I didn't want you trying to find me and win me back. I want it to be clear—I'm not coming back."

A car had honked outside.

"Well, there's my ride."

She had stood up and walked out of the room, and he had not heard from her since. He had seen her picture in the newspapers, in the gossip columns. She was a young heiress, beautiful and wild.

He looked at the pile of mail in the basket next to his chair. He had not opened a thing in a month. It was all he could do to take care of David. If it were not for his son, he truly was not sure what he would do.

James noticed a legal-sized envelope in the basket. He recalled that when he had pulled it from the mailbox, he thought it might be from Cynthia's lawyer and hadn't wanted to open it. *Coward,* he thought as he ripped open the envelope and read the cover letter. It was from a lawyer, but not Cynthia's.

The local law firm that sent the letter represented Joseph Levy. There was an apology for delay in forwarding the enclosed contents to James, along with an explanation that, due to the increased amount of litigation and the loss of some significant partners, the disappearances had significantly impaired the firm's ability to fulfill its duties.

James opened the smaller envelope that accompanied the letter. Inside was quite a long letter, handwritten. Within the first two sentences, he knew it was from Joseph. James had tried to find his former mentor after the wedding, when so many had disappeared. He was not surprised when he could not find the older man at his apartment or the café. No one had seen Joseph since that day.

James sat reading the letter from his friend, the last words he would ever have from him, words about love, friendship, and faith. There was a moment, as the words sunk in, when the veil was pulled away and he saw the perfect love and holiness of God. He felt un-done. Sobbing quietly, he fell to his knees. He finally knew the truth. He had known it since the day he and Cynthia had married and her family had disappeared, but in the stubbornness of his heart, he had turned away from it.

Now he could see that the truth was not danger to be avoid-ed, but was life itself. Through his tears he prayed to the Savior. Lay-ing down all of his selfishness and sin, he took hold of the forgive-ness being extended to him. He sat there, basking in the peace and overflowing with thankfulness, for a long while.

David's cries interrupted his thoughts. James picked up the child and went to the kitchen for a bottle. After warming it up, he went back into the living room and sat in the chair, rocking David and watching him suck down the warm milk. James had a pretty good idea of what lay ahead; not much of it was good. Earnestly, he prayed for his young son—and for himself.

18

A YEAR LATER

Elena pushed the baby stroller along the first floor of the Mall of the World. It had opened three months before, but this was her first time here. She had never seen anything like it. She stopped in front of the Phantasmic Fountains and watched as the synchronized lights changed color with the rhythm of the music. She smiled when she noticed Olivia's rapt attention. Nothing in the world was as amazing to Elena as her granddaughter, and she was thankful Teo and DC needed her help so much. DC had his job, and Teo had begun working on opening a new clinic for Arturo in New Babylon. She and Stephen Amona had been spending a great deal of time finding the right spot to build the state-of-the-art clinic. The fact that the fertility clinic also provided abortion services had been the subject of quite a few sharp conversations with Teo.

Elena said a silent prayer for her daughter and for DC. He had been so enthusiastic in his new faith in Jesus that Teo had been put off, and an observable breach had developed between them. It hadn't helped matters any when DC shared his concern that Billings Mason was the "false prophet" foretold in Scripture. Teo loved Billings, now Pope Peter II. He had performed her own private miracle, restored her husband's health, and made the birth of Olivia possible. No amount of arguing from DC could convince her that the new pope was less than what he seemed. Thankfully, six full months of DC's focused attention on loving his wife was strengthening their relationship. DC had changed a great deal in the last year, Elena had noticed. Everyone had noticed, actually. He was more humble and sincere. He had always been a kind man, but now there was a depth to him that had previously been missing.

Elena sat down on a bench, pulling the stroller up next to her so she could catch the expressions on Olivia's face. Soft, brown curls framed the little girl's chubby checks and gold-green eyes. It was hard to believe Olivia was about to have her first birthday in little more than a month.

Elena looked beyond the fountains and noted the stores. On this level, they were all top-end retailers: Gucci, Marc Jacobs, Vuitton, Prada. Once she had loved to buy from those designers. She bought whatever she wanted and never questioned the price. *How vain!* she thought.

The stores on the second floor in the north wing showcased art, crafts, and goods from all over the world. She was especially interested in exploring those because she'd seen a special report about them on the news. Many nations had opened shops in that part of the mall and were promoting goods unique to their cultures.

The west wing of the Mall of the World had a section especially for children, with an aquarium, a theme park, and even a science museum. Olivia was still too young to enjoy all of it, but Elena thought it would be quite fun in the next year. *If we are here next year,* she thought with a pang of worry.

She and DC had learned a great deal about their faith in the past year, particularly about the coming Tribulation. It had not been easy for either of them to find much information in the past few months, though. The search engines on the Internet were now under the control of New Babylon. The World Union had put legislation in place to discourage faith offenses throughout the nations. The intent of the laws was to encourage unity, to educate about and promote the common teaching of the Globalization Initiative, and to prevent the Internet from becoming a tool of subversion or of terrorists. The result was actually a form of censorship, many agreed. It had become difficult to search for any Christian content on the Internet, except on 1Faith, which was run by Interfaith Global Union. The content on 1Faith had been heavily modified though, and DC had pronounced it untrustworthy.

The Interfaith Global Union, a new ecumenical religion, had been ushered in by the new Pope Peter II, with the full support of all the cardinals of the Catholic Church as well as the World Council of Churches. Various Muslim groups, the Dalai Lama, and other religious world leaders had also led their followers into the fold. The union's headquarters would be in New Babylon. Modeled after the form of the World Union, the Interfaith Global Union had delegates elected from every major religious group in the world. Rather than political issues, the Interfaith Global Union had authority from the World Union to promote religious tolerance and unity. Pope Peter II had been unanimously elected as president of the new organization of the faithful.

A giggle from Olivia turned Elena's thoughts from the profound to the mundane. "Isn't that pretty, Livie?" Elena asked.

"Nana," the baby squealed.

New Babylon, Iraq

"If the riots in London, Paris, and other cities throughout the EU, North America, and the Middle East have taught us anything, ladies and gentlemen, it is the need we have to humanely deal with multitudes of dissidents," pleaded the Italian ambassador, Luca Giamo. "I have lists of human rights violations here, many of them due simply to the lack of space local officials have to detain people."

He picked up a stack of paper, then put it back down on the podium. He began reading from the list in front of him. "A sixteen-year-old girl was kept in handcuffs for ten hours while other detainees were denied essential medicines and medical care. Another young woman went into preterm labor and gave birth on the floor of her jail cell. Other detainees called for help for hours, but their cries went unanswered. Two men had heart attacks, and no medical help was given. Both men died in the overcrowded cells in which they were locked." He looked up. "The list of violations goes on and on. I do not fault law enforcement officials. Local authorities simply do not have the facilities to adequately address this sort of civil unrest."

Luca looked around the room at the desks of the ambassadors set in concentric circles before him. He caught the eye of the Mexican ambassador. "Estos abusos deben abordarse." The ambassadors who spoke Spanish murmured approvingly.

"Chaque nation doit être équipée et il ne devrait y avoir aucun retard," Luca said, nodding at the French ambassador. Then he proceeded to speak in each of the sixteen languages he was fluent in—Arabic, Cantonese, Russian, Hebrew, and others—pleading with the ambassadors in their own languages to provide funding for an adequate number of civil, humane containment centers in each major urban area within the World Union. By the time he had finished his speech—the first of his career as ambassador—the entire room was standing and applauding.

He waited patiently for the clapping to die down before he began to speak again. "Ah, I am only sorry I cannot address each one of you in your mother tongue yet." He chuckled. "I am thankful for the facility I have with languages. I believe it has helped me to understand my fellow men—and women—much better."

The other ambassadors took their seats, and he began again. "I implore you to pass this bill to fund the much-needed facilities worldwide. We are beginning a new chapter in our history, and it is only fitting that even those who are protesting this change be treated humanely."

From the enthusiastic response, Luca was certain his bill would be funded. He looked into the camera and smiled humbly, his dimples creasing his young face attractively.

ONE WILL BE TAKEN

New Babylon, Iraq

Teo checked the last of the figures in front of her and sighed. *Finally!* She couldn't wait to get home and cuddle with her little girl. Smiling, she thought of the preparations for Olivia's first birthday. Her father would be there, and her brother Luca. She had also invited Stephen. They had grown so close in the last nine months of work. He was also a great friend to her brother, a mentor of sorts.

Luca had volunteered to host the party at his mansion. He had asked her somewhat sheepishly if she minded if there were just a few members of the press there. The Italian ambassador had become something of a celebrity, due to his good looks, intelligence, and charismatic appeal. Teo had laughed at his expression. She could see the whole thing was embarrassing to him. Of course she had said yes.

She had wanted to ask him to invite Pope Peter, but she was afraid of what might happen with DC if she did. Her head started pounding. It was not that she minded DC becoming religious; she minded him becoming a fanatic about it. *He does seem better now,* she thought hopefully. All of the talk about the Antichrist and the Rapture had worried her and had only served to widen the breach between them. Then her mother had "believed," too. Thankfully, Elena had kept her newfound faith quieter than her son-in-law had. Elena was such a great help with Olivia, but if she had gone off the deep end, Teo would have had to find other childcare. She sighed. *It's getting better.*

Listening to the pope's daily teaching program each morning had really helped Teo through the stress of the last few months with DC. The pontiff spoke of the many people throughout the world who were now embracing what they called "true Christianity." The intolerance of these "One Way" Christians was upsetting whole families. The pope had helped her to see that these Christians were just lost, confused people. Many of them, like DC, had lost family members in the mass disappearance. Rigidity of thinking helped the survivors to cope with their loss. DC had lost his entire family. She sighed. She needed to be more patient.

Last month, when she and Stephen were on a business trip to Rome, he had taken her to the special Mass the pontiff had held in the Stadio Olympico. Inside, the stadium had been filled to capacity. Speakers had been mounted outside of the stadium, along with huge LED screens so the crowds could see the popular leader.

She and Stephen had sat in a private box overlooking the midfield, watching as ambulances drove out onto the field, silently, with lights flashing. Each had unloaded one or two patients and then driven off. This went on for almost an hour, until the entire field was covered with people on stretchers, each accompanied by family or friends. The crowd watched, murmuring.

Then the pope had entered the field. The crowd went wild when they saw him, dressed in simple cleric's garments, walking onto the field alone. Teo had watched expectantly as he approached the stage set in the center of the field.

Billings Mason, the new Pope Peter II, stood in the middle of the stage. The cameras caught his image and broadcast it through-out the stadium, inside and out, and on international television. He raised his arms out to his sides and slowly turned in a circle before the roaring, applauding crowd. He stopped and bowed his head. The audience grew quiet.

"The unity of mind and spirit we celebrate now flows from our common heritage. Mankind has come to the verge of a new world, a brave new world where peace and prosperity reign. In the next few months, a new source of power will be disclosed. Oil will still be of use as we transition to this new, clean energy. It is a gift from the true fathers of mankind, our ancestors."

The mass of humanity in the stadium was still and solemn with joy and hope as the pope continued. "No longer will nations have to suffer the inequalities of resources. There will not be a third world, or a first. All nations will share level ground in economics, in resources, in freedoms. The united government we have created will begin to bear the good fruit of unity, peace."

At this, the crowd erupted in cheers. Teo looked around at the people in front of her as they hugged one another and jumped up and down. It was several minutes before the pope could speak again.

He smiled benevolently. "Tonight, these unfortunate souls on this field, victims of tragic illness, accidents, and violence, will all be healed. This is to demonstrate their acceptability before the True God, who loves each and every one of us." He raised his hand. "To those of you who suffer, I say, be healed!"

Teo had sat in shock as camera shots showed burn victims being healed completely, their disfigured skin becoming smooth before their very eyes. A man with withered legs had screamed in delight as his limbs became full and muscular. He had stood and embraced the woman next to him. The camera had panned to a little boy who sat in a wheelchair. His rigid, contorted body seemed to collapse at first; then he had stood up from his wheelchair and begun to dance.

Teo smiled again as she remembered how each person in that field had been healed. The crowds had erupted in jubilation, and she had embraced Stephen with great emotion. They had watched as other religious leaders entered the arena, led by a scarlet-robed choir, singing. As the leaders took to the stage, arms raised high in praise, the words to the song appeared on the screen, inviting all to join. The unity of that moment still warmed her heart.

Smiling, she pushed away from her desk and stood up, ready to go home to her little girl.

ONE WILL BE TAKEN

Paris, France

The light of the morning sun began to warm Arturo as he sat outside the café and sipped his coffee. Idly, he watched people walking past, on their way to work or to the shops. He loved to visit Paris in the spring. Judith was back at the hotel. She had not wanted to get up so early.

He grimaced as he noticed a man setting up a small stool in the park across the street. Another man placed a box next to the stool and a woman sat down on it. Arturo saw her bow her head. All he had wanted was a cup of coffee and some peace—and now this! These people were all over Paris. The entire week he and Judith had been here, in every place they visited, they had seen at least one small group of street preachers. Even at Versailles!

The waiter came to refill Arturo's cup. Arturo nodded to the small crowd gathering across the street. "Are they here every day?"

The young man looked toward the park and nodded. "*Oui, sir.*" He stopped and listened as one of the men began to talk, his voice carrying across the street quite clearly.

"We are entering into the last days of mankind. The time is short and you must decide whom you will serve! Even now the False Prophet has begun the deception. Neither aliens nor any extraterrestrial ancestor took those who disappeared. They were taken by the Lord Jesus Christ. When He left for heaven after His resurrection from the dead, He promised that one day He would come for His own. Listen to these words He spoke Himself, from the book of Matthew in the Bible: 'Then there will be two men in the field. One will be taken and one will be left. Two women will be grinding at the mill. One will be taken and one will be left. Therefore, be on the alert, for you do not know which day your Lord is coming.'

"Each person who was taken was a believer in the Lord Jesus

Christ. Those who were left remained because they had not believed on the Lord Jesus Christ." The man perched on the box spoke forcefully.

Arturo and the server watched as a large man barrelled his way toward the speaker. "You lie! I believed and I am still here." The large man towered over the street preacher, even though the preacher stood on the upturned box. Arturo smiled, expecting some entertainment after all. His server moved closer to the patio railing.

"I believed," the belligerent man continued. "I went to church every week. I took the Communion. I gave money. I prayed. It was all a lie! My wife and children disappeared. A good God would not have left me here alone!" He shook his fist in front of the smaller man.

Amazingly, the street preacher did not back down. He looked up into the man's face with compassion. "I, too, went to church and prayed and did good works. I also lost my family when they were taken. Jesus said there will be many who will say to Him, 'Didn't I do this or that for You in Your name?' and He will answer, 'I never knew you.'

"The truth is that Jesus did not fail us, my friend. I know that although I intellectually agreed with the gospel message, I never submitted to God myself. I never acknowledged, nor did I truly see, that I needed a Savior."

Arturo snorted. The sound caused the server to turn around, and Arturo noted the tears streaming down the young man's face.

"Oh, please, why are you crying?" Arturo asked impatiently.

"Because, sir, he is speaking the language of my mother's people. I have not heard Ket spoken since my mother passed away." The server continued to cry.

"What do you mean, young man?" Arturo demanded. "He's speaking in English."

The server stopped crying abruptly. He turned to a woman seated at a nearby table who was also watching the scene across the street. Arturo could not hear the whispered words the server spoke to her, but he watched in amazement as the young man vaulted over the railing and ran across the street. He made his way through the crowd and knelt before the street preacher. Arturo could barely hear the waiter say, "Sir, please, what do I do to be saved by Jesus?"

Arturo tapped the shoulder of the woman next to him. "Excuse me, madam, what did that young man ask you?"

She turned to him. "He asked me what language the man across the street was speaking and I answered, 'French, of course!' Then he took off over there." She shook her head and picked up her newspaper to read, remarking, "These people are disturbing all Paris."

Washington Dulles International Airport

John Foster stood impatiently in line, waiting for the next customs agent to acknowledge him. He was used to just having his retina scanned and making his way quickly through the process, but the AGs had blown up a section of Dulles Airport near Washington, DC. Security was extremely tight now.

He had just flown into Washington from New Babylon, hoping to interview some AG members. One of his contacts in the movement had indicated he might be able to arrange an interview with someone in leadership.

John sighed heavily as he waited for the agent to finish interrogating the heavyset woman in front of him. He mentally reviewed the details of the AG group. They had a disruptive presence in almost every city in the former United States of America. They picketed, stopped traffic, and sometimes became violent. They were always masked. The Anti-Globalist, or AG, movement was also erupting in other places in the world, usually where the nationalist identity had been particularly strong. The World Union had begun sending troops, culled from the armies of its members, to supplement the member nations' homeland security forces, which had been kept in place for situations like these.

The customs agent finished with the woman and nodded to John. After a few questions, John's passport was stamped, and he pulled his bag along as he went in search of the rental car company. Within a half hour, he was on his way to his hotel.

He could not believe how much the Washington, DC, area had changed in the time he had been in New Babylon. The US flag no longer flew from the flagpoles of various buildings as it had for so many years. The blue flag with the green world, the official flag of the World Union, now flew in its place. Something about that disconcerted him. What really seemed strange, though, was the absence of the traffic that had been characteristic of the area. Very few cars were on the road. Many people had moved away after the terrorist attacks a few years back. The capital city was a target, and for many folks the risk had become too great. The whole DC metro area had suffered after the disappearances as well. Any honest person would have to admit that the former United States had been severely affected by the disappearance of millions of people; the southern portion of the country had been especially hard hit. It would take decades for the country to recover, if ever it could.

In addition to the impact of the disappearances, the North American continent continued to be troubled with floods, earthquakes, tornadoes, and other disasters. John supposed that all of the upheaval had led to the AG movement. Many of the group's members were convinced that the globalization of the nations had adversely affected the economy of the former United States.

The AG condemned the World Union for not sending in more personnel to fill in the large gaps left in the population after the disappearances. There simply were not enough extra skilled workers in other nations to send to meet the needs of North America. There had been a call for volunteers, but few of those who did have the skills wanted to go to the continent experiencing the worst natural disasters in recorded history.

John pulled up to the Marriott and was greeted by the valet. He took the ticket offered to him and removed his bag from the backseat. Checking in was fairly painless, and he went to his room to take a nap before his meeting. He thought about calling Elena, but decided she would be asleep. He would call her later. They'd had an argument before he left and he was not anxious to resume it. Elena had become very passionate about her newfound faith, which would be fine if she left him alone about his own beliefs and did not pressure him. A little time and distance would make their next conversation easier.

Guildford, Surrey, United Kingdom

Kate Havenstone stood and looked out toward the pasture down the pebbled lane. The sun was just rising. Pink streaked through the darkness, bringing light. It was wonderful to see it after the many months of darkness they'd had before because of the volcanic ash. *Then the disappearances.* She set her coffee mug on the lace doily that covered much of the table's surface. She thought of Granny, who had crocheted the doily for her, and wondered if she would be impressed with her granddaughter's home in the Downs. It wasn't an overly large home, but it was charming, and every room looked onto the Downs, a garden, or a pastoral scene. Kate decided Granny would have loved the natural beauty.

Kate caught her reflection in the mirror above the fireplace and smoothed her blonde curls. Her good looks had surely helped her in her career, but her quick wit and intelligence had ensured her success. Kate was constantly rated the top newscaster in the business—worldwide. She wished that fact translated into more leeway on what she covered. But in the past year, the restrictions on what newscasters were allowed to broadcast had alarmed her journalistic sensibilities.

She moved over to the grand piano, which held a large collection of photographs of Kate and her family, Kate with celebrities, Kate with world leaders she had interviewed over the years, and awards she had received. There were so many that the collection had spilled over to the floor-to-ceiling bookshelves behind the piano. It was her own variation of an "I love me" wall, according to her ex-husband. She picked up the latest photo, taken of her with the pope.

Billings Mason, again. Most now called him Pope Peter. Whatever name they used, people flocked from all over the world to see him. Many came to be healed, but many more came to worship as he led lengthy services. The most popular services were the ones he held in the countryside. There, he would provide food and even wine for the masses. That was only one of the many miracles performed at these "reunions," as they were called. The attendees expressed wonder and awe for days and weeks afterwards; she knew because she had interviewed quite a few of them. Membership in the Interfaith Global Union, or IFG, was increasing dramatically. Billings had led the entire Catholic Church into membership, and shortly after, he had been elected IFG's leader.

She thought back over the past year since Billings' dramatic promise of a new source of energy. True to his word, Global Energy, a new government agency, had been supplied with new technology. Kate did not understand much of the science behind it, but nanotechnology was now able to produce small solar cells that actually utilized a virus to replicate themselves. Oil was still used, of course, but the transition to the new energy source was definitely taking place. New Babylon was now completely self-sufficient energy-wise; the rest of the world would soon follow.

Raising the dead, healing the sick, feeding the masses. Kate looked at the image of Billings Mason in her hand. "It's almost like you are Jesus Christ Himself," she said aloud. She could almost hear Granny scolding her for blasphemy. Blasphemy. Kate wondered. Personally, she did not buy into the whole one-faith-and-coming-savior story. Although there were plenty of signs and wonders surrounding Billings, and the promised technology had been given, there had been no signs of superior beings showing up anywhere. One of her researchers told her that, as far as he could discover, the people who disappeared had all been Christians. No Muslims, no Hindus—no one with any other belief system. However, not all Christians had been taken. This had puzzled him. It puzzled her, too.

Granny would have an answer for that. Kate thought back to the many Sunday mornings she had gone with Granny to the small evangelical church. The older woman used to talk to Kate about the sermons and would explain the gospel message to her over and over.

What was that she used to say? Something about standing in a garage doesn't make you a car and going to church doesn't make you a Christian? Kate put the picture frame down slowly. What if all of Billings' messages and miracles were blasphemy? Vague memories flooded her mind of Granny warning her about the end of days and the spirit of the Antichrist.

One of the traits Kate prided herself on was truthfulness. She tried to be honest and forthright in her reporting, and in her personal life as well. There was something going on that had been troubling her for months now, something not quite kosher about Billings Mason. It was not what he did that bothered her so much as the stuff he said. No doubt, the masses loved him—and that alone was troubling.

What if Granny was right? Kate wondered. It was far-fetched to believe that there was going to be some sort of apocalypse, some Antichrist, and all those weird ideas her grandmother had bought into. But raising the dead, healing the sick and crippled, feeding masses of people, and finding a new energy source for the world was a bit otherworldly too. She needed to find out what was true.

19

NEW BABYLON,
IRAQ

The heavy oak door opened with barely a sound. Billings Mason turned.

"Yes?" he inquired of his personal assistant.

"Your Holiness, Ambassador Giamo is here for his private interview."

"Very well. Please show the ambassador in." The assistant bowed and left the room. Within a moment, he ushered in Luca Giamo, the Italian ambassador to the World Union. The door clicked shut behind Luca.

"Luca! It is a pleasure to see you!" The pontiff knelt down before the young man with great reverence. Luca helped him up with his strong arms and embraced Billings with evident affection and warmth.

"I was glad to have a chance to see you, Billings. Things have been very busy lately for both of us." Luca turned slowly, looking at the expansive room around him. A stunning monolithic fireplace rose two stories at the other end of the room. Its coppery surface rippled with reflected light from both the fire inside and the light steaming in from the floor-to-ceiling windows. He chuckled. "A fireplace, Billings? Really?"

Billings grinned. "Hey, I have a devoted follower who is a sculptor. He designed it for the new Interfaith Global Union headquarters. I couldn't say no. Besides, it's quite the conversation piece, wouldn't you say?"

"It sure is. There aren't many fireplaces here in New Babylon."

"No, indeed! Won't you sit? I have some Romanee-Conti 1990, along with a small selection of cheeses and pâté. Would you care for some?" Luca nodded and Billings judiciously poured the expensive vintage into crystal glasses.

"Well, I certainly feel honored, Billings. Isn't this wine over a thousand dollars a glass?" He swirled it in his glass, admiring the brick cast of the brilliant liquid. Tipping the glass to his mouth and sniffing appreciatively, he noted the scent of dark berries and something akin to grapefruit. "It's amazing, Billings. It has quite a long aftertaste, with a bit of a bite."

"It's a wine fit for a prince, Luca, which is what you are!" Billings patted Luca on the shoulder. "Why don't we sit?"

After the men settled down in front of the fireplace, Luca began. "I'm quite impressed, Billings, really, with all of the new memberships in the Interfaith Global Union. The initiative for developing a world faith is coming along quite well."

"Thank you, sir. I have been pleased as well." Billings accepted his master's praise with deference.

Luca set his glass down carefully. "However, I am not pleased with the number of *Christian* converts. Billings, this revival has to be stemmed."

"It is disconcerting, but I really don't see that we have any recourse right now, Luca. Once you are in power, yes. Right now, there is not much that we can do," Billings said, gesturing with his palms upward, his hands communicating his lack of control over the situation.

"That is where you are wrong, Billings. There is much discord in the world that we can begin blaming on Christians. Of course, this must be done subtly, with finesse." Luca paused to sip his wine again with noticeable appreciation before continuing to impart to Billings the pressing nature of the issue. "The anarchy of the riots in the North American sector can be linked to those with Christian roots,"

Luca said, smiling. He drank the rest of the precious vintage with relish.

"I'm unsure of how I can help with this, Luca," Billings said. "I have no political power."

"Not political, but spiritual. You have great influence with the masses, Your Holiness. Begin to use it by planting seeds. We don't need to harvest the crop yet, but we must focus on sowing in the minds and hearts of the unaffected seeds of distaste and distrust for those Christ-followers. In a little while, we will see those seeds come to fruition. Some tenfold, some a hundredfold," Luca said, steepling his fingers in front of him and tapping them together with pleasure in his sagacity.

Billings nodded thoughtfully as he crafted his response. "I think I understand the way it needs to be done, Luca. I have heard that the first humanitarian center has opened just outside of New Babylon. This is promising for your plans, is it not?"

"Yes, of course. There must be a place to house dissidents humanely. The centers in North America are almost complete as well."

Billings stood up and refilled Luca's glass and his own. "A toast then, Luca, to your plans being realized easily and efficiently!" Luca raised his glass. "Thank you, Billings, but the plans are not my own. They are my Father's plans."

New Babylon

DC sat on a bench in the shade of a palm tree in Children's Park, New Babylon. Scores of children played, most of them supervised by mothers or nannies. Olivia sat by him in her stroller. He grinned at her as he admired her soft, chubby cheeks. She had on the goofiest bonnet, handmade by a friend of Elena. Both Elena and Teo had insisted that Olivia wear it, along with the hand-smocked dress the same friend had stitched so lovingly.

"Oh sweetie, that silly hat they make you wear makes Daddy laugh," he said affectionately, his voice rising into a singsong, high-pitched tone that elicited a wide smile in return, showing several teeth. He missed the Gerber smile, but this one was adorable too.

If only life were no more complicated than tussles over bonnets. He sighed and turned back to his computer. He was glad he could get an Internet signal here to pass the time while he waited for Waleek. The park was the only place in New Babylon where he could be sure their conversation would not be monitored. Waleek was an Egyptian. Raised by Coptic parents, he had turned his back on his family's beliefs—until his family disappeared.

Just like me, DC mused. He thought about how much his parents would have doted on Olivia. They would have adored her.

He and Elena had met Waleek one sunny afternoon in this very park. Teo had been out of town, and DC and his mother-in-law decided to take Olivia for a picnic. Elena was dishing out the food and drinks just as Waleek approached them.

"Excuse me," he had said tentatively. "I was told to meet a man named DC, along with his mother-in-law and young daughter, on a picnic here this afternoon."

"Who told you to meet us?" Elena asked with marked worry in her voice. "We just decided to come here for lunch an hour or so ago." DC nodded in agreement as his gaze scanned the park for anything suspicious.

"God did."

Over the next two hours, Waleek shared the message he had received from God that morning. He was to find them and introduce them to other believers in New Babylon. The church was not completely underground, but members were extremely cautious. They met in small groups in various homes throughout the city. The pastor of their congregation, Youcef, also trained other men and women to lead these groups. The leaders uploaded a special program to their laptops or e-readers so that they could access Youcef's sermons whenever they had the opportunity.

"There are some the Lord has called to be evangelists, who proclaim the gospel publicly. Others of us simply share where and when the Spirit leads us," Waleek had explained. "Persecution has not begun yet, and we are thankful to the Lord for giving us a time of relative peace to prepare. We know the False Prophet, this pope, but the Man of Perdition has not yet been revealed."

DC recalled Waleek had lamented the fact that there were no "mature" Christians now. Though some, like DC, had grown up in Christian homes and knew a bit more than others, no one knew very much about the times they were currently encountering. Waleek shared how his pastor spent a great amount of time each day studying Scripture. He had found a passage warning of Babylon's destruction, calling for God's people to "come out" before it was too late. Its destruction was not imminent, but it was certain. DC remembered his mother telling him that in that scenerio, the only Jews to escape the destruction of Jerusalem were the Hebrew believers in Jesus. When they saw the city surrounded, and the Roman general in charge removed his troops for a while to shore up his supply lines, all of the believers heeded Jesus's warning and fled the city, settling in a place called Pella. This situation was similar. An enemy surrounded them in New Babylon. They were going to flee, too.

DC and Waleek were meeting today to discuss evacuation plans.

Olivia cooed a greeting, and DC turned to see his friend. Waleek was a big man, about six foot four and built like a lineman.

"Hey, brother!" DC said, rising to embrace Waleek.

"Sorry I'm late, DC. I had to stay after work a bit." Waleek turned to Olivia, who had lifted her arms up toward him.

"Eek, Eek!" she squealed with delight as he picked her up and buzzed her cheek.

"She really loves you, Waleek!" DC adored seeing his daughter interact with others.

"Yes, and the feeling is mutual." Waleek sat down and put the infant on his knees, bouncing her gently.

"Listen, I have to get home soon," DC said. "Teo is planning on dinner together with her father. What is our assignment?"

"Pastor received word that a wealthy brother has purchased a hotel near the entrance to Petra. Over the next few months, we will leave in small numbers to avoid drawing undue attention. You are to ask to be reassigned to security at Petra. There is a believing sister in the Ministry of Antiquities who will insure your acceptance, giving you and your family a legitimate and public reason to leave," Waleek explained patiently.

DC thought about it for a minute. There was no way Teo would agree to leave New Babylon. She loved it here. He looked across the park to the hustle and bustle of the river, the warm sun glinting off its current. He could see barges bringing goods from all over the world. Just in the short time he had lived here, more apartment buildings, stores, and restaurants had sprung up outside the city center. There was virtually no crime in New Babylon, and there was plenty to see and do. It was an amazing place, truly a world wonder. He could only imagine Teo's response when he told her that he wanted to be reassigned to Petra, a dead city in the middle of a desert.

"Waleek, I don't think I can pull it off," DC said warily. "Teo will never agree. Look, we still aren't sure when that prophecy is supposed to be fulfilled, right?"

"Pastor has said that he is unsure, but he feels the Lord would have us move and prepare a place. I too have prayed and feel that the Lord wants me to go to Petra. I've been reading and studying, and I think it will be a place of refuge when the Wicked One begins persecution."

DC rubbed his chin. He just did not see it working.

"Why don't we pray, DC? If God wants you to go, He will make the way clear," Waleek said, bouncing Olivia, and then leaning forward to kiss her forehead. She giggled.

"Okay, let's pray," said DC. He smiled at his daughter and

began to pray. Both men took turns praying, being careful to appear in casual conversation with one another.

Washington, DC

The room was still dark when John woke up. He rolled over in bed and closed his eyes for a moment. It seemed like he had just lain down to sleep a few minutes ago. Stretching to reach the phone, he ordered some coffee and food from room service.

He got out of bed reluctantly and took a shower. He finished just before a knock on the door announced the arrival of his breakfast. Opening the door, he moved to the side to allow the man to push in the linen-covered trolley. The silver-plated coffee urn looked promising. John tipped the man and closed the door behind him.

As he sat on the edge of the bed and ate, he read the newspaper he had bought at the airport. None of it was good news. America was no longer what it had been. The economy had collapsed after the disappearances, and one natural disaster seemed to follow another. The World Union had to forgive much of the debt the former United States had owed; the nation simply had no way to repay the trillions of dollars of debt it had incurred.

The fact that North America was a mere shadow of what it used to be was the motivation behind the Anti-Globalist movement. AG members blamed the new world government for all the problems they were facing now in the former United States. There was a lot of anger at the shift in the balance of power too. For many decades, the United States had been the leading world power, but now control had shifted to the Middle East. John Foster had foreseen this shift long ago, but for different reasons. He could not have known so many people would just disappear in a single day.

Elena believed it was God, which to John was just as likely as the alien theory, the fifth-dimension theory, or any of the other crazy ideas being promoted now by those who needed an explanation. What surprised John was how many people just didn't care why the disappearances happened. It seemed that a lot of people, unless they had personally lost family or friends, dismissed the occurrence as a mystery and wanted to move on without examining the issue. For a moment, he wondered why he had not spent much time over the last year looking into it himself. Life in New Babylon was interesting and pleasant. He supposed covering the wider issues of the world governing body had distracted him from giving the disappearances much thought.

Looking at the clock, he realized he needed to leave now if he was going to meet his contact. He called down to the valet to have his car brought to the front of the hotel lobby. He decided to give Elena a quick call before he left. He knew she would have her phone turned off, but he wanted to leave her a message to let her know he had made it safely and that he loved her.

He got to the lobby just as his car pulled up outside. Tipping the valet, he got in and made his way to the shops in Crystal City. He was picking up his contact, Blake Preston, outside of a restaurant there. Blake had made John promise that he would be careful he was not followed. John looked in the rearview mirror dutifully, though he was sure no one was following him. The streets were strangely empty for a Friday night. Of course, there was no telling how many cameras on the streets were recording his movements.

He pulled up to the restaurant and turned on his left turn signal to let Blake know it was safe to come out. He looked through the window of the small establishment and was surprised to see the restaurant was full. Concrete barriers had been placed along the sidewalk to prevent potential car bombers from getting too close to the restaurant and shops beyond. John noted the police officers by the front doors inspecting a woman's bag. Other patrolmen strolled along the streets, semiautomatic weapons in hand. *Things have definitely changed,* John thought.

There was a tapping on the passenger window. He hit the

unlock button and Blake Preston got in.

"Blake! It's so good to see you again!" John shook his friend's hand.

"Let's go quickly, John," Blake said, nodding toward the policemen. "We don't want to attract attention, and no matter how much the world has changed, a black man in Washington, DC these days is still suspicious to the police."

John pulled carefully away from the curb. "Where do we go from here, Blake? I can't tell you how much I appreciate you setting this up for me."

"You may not be when all is said and done, John." Blake's voice sounded a bit grave. "Things are getting much worse. The AGs used to be about protesting, calling for our needs to be addressed and our rights as Americans to be restored. There is new leadership now. Acts of violence I never thought would even be considered are underway. The bombing at the airport—that was just practice, John."

"Practice for what?"

Out of the corner of his eye, John could see Blake shake his head. "I don't know. Listen. There is something I have to tell you, John. My wife, she's been visiting this church in Arlington for about six months now. All she does is talk about Jesus and the Bible and stuff."

Sounds familiar, John thought.

"Anyway, she had a dream about me last night. She has no idea I'm in the AG movement. I'm real careful to keep that a secret. Somehow she found out from this dream. She's all freaked out about me being in danger. She knew enough details about the people I'm working with to convince me that this is no ordinary dream. She made me promise not to take you to the meeting tonight."

John pulled the car over to the curb and stopped. "Are you kidding me, Blake? I flew all the way from New Babylon to get this story. This movement is growing expansively throughout the world. It's big news! There are demonstrations, riots in various places, and they are increasing. The center of the opposition is here in North

America. I want to get this story. I need to get this story."

"John, I've known you for a long time. Have you ever known me to not give you good leads or to lie to you?" Blake asked.

John thought about the many times Blake had provided him with information over the years. Blake had worked as an aide to a senator and had passed John a lot of helpful insight.

"No," he admitted.

"Ashley, my wife, she didn't just dream about me. You were in the dream too, John."

"Me? I've never even met your wife, Blake."

"No, you haven't, but she knew you anyway. And when I got in the car, I knew for sure that what she was telling me was true."

"Why is that?"

"She said you'd be wearing one brown shoe and one black shoe. She noticed it in the dream. After they shot you, the AG guys picked your body up and threw it into the Potomac. That's when she saw your shoes."

John Foster looked down at his feet, about to protest, when he saw that he did indeed have on one brown shoe and one black. Something like fear made his stomach lurch.

Arlington, Virginia

James sat in the chair facing his son's crib, his laptop open before him. He typed quickly, taking short breaks to think before typing again. The past year had been extremely busy for him. After truly giving himself to Jesus as his Savior instead of trying to earn his way to heaven, he had found himself having incredible experiences. On walks with David, at the store, at the library, everywhere, it seemed he literally could not go out without sharing the gospel message with someone and leading that person to faith in Jesus Christ.

All of his training as a priest led him to see the need for

community. What he studied in the Scriptures caused him to see the desperate need new believers had for discipleship. These new Christians would shortly be facing a time of unbelievable suffering. He had taken to heart the advice his friend Joseph had written to him, and had spent hours each night reading and studying the Bible. What amazed him was the ease with which he could comprehend even deep theological issues. His memory had always been excellent; now it was practically photographic. He began having weekly Bible studies at his home, and he currently had at least two or three meetings a week. The number of converts had rapidly increased to the point where they had to rent a warehouse in Arlington, Virginia, to meet.

A few of his new congregants were what he liked to call technocrats. One of them, Eric, had been a hacker of some intense skill before his wife had disappeared in the Rapture. James had met Eric shortly after James's own conversion experience. Eric had been at the pharmacy at the same time James was there getting a prescription filled for David, and Eric had overheard James sharing the gospel message with the pharmacist. Eric had followed James and David out to the parking lot and asked James many questions. Eric put his trust in Jesus that day and soon become an integral part of the ministry.

Knowing the new believers only had a short time of peace before the coming Great Tribulation, Eric wanted to provide a way for the Christian community to communicate securely across the world. He had been able to create another Internet using methods similar to those employed to set up undetectable proxies in the past. Eric's mesh network design would use other Internet service providers until the new network grew large enough to operate completely on its own. It was designed to be undetectable, and so far it was proving to be. Eric had named the new network "HisNet." Its use had already spread out from their congregation to hundreds of thousands of users.

Many websites had been developed by believers who had

been caught up, and Eric and his friends had switched these sites over to HisNet before censors could delete them. So far, much of the Internet was free, but that was beginning to change. James and other pastors had their own websites and blogs offering teaching and mentoring programs. Many prayer groups and even social groups were on the network too.

James wrote daily, teaching over the Internet, in addition to the weekly meetings of his own congregation. He took seriously his calling to equip his congregation for the works God called them to do and to get them ready for the terrible days ahead. His congregation had numbered over five hundred people by the end of the year, and in the last two months, that number had doubled. Many, many more logged onto his website and blog. Friends and family passed the access on to their loved ones, and Eric made sure that the sites stayed safe. That was his gift. So far, North America was fairly free in religious matters, but it was only a matter of time before that changed.

James's eyes felt heavy. He realized he could hardly keep them open, so he stopped writing for the night. He thanked the Lord quietly and closed the laptop. He got up and stood over David's white wooden crib. David was laying on his side, clutching his "Duddy," a much-loved stuffed dog. Carefully, the young father stroked his son's cheek, not wanting to wake him. As James stood there, he prayed for David. Tears ran quietly down his cheeks.

James walked out of the bedroom and into the small kitchen. He had moved out of the house he shared with Cynthia a month after she left. There were simply too many memories there that haunted him. He prayed for her every day and sent her photos of David and notes about his milestones: his first tooth, his first steps, and his first words. There was no response. Nothing had been returned. He made sure she knew their new address, just in case she might want to see David. James knew that she was fine, so he wasn't worried, just sad. She was often in the news for her appearance at one celebrity event or another. Despite all the upheaval the United States had faced, Hollywood was still going full steam. Movies and television were still in demand. People wanted an escape.

As he washed the dinner dishes from earlier in the evening, James thought about something one of the young women in his congregation had told him after their meeting on Sunday. Her father was the head of security in the Capital Police Force. Over dinner, her father had told the family that five new detention centers staffed by World Union soldiers were ready to be opened around the city. This unsettled her father, because the facilities had been built and staffed without his knowledge. He knew nothing of their existence until they were operational. She said her father was quite upset about the secrecy. She was upset, too, because of what it might mean for her future. She was afraid of the coming persecution. James had done his best to reassure her, but it was surely coming.

Earlier in the year, he had seen the broadcast from the capital of New Babylon that showed the young Italian ambassador pleading for humane centers for detention. When James saw in a magazine at the pediatrician's office a photo of the ambassador in the background at the papal coronation, James realized who young Luca Giamo must be. It made sense. There was no question in any true Christian's mind that Billings Mason was the False Prophet, whose role was to deceive many. There were only two sources for the sort of power he possessed. Since he rejected Jesus as the Messiah, Billings' power had to come from the Evil One.

James was unsure how much time there was before the seven-year Great Tribulation, foretold in Scripture, would begin. Right now, apart from the upheaval of protestors, the world was at peace. That would change, he knew, but he had no idea when. In the meantime, his job was to raise David and teach the believers God placed in his care.

ONE WILL BE TAKEN

≈

New Babylon, Iraq

Elena woke up with a start. *John!* She had been dreaming about John. Some men had shot him. She picked up her cell phone from the nightstand and saw he had not called her. That was not like him. Quickly, she dialed his number. His phone rang but went over to voice mail right away. She tried texting him and waited several minutes for an answer. *I wonder if he's still mad at me.* She put the phone down.

She knew better than to push when it came to her faith in Christ. She had not thought leaving books around the apartment, with key parts underlined, would be offensive to him. She had found some good books about finding faith in the Savior that were written by a man who had been a reporter, just like John. The research, writing, and arguments were so compelling; she thought they would help John see. For some reason, he had responded in a mocking way.

"I don't get it, Elena," he had said. "First, you're all sure that Billings Mason is the Messiah, some sort of God, and now you're claiming it's Jesus. I don't know how I can keep up. Maybe next month it'll be someone new."

She curled up in a ball on the bed as she remembered her own hot-tempered response to his sarcasm. Closing her eyes, she prayed for her husband and for peace between them. She had spent the whole afternoon since he left with her Bible and a colored pen, marking whatever she could find that pertained to wives. She was determined to focus on her part in their marriage, the same way she had seen DC do with Teo over the last months. From what she read, she began to see that God was not interested in her convincing John that Jesus was the Savior. That was His job. Hers was to love her husband and demonstrate respect for him, not to try to argue him into the faith.

The fight she'd had with John reminded her of some of her battles with Arturo. Almost as if she were viewing another person, she saw herself clearly. She was not wrong about the things Arturo had been doing, but the way she had responded had driven him away from her. Haranguing him continually had not changed his thinking but had hardened him in it. And she, too, had become hardened. Bitterness had made her an unpleasant, lonely woman.

She thought of John. His love had helped soften her heart. Looking back, she could see that God had begun to draw her to Himself, and He had used her husband's love to help her see His love for her.

How can I blame John for thinking I'm not stable in my beliefs? It must seem to him like I am confused. She sat up and walked to the bathroom. She looked at her reflection in the mirror above the small porcelain sink. "Lord, just let me reflect You."

London, England

Kate stood in front of the camera and nodded to her cameraman that she was ready. "Ladies and gentlemen, I am standing across the River Thames from Jubilee Gardens. You can see from the flames and devastation behind me that a bomb of some sort has destroyed the London Eye."

She turned to face the scene, and the camera zoomed in on the destruction. Firemen and first responders were working to rescue any survivors while boats in the river were navigating closer to the wreckage. The London Eye was raggedly broken in two. The bottom section was still intact, but parts were in flames. The upper section had been thrown into the river.

Kate waited until the camera panned back to her. "It has been about thirty minutes since the initial explosion at about two o'clock this morning. We are as close as we can get right now. Security has closed off the bridges, and militia has enclosed the entire area. Just seconds before the explosion, emergency services were bombarded with calls warning about the bombing, claiming that the AG group was responsible."

Kate's blue eyes sparked with anger as she continued. "Each of the calls also warned of further attacks from the AG group. Citizens are encouraged to stay in their homes. The government wants the people of London to be assured that it is doing everything possible to find the terrorists responsible for the deaths and injuries today, and officials are working hard to restore the security of London. Thankfully, few people were out on the streets at the time of the explosion. Authorities are hoping the loss is minimal."

She heard her producer speaking in her ear bud, so she put a finger to her ear to indicate to the audience that she was listening. Her face grew pale. "We have breaking news, so we are returning you to the news desk and Brian O'Donnel."

The red light went off. Christopher, her cameraman, lowered his lens. "What is it, Kate?"

"There have been other attacks," she said as she walked quickly to the News 2 production truck, Christopher following. Valerie, her producer, was inside.

"What's going on?" Kate asked, her voice shaking. Valerie pulled her headphones off.

"There have been other attacks, Kate. The Eiffel Tower sustained some damage in an explosion. Washington, DC, is reporting some sort of missile hit on the Washington Monument. No one was injured in either attack." She put her headphones back on.

Stepping out of the truck, Kate moved in her assistant's direction, and he handed her a bottle of water. Kate took a drink though she barely felt thirsty. Christopher sat down on a stool next to the truck.

"I wonder what's changed," he said.

"What do you mean?

He looked up at her. "This group used to just protest globalization. They wanted to keep their national identities. Sure, their arguments and ideals were dumb, but they weren't violent. I'm wondering what's happened to change that."

Kate looked across the river at the devastation. "I don't know, Christopher, maybe it's because we finally are making peace a real possibility by setting aside our cultural differences and prejudices. I can actually understand it in North America. The United States was a superpower; now it's not. This movement started there."

"Yeah, but it's spreading. Why can't we learn to just live at peace? Why this anarchy? Things are changing—really changing—for the good. My wife's family came here from Sudan because there was no hope for their future, but now even the third world is beginning to thrive. This World Union has not been in power for more than a year, and great changes are taking place."

Kate thought about that for a minute. "I think some people have a hard time losing what is familiar, what was unique to them as a people. And cultures *do* evolve for different reasons. I'm British. Our culture has transformed quite a lot since the time when my parents were born. Low birthrates and immigration are two of the reasons why that happened. A third reason is that, along with a more global mindset, we have learned the importance of unity as humans." She crossed her arms and looked away to the side of the truck, her eyes tracing its outline as she spoke.

"Have you noticed, Christopher, that there has been quite an increase in crime since the disappearances? There seems to be something that has changed."

Christopher thought a moment. "If you had asked me that a few months ago, I would have said no. But now that you mention it, I suppose we have had a lot more murders, rapes, and robberies than the average by this time of year. Why do you think that is?"

"I don't know, Christopher. It is just something I noticed. When I went back over the figures for crime this year, I had one of my researchers graph the trends for me. Every single area of criminal activity has increased dramatically. Groups like the AG that were initially fairly peaceful have become more violent. I have no answers, just a growing list of questions and a sort of niggling feeling I can't shake."

Christopher stood up and grinned from ear to ear, jovially thumping Kate on the back with his hand. "Kate, I love your niggling feelings! Those niggling feelings got you the Pulitzer." His expression changed as he saw the bright explosion across the river a moment before he heard it. He cursed and grabbed his camera. "Come on, Kate . . . we're back on!"

20

WASHINGTON, DC

There was a bright light and numbing explosion to their left. John slammed on the brakes to avoid hitting the car in front of him. He stopped just short of the bumper. His ears rang.

"What was that?" Blake shouted. All around them, cars came to a screeching stop. People got out of their vehicles and crammed to the side of the Fourteenth Street Bridge. John and Blake got out of the car too and joined the group that had converged.

"It's the Washington Monument!" someone exclaimed. "It's been blown up!" The crowd began cursing and crying, and people were fumbling for their cell phones.

Blake pulled on John's sleeve. "We have to get out of here, man. Right now."

John didn't ask why; he just followed Blake back to the car and got in the driver's seat. With a little maneuvering, he was able to get out of the snarl of cars and make his way across the bridge.

"Turn back toward Arlington right now!" Blake yelled.

"What's going on?" John asked more calmly than he felt. Something was off.

"Listen, man, I just wanted to make life better for myself, you know? I didn't think about anything else. I didn't know they were going to try and kill you."

"You told me that already. What else is going on?" They had driven around for almost two hours after Blake had revealed his wife's dream. He had been too afraid to let John go back to his hotel and had thought it best to just keep moving. Blake had not given John any details.

Blake was silent for a minute. Then he wiped the sweat that was streaming down his face with his left hand. "My mom, she taught me better. I knew it, but I just put it down in my mind, you know? Listen, I knew they were going to do something tonight to divert attention."

"Attention from what?" John turned the car to cross the Potomac on the Memorial Bridge. He could hear sirens wailing.

"They are going to rob the Bureau of Engraving and Printing and get the plates for that new funny money so they can print their own. I was supposed to meet them earlier, with you, at Roaches Run. I honestly thought they just wanted to get their viewpoint out to the international press. I had no idea about . . ." Blake looked at John. "I swear, I would not put you in danger, John."

"I know that," John assured him.

"We have men on the inside of the bureau. The plan was to have one group make a diversion. I wasn't in on the plans for that. AG leadership runs the group on a cell model. One cell doesn't know who the other cells are or what their missions are. I was part of the cell that was to hit the Treasury tonight," Blake said, then sighed and went silent.

"What is it?"

"I didn't show up. I don't know what that means, except some kind of trouble. They know I met you tonight. I had a partner watching out for me in case there was any trouble. He saw me get into your car, so they know I didn't follow through with the plan. That means consequences," he said, his voice more tense with panic. He spoke quickly and anxiously. "Listen, you've got to drive me home right now, John. I have to get to my wife. They know where I live. . . ."

John agreed and turned the car, following Blake's directions. They drove through the quiet residential streets of Arlington until they came to a small bungalow. John pulled into the driveway and

228

noticed the clock on the dashboard. It was after eleven o'clock, yet every light in the house was on. They jumped out of the car. Blake jogged to the front door and stopped abruptly in front of it. It was ajar.

Blake opened the door cautiously, and they walked into the living room together. It was neat and tidy. Anxiety made John hold his breath as they went to the right, through a small dining area, and into the kitchen. A woman was slumped over, her head and arms resting on the table.

"Ashley?" Blake whispered.

The woman lifted her head from the table. She had been beaten severely. Her face was bloodied and bruised, and one of her eyes was completely swollen shut. "They were looking for you. They want you to know that they will find you and kill you for betraying them. That was the message they wanted me to give you. Honey, I was so afraid they would find you first."

Blake rushed over to his wife and scooped her gently into his arms. "John, go look in the bedroom closet. I have a backpack there. Grab it, and let's get out of here fast."

John did as he was told and was back at the car just as Blake closed the back door gently. His wife was lying on the backseat of the car.

"Where are we going?" John asked.

"I don't know yet, but we need to find another car. They have this license plate number. AGs are big now, really big. They have many in the local police force and militia on their payroll. We have to find something else—now."

Blake paused as he seemed to be mulling things over in his head. "I know. Head over to Tenth Street on the east side of town. One of Ashley's cousins has a used car dealership there. I know the security codes and the combination for the safe. I worked there a while back."

"I don't understand," John said. "The AG movement has been a fairly nonviolent protest movement. What's going on?"

Blake licked his lips nervously as he glanced at his wife lying in the backseat. "We have a new leader now, John. I haven't met him yet, but he's consolidated a lot of power over the past year. He doesn't like the global government at all—in fact, he has made it his duty to restore the United States to its former power and even unite with Mexico and Canada. I know he controls everything on the East Coast—drugs, prostitution, gambling, and the black market. Most of the cops in the metro areas are in his pay, too. This dude has got connections. When he joined the AG movement, he brought in lots of money. You saw my house. That was a reward."

"For what?" John asked.

"I was the one who got the inside men in the Bureau of Engraving and Printing. I found out their weaknesses and threatened to expose them to the local authorities. One of them is a pedophile, so blackmailing him was incredibly simple. I had heard about the new leadership in the AG movement and saw this as my opportunity to advance myself. I knew one of the guys lower down in the organization, so I took my offer to him."

"And that's how you joined the AG movement?"

"Yes, I've been with them for about six months now. I only know one of the lieutenants, but that's enough to have them come after me tonight because I know his face and his identity. Hey, pull in ahead on the right."

John pulled the car to the sidewalk and stopped. Blake opened the door slowly after looking around. No one was on the street. He turned to John. "Listen, I got you into this mess, you and Ashley. I'm going to get you out."

New Babylon, Iraq

Elena tried dialing again. John's phone didn't even ring; it went straight to voice mail. She was trying hard not to panic, but her hands were shaking and her mind was racing. It was almost six o'clock in the morning and she knew DC got up around this time. She went to the kitchen, poured another cup of coffee, and forced herself to eat a piece of toast.

Elena knew John had brokered a private interview with someone in the AG movement, though he had not given her much detail. Sitting in front of her computer, she perused the news sites she favored. She was horrified to learn of terrorist attacks in London, Paris, and other former capital cities—including Washington, DC. Each attack had been followed up with sniper fire on the first responders or with bombs. The AG group took credit for every attack.

Picking up the phone, Elena dialed her daughter's apartment. DC answered. "Hello?"

"It's me, DC. Can you come up here, please? I can't get a hold of John and I'm very worried."

"I'll be right there."

Elena plugged the phone into the charger. She and DC had always enjoyed a good relationship, but since they had both put their faith in Jesus Christ, DC was truly like a son. She appreciated the changes she had seen in his character over the past year. He had always been a fine man, but now he was a man with resolve and certainty. Hopefully, Teo would see the truth, too. Elena said a quick prayer for her daughter.

Hearing a soft knock a few minutes later, she walked briskly through the spacious apartment to the front door and opened it. DC came in and gave her a hug.

"So what exactly happened?" he asked. He had a manner about him that was already comforting. It was nice to not be alone.

"I woke up last night; I don't know the exact time. I had a dream that John had been shot. I tried to call him but got no answer, so I started praying for him. Have you seen the news this morning?"

"Yes. The AG group has just graduated to terror attacks. But no one was injured in the attacks in Washington, Elena."

"I know, but that was where John went. And he went to interview one of the leaders of that group."

"But why would they want to hurt John, Elena? Maybe you just had a bad dream. It doesn't have to be an omen," he reassured her.

"I thought of that, of course, but it was a different sort of dream, DC, and John is a very popular journalist. He is someone who believes in globalization and who has written many articles promoting the World Union. Maybe they want to make a statement using John," she said, her voice breaking.

"I'll go in to work and see what we can find out there, okay?" DC turned to leave. "I'll let you know what I find out. Try not to worry."

"I'll try. If you can find out anything, let me know as soon as you can," she said, giving him another hug. "Tell Teo I'll be down at eight to watch Olivia."

New Babylon, Iraq

Sweat glistened on Luca's smooth brown arms as he easily curled the 140-pound weight for the sixteenth time, finishing his four sets rapidly. He racked the weights and headed to the kitchen to grab a bottle of water. Clicking on the television in the kitchen, he sat at the counter and watched the news coverage of yesterday's coordinated attacks.

Former capital cities had been targeted. The casualty rates were not very high, at least for the first round of attacks. The second rounds seem to have targeted police officers and other first responders.

Maybe they won't be so quick to respond the next time! He leaned back in his seat and drained the water with pleasure.

He had selected with care those people who would best serve in taking things to the next level. His plans were unfolding precisely as he intended. The radicalization of this particular group, and others, would assist in the need for troops to be deployed by the World Union. Further terror attacks would increase the need for more control from the central government. Flooding the markets with global dollars would bring about severe inflation. When the time was right, he would have his ten cohorts assume their roles. Each of them was already in a position of authority, and each would use the time in the next few years to consolidate his power, employing bribery or intimidation to do so.

Luca was a bit concerned about his friend in North America, "Mister Smith." *That one is apt to improvise too much. I'll have to keep an eye on him.*

Andres Quinteros was a cunning man. He'd married into one of the largest drug cartels in Mexico. Within a few short years, he had ruthlessly rid himself of any competition, including his father-in-law, and still managed to keep his name clear of any suspicion. In the past year, using information and money supplied by Luca's intermediary, Stephen Amona, Andres had garnered power throughout much of the North American continent through drug running, prostitution, and the AG movement. He was a sociopath with no scruples, with allegiance to no one but himself.

Luca put down his water bottle and headed up for a shower. Juanita, his housekeeper, would arrive in a few minutes and begin preparing his breakfast. He wondered if she was bringing her young daughter to work with her again. She was such a pretty child.

Rome, Italy

Judith finished her last lap in the pool while Arturo looked on indulgently. He was glad to be back in Rome, glad they had been there almost a month in safety when the Eiffel Tower was bombed in Paris. He was thankful for his private jet that enabled him to travel so easily. Since the last AG attacks, the government had been enforcing stringent security methods to quell the movement, one of which was to restrict travel, especially air travel. No one was quite sure how those terrorists had smuggled weapons onto commercial flights, but they had—and everyone else was now paying for it.

Arturo let out a frustrated sigh. He was at the time in his life when he just wanted to enjoy himself. He had worked hard. He deserved to relax!

"Why the sigh, darling?" Judith inquired as she wiped her face on a towel embroidered with the Giamo crest.

"Just the world situation. You know, I am quite proud of the way my Luca is working to bring peace to this chaos. He is quite a fine young man, isn't he?

Judith poured herself some coffee from the urn sitting on the buffet table and took a seat at the table next to Arturo. She forced herself to agree pleasantly with her lover. *He is such a fool,* she thought. She stifled a shudder when he ran his hand up her thigh under the cover of the tablecloth.

"You know, he is so much like I was at his age . . . although I did not choose a political life to serve humanity, but medicine."

"And look at all of the good you accomplished, my love," she purred. *The man has only two things on his mind: himself and his pleasures.* She squeezed the hand on her thigh meaningfully.

"He was the youngest man elected to the Chamber of Deputies here in Italy. He is the youngest ambassador in the World Union. He has such mental acuity, my Luca! When he gave that speech a while ago and spoke to the other ambassadors in their own languages, I promise you, tears ran down my face." Arturo shook his head at the memory. "It still amazes me when I see him. Such charisma, and not only because he is good-looking. There is something that sets Luca apart from any other person. Wouldn't you agree?"

"I do agree with you, darling. Luca is unlike any other man." She thought wistfully of her one encounter with the handsome young man aboard Arturo's yacht a year ago. Luca had thanked her in a very personal way for taking his father's attentions away from himself. She hoped to be thanked again. There was a chance when she and Arturo attended young Olivia's birthday party.

"Arturo, what about little Olivia? Have you settled on a gift for her birthday yet?" Judith changed the subject.

"Oh, yes. I think Teo will be quite happy with my choice," he confided in his mistress. He went on to describe his purchase in detail, bragging shamelessly about his gift for his first grandchild. Judith desperately tried not to yawn.

New Babylon, Iraq

DC hung up the phone. Another dead end. It had been a month, but there was still no sign of John. Elena was terrified that something awful had happened to her missing husband. She expressed her trust in the Lord, but DC knew she had to be frantic. He would be.

Teo walked in the room. "Olivia is fast asleep, honey. She fell asleep while I was rocking her."

She walked over to the desk and put a delicate hand on his shoulder. "Any luck with the lead on John?"

DC swiveled his chair around. "No. I hate to disappoint Elena again."

"I have to say that my mom has impressed me," Teo said as she sprawled herself out on the couch.

"How is that?"

"Well, growing up, she was always such a control freak. She'd get really upset over the smallest thing going wrong. I know how crazy in love she is with John; I've never seen her so happy. She has responded to his disappearance with a lot of, well, grace."

DC wanted to jump on Teo's statement and explain the peace the Lord could give to anyone who came to Him, but he restrained himself. He just looked at his wife and smiled.

"I know what you want to say," she began to protest.

"Hey, don't I get some credit for not saying anything?" he chuckled, moving over to the couch and wrapping his arms around her. "I am glad that your mom is doing well with this situation. I'm becoming very concerned that we might not find out what's happened to John."

Teo rested her head on his shoulder. "I remember when I thought I'd lost you. I would not have made it without you. I was a wreck. I could never handle what mom is going through the way she is now. Do you think we can do anything else to help her?"

"I think all we can do now, Teo, is pray. It looks like only God knows where John Foster is right now." He held Teo closer.

"Would you pray now, DC?" she asked. He closed his eyes and prayed for Elena and John out loud, and silently for his beautiful wife.

Jerusalem, Israel

Kate Havenstone pulled a scarf from her bag and wrapped it over her hair. She turned to remind her producer to do the same before they got out of the van, as close to the Temple Mount as they were allowed. Israel was one of the few countries that had declined to enter into the World Union, and its own soldiers guarded the Temple Mount. The dress code was strictly enforced, and not just by the soldiers. Kate had heard of quite a few attacks by ultra-Orthodox Jews on women who were not deemed modestly dressed. She had no intention of drawing any negative interest.

"Wow!" Valerie exclaimed. "I had no idea it would be so massive!" She and Kate walked along the wall of the new Temple, followed by Christopher. Dedication ceremonies would happen later in the week. The massive Temple had been rebuilt in exacting detail, and the resulting structure was breathtaking. Many years before the meteor hit, groups had been working to ready the items necessary for building the Temple, the articles inside of it, and the priestly garments. Because of their foresight and faith, the building process went fairly quickly.

"It's much bigger than I thought," Kate agreed as she took in a panoramic view. "Look, Val, I'd like Christopher to get a shot of how they have incorporated the old Wailing Wall into the fabric of the new wall." She pointed ahead. The Wailing Wall had been left in its place, memorialized. "The Israeli government has tried to keep the archaeological ruins in place, while still meeting the Temple's spatial needs. I want to highlight that in my coverage. I have one of the archaeologists who worked on the preservation scheduled for an interview tomorrow. His name is . . ." she checked her notepad, "Michael Benari."

The three of them chatted for a few minutes about sights they wanted to record. Christopher talked with one of the guards and found the place their network was assigned for the opening ceremonies. Of course, all the media had to stay outside of the Temple itself.

Kate left Christopher and Valerie so she could explore a bit by herself. She made her way up the Mughrabi Gate. As she went, she had to pass through two checkpoints, where her bag was searched, as well as go through several metal detectors. Guards with dogs walked along the line of people waiting. Kate assumed that they were trained to sniff out potential terrorists by smelling things like explosives. She turned and looked down to her left just before she entered the gate. The area below was full of people praying in front of the Wailing Wall. The arches to the north were barely visible through the crowd. Thousands of people, Kate guessed. Although the Temple was finished and worship would begin there soon, the Jewish people still viewed the Wailing Wall as a particularly holy spot.

The Temple on top of the mount was stunning. She had been to Israel as a child with her grandmother and remembered seeing a model somewhere else in the city. This new Temple looked much like it. Kate wandered around the Temple Mount. She could not believe how different it looked now! There was absolutely no visible sign of the Muslim occupation of this site at all. Of course, the Dome had been destroyed, but she remembered there had been smaller shrines all over. They were all gone. She looked around and could see not one Muslim on top of Mount Moriah.

She thought about all of the conflict still going on between the Israelis and the Palestinians. After the meteor had hit the Dome of the Rock and the armies in the north were destroyed on the same night, many in the Middle East had turned to Christianity. For a while there had been security and peace in Israel, but along with the increased problems in the rest of the world, the Israeli-Palestinian problem had reemerged.

She looked over the railing and saw Christopher making his way through the queue at the Mughrabi Gate. Valerie was below by the old Wailing Wall, talking with one of the guards. Kate watched as a mother with a baby on her hip approached the guard talking with Valerie. There was something odd about the woman's expression, and for a moment, Kate wondered if the guard was doing something inappropriate by talking to Val. Suddenly a piercing scream ripped through the air, and the group below Kate exploded, sending human limbs flying through the air along with bits of metal and stone. Christopher had just reached her when the bomb exploded. He grabbed her by the arm and pulled her back roughly from the rail. They fell to the concrete ground together, clutching each other desperately as the blast wave passed over them.

Kate could hear other explosions ripping through the air. She tried to stand up, but Christopher pulled her back down. "Look, the guards up here have it under control. All of the explosions are below us, not here on the Temple Mount itself."

Kate suppressed the horror rising within her at the carnage around her and tried to think clearly and practically. She knew she should hate herself for suggesting it, but she said it anyway: "Do you have a camera with you?"

Christopher rubbed his forehead. "Yeah, here in my back-pack."

21

ALLEGHANY COUNTY,
VIRGINIA

John Foster sat on a sleeping bag in a bare room at the back of the cabin. It had been more than a month since he, Blake, and Ashley had escaped from Washington, DC, along with Ashley's mother. Blake had "found" another car for them, and they had left the city right away. They had gone to stay with Ashley's mom outside of Baltimore, but after only a few days, Blake had spotted some of the AG crew gassing up their car at the station on the corner. He had come tearing into the house and hustled them all out the back door. He had boosted a minivan. They all got in and took off, leaving everything behind.

John had tried to reason with Blake. "Surely they've forgotten about us now and it's just a coincidence," he said.

Blake had snorted. "Yeah, you don't know the guy running this show, Mr. Smith. He seems like a real gentleman—smart, well dressed, you know. But he's ruthless. He once castrated a guy because Smith's wife had remarked on the guy's good looks."

Ashley gasped. "Blake, why did you get involved with those people?"

"I didn't think they'd get this violent, Ash. Look, John, I think Smith was planning on killing you. I didn't deliver you like I was supposed to, or show up to boost those plates. Failure is as good as actual betrayal to Mr. Smith." Blake turned onto the highway and headed north. "I know a place in the mountains that belonged to a friend. We can stay there for a bit, see which way things are going."

They used the stolen minivan to drive all the way to the cabin. Set in the middle of a clearing in the woods, backing up to Jefferson National Forest, the small wooden house was in the center of 120 acres. A trout stream ran through the property and was lined with old growth trees towering hundreds of feet in the air. When the minivan pulled up, John saw a small black bear lumber into the woods. The property had its own well and septic system as well as solar energy. The barn behind the house was fully stocked with canned foods and MREs.

The place looks like it belonged to a doomsday prepper, John thought. *Guess they really were on to something,* he mused wryly.

After taking stock of the supplies, Blake announced that he and John were going to head out to get more provisions. They left Ashley and her mother, Celia, to sort through the house. As Blake drove the van down the dirt road away from the cabin, he and John discussed their situation.

"What friend owns this cabin? What if he shows up?" John asked.

Pulling the car over, Blake stopped the engine. "Look, I'm going to level with you, John." He rubbed his eyes and leaned back in his seat. "I was working undercover for Global Security. They were keeping an eye on Mr. Smith's operation. My job was to get into the operation and identify Mr. Smith. It was a potentially deadly assignment, one I didn't want. Before I took it, I insisted on being paid a lump sum of cash—to provide for Ashley in case I died. See, Global Security promised to drop some outstanding charges against me. Those charges could put me in jail for the rest of my life, John. I had no choice but to work for them to get the charges cleared, and the whole thing was top secret. I signed all kinds of nondisclosure papers. But I didn't trust Global Security any more than I trusted those Anti-Globalist terrorists.

"I have a backup set of documents I bought a long time ago. I took all of that cash and my alter-identity, rented a car, and drove up here. I figured it's close enough to civilization but remote enough to allow me to get supplies when I need to and still stay off the radar. So I approached the owner of the cabin and offered him a cash settlement, under the table. We worked out the proper papers together with the help of a lawyer I knew in Roanoke who owed a friend of mine a favor."

John had turned and looked Blake full in the face. "So this is your place? And you don't think anyone can trace it back to you?" He wasn't even remotely expecting this.

"No, I worked hard to cover my tracks in case I needed a safe place to hide. Now you and I are going to drive down to Marion. There are a couple of hunting supply stores in the area, and we're going to borrow some guns and ammunition. Do you know how to shoot?"

"I served in Afghanistan. Sure I do. But I'm not planning on staying with you. How about you leave me in Marion, and I'll make my way home? I haven't talked with my wife in almost two weeks. She's got to be frantic."

"I'm not too sure you'll be able to do that. See, I really can't take the chance that they'll find you and you'll lead them back to us here. I've got to protect my own wife. I don't want to keep you here forever, but I just have to make sure we can get you to safety without jeopardizing our own."

John tried to keep calm. "Look, Blake, I can't stay here forever. I need to get back to New Babylon. People are looking for me by now."

Blake put the car into drive. "Yeah, they're looking for you all right. You don't seem to get it. Things are about to change big time here in North America. There's a civil war brewing. Don't you get it? Global Security has been watching the AG group for some time. It's a power play. Smith has been consolidating his power base. He has a plan. He is not going to take the chance of you or me messing up his plan in any way."

"Why me? I'm not the most well-known journalist. I don't know Mr. Smith. I don't know his plans. I don't get this!" John shouted and hit the dash with his fist. This was not fair.

"I've been thinking about that, John. You work for the *New Babylon Post*. You're one of their top journalists and you've become a big promoter for the World Union. You've interviewed all kinds of world leaders in the past year. Maybe you've become a target for the Anti-Globalist group. All I know for sure is that I was supposed to deliver you to Smith. If it wasn't for Ashley's dream, I would have delivered you and you'd be dead. Hell, I might be too."

Their conversation had ended there, and they'd driven to Marion in silence.

That had been over a month ago. John looked at the small radio next to his sleeping bag and thought about the weeks since they had gone into Marion. Things had gone from bad to worse in a short time.

The few stations he could get on his radio reported riots breaking out in many of the large cities all across North America. World Union troops had been sent in to subdue the violence and re-gain control. But the AG movement was ready. Roadside bombs had been placed at strategic places. Snipers hid and shot at troops when they left the military bases. It seemed as if there was no safe place because fighting broke out sporadically in all types of locations.

Civil war had indeed begun. Many people had left the city areas and retreated to rural locales. All civilian airports were shut down. Provisions had become scarce in many places because of the violence. Grocery stores opened for just a few hours each day, if at all, and armed guards searched customers brave enough to queue up.

I should have gotten out earlier, John thought. He still could not figure out why anyone would want to kill him. Sure, he had seen lots of hateful comments below his online reports. His e-mail ac-count at work often had negative content in it, but he just deleted it and dismissed it from his mind. He had been sheltered by the wealth and security of living in New Babylon. He realized now that the me-dia in New Babylon had been strongly controlled and censored. He didn't know it at the time, but only certain information was made available. He had no idea things in North America had become so volatile until he had personally arrived in the former US capital.

Blake, Ashley, Celia, and he had fallen into a simple routine. The men had taken to hunting and fishing to supplement their canned food supply. Celia and Ashley had cleared out the overgrown garden that was fenced to keep out the deer. They had some things growing now, enough to keep their diets balanced and nutritious.

John looked out of the window. Dawn was just beginning to breach the darkness. He cranked up the radio he had taken from the hunting supply store in Pikesville that night. A few pirated stations broadcast news sporadically with quite a bit of static. One of the broadcasts was a Christian guy from somewhere in the north. Ashley had first heard him broadcasting a few weeks ago. He was someone she knew, her pastor. John thought he remembered her saying his name was James Martin.

New Babylon, Iraq

"Mom, I want you to know I honestly admire the way you've handled yourself since John went missing," Teo said, patting her mother's hand. "DC and I have been praying for you both. It's not something that comes easily to me, but DC is a natural!"

"I appreciate your prayers," Elena answered. "I know God is in control. He knows where John is. I just wish I did, too! With all of the violence and upheaval going on in North America right now, I'm sure he is just hunkering down. He would get ahold of me if he could."

"DC said that the authorities are jamming cell and Internet capabilities in the major cities right now in an effort to keep the AGs from coordinating more attacks and to prevent IED explosions. That makes it tough for us and for John."

Elena smiled as Olivia crawled over to her lap. The older woman picked up a toy tea cup and pretended to take a sip. "Hmmm, this is so good, Livie, honey. Nana loves it." She handed it to Teo, who also pretended to take a drink, then smiled at her daughter.

"Olivia, this is the best coffee! Thank you, sweetie!" She playfully handed the cup back to Olivia.

"This makes it easier," Elena remarked, "being with you and Livie and DC. But I feel like I need to *do* something, you know? I wish I could get to Washington and look for John myself."

"It's just too dangerous right now, even if there were some way you could get there."

"I know, I've seen the news reports too. All I can do is pray for him right now," Elena sighed and then changed the subject. "Are you all ready for Olivia's big party?"

Teo chuckled. "I know we—I mean I—am going overboard with the party. It was going to just be a smallish sort of affair, but then Luca got involved when I asked to use his house. This small apartment just won't accommodate all of Olivia's friends from her playgroup and their parents. Luca said the whole event would help him politically by showing off his family. He's young, and a lot of people think that means he isn't grounded."

"Well, it was kind of him to let you use his home, anyway. I have to tell you, though, that I do think it's too much. A menagerie? Really? I just baked a cake for your first birthday and let you have at it."

"I know it seems a bit over the top, but not in the circles I travel in now with my job—and with a brother who is Italy's ambassador to the World Union. Luca and I are finally becoming close. He is an amazing person. It's very generous of him to want to throw this whole party for Olivia," Teo insisted.

"I know you're growing close to your brother," Elena said quietly. Teo did not share the older woman's intense concern. Elena had honestly liked the young man when she had first met him. He had brought Billings Mason in to heal DC, and she rejoiced in that—

and in Teo's healing. She looked at Olivia, for whom she was truly thankful to the Lord. But since becoming a believer in Jesus Christ, a true follower, she knew Billings' power did not come from God.

Elena had voiced her worries to DC one morning after Teo left for work. "I am confused, DC. Life is a gift from God, but Billings Mason is definitely not from God. I can't tell you how much it sickens me that he was made pope! Every time I see him perform his miracles, my stomach turns."

DC had thought a moment. "I've been thinking about that as well, Elena. Whatever Billings' motives, or his source of power, God is sovereign over all. I believe He allowed Billings to heal Teo and me so we could come to know the Lord. All life is from God. Olivia is from God, no matter whom it was He allowed to heal Teo."

Elena turned to look at her daughter sitting next to her on the couch. Teo had softened in the last month, and this encouraged Elena. She silently prayed that her daughter would turn to the Lord and believe. She smiled when she saw Olivia pick up her doll and hold it close.

"I wonder if Olivia is going to enjoy seeing all the animals. She loves dogs and cats. Luca said the menagerie has a cheetah." Teo laughed aloud at the thought. "Can you just picture the look on Olivia's face when she sees a big kitty?"

New Babylon, Iraq

Billings Mason sat on the edge of his desk, hands opened in an appeal to viewers. He grinned, his white teeth gleaming in contrast to his tanned face. The red light on the camera blinked steadily. "And in our meeting yesterday, the Truth Congress ratified our basic tenets. As you know, for centuries, mankind has been held captive to various philosophies and superstitions. We followed the truths we were taught, hoping to please God or to placate Him.

"We lost our way. Once, long ago, we held a common language and faith. When that language was lost, as we traversed the earth looking for new fields and hunting grounds, we also lost that true faith. To be sure, though, even through all the centuries, bits of truth remained in each culture."

As he stood up and moved a bit closer to the camera, his smile grew larger. "It has been so exciting for us in the Truth Congress to discover those roots of truth together. We've collected our findings into a new book that celebrates the unity of truth. My hope—our hope—is that by using the five key truths in this book, you will begin to discover that knowing the godhead is not following a limiting list of do's and don'ts, but finding freedom in expressing your individual gifts, needs, and desires."

Billings picked up a slim leather book from the desk and held it up for the camera. "This is a wonderful book, *Prepare the Way*. Sri Gupta, Hinduism's representative to the Truth Congress, wrote it. This is a fresh revelation and a very real comfort in these times of conflict, which are really just the birth pangs of the coming peace. The true Savior of mankind will, most certainly, usher in that peace we all long for. Every major religion has at least a hint of such a savior in its teachings. There have been some men who indeed may have brought in the new age—if only we had been ready. We want to be ready now. At the end of the program, you will see a number you can call and a website you can visit. We want this book to bless you, so it's yours, free. We can send you a hard copy, or you may download it digitally."

The camera zoomed in on him. "As you know, I have been privileged to experience some amazing spiritual encounters. Despite the troubles caused by the terrorist group AG, we will see a new world order succeed." His eyes glittered with joyous tears that ran down his handsome face. "We are on the cusp of a new world. Not a 'brave new world,' as the anarchists accuse, but a compassionate world fueled by true faith and respect. As we learn to express tolerance and acceptance of one another—because the true way of love does not insist on being right—we will become all that humanity is meant to be."

Billings wagged his finger at the camera. "Don't miss the broadcast next week. I am going to interview a special group of young people. You do not want to miss it! Until then, go with my blessings."

The red light went out on the camera.

Jerusalem, Israel

The morning light was just barely visible between the two curtains. Kate had not closed them all the way the night before. She rolled onto her back and put one arm over her eyes. She and Christopher had not left the bar downstairs until almost three o'clock in the morning. Her head was pounding and her voice already felt hoarse.

Reaching over the edge of the bed, she felt around for her purse. She rummaged through it until her hand found the round plastic bottle. She popped the cap, shook two pills into her hand, and swallowed them both without water. Usually she took them for migraines, but they would work for her hangover.

I don't even want to think about how much I drank last night, she thought. But thinking about that was better than thinking about Valerie and all of the other victims of the bombings yesterday. She and Christopher had taken quite a bit of footage of the initial carnage before they were asked to leave the Temple area.

That's when it really hit the fan. They were just pulling their van away from the curb when multiple explosions detonated, shaking their vehicle violently. Christopher was driving, thankfully, because he had been in Jerusalem on assignment several times before, so he knew where he was going. He had driven like a madman to get away from the area. The entire Temple Mount was attacked, and snipers targeted first responders. Bodies were everywhere.

She and Christopher made it back to the hotel and headed straight for the bar. Kate was pretty tough, but seeing the body of someone she knew had been more than she could handle. She and Christopher claimed a table at the back of the lavish establishment and downed shots and drank beer while watching the news on the television behind the bar. Kate tried to ignore the fact that she still had some blood spatter on her once crisp white shirt.

Live footage showed that the Temple Mount was still under attack by crowds of men, faces wrapped to prevent their identification. Missiles were being launched into Israel from the Gaza Strip. Kate watched the devastation on the big screen until she got so drunk she had to go upstairs to her room.

The phone rang next to her. It was her wake-up call. She picked it up, replaced the phone in the cradle gently, and headed to the shower. "Ain't no rest for the wicked," she sang softly to herself.

An hour later, she left her room and jogged down the stairs. Christopher was waiting for her in the lobby.

"Hey, you doing okay this morning?" he asked.

"I'm fine. Just sick about Valerie is all."

"Yeah, I got all of the video uploaded to the network. The boss is thrilled with the footage we got." He slung his bag over his shoulder and opened the door for her.

"Well, I guess that makes it all right then, huh, Christopher? That jackass ought to be glad I'm not there right now."

Christopher did not answer, just shrugged his shoulders. They both climbed into the van.

"Where are we supposed to meet this Dr. Michael Benari, anyway?" she asked.

"At the university, Kate. Valerie thought that some of the interview should be done in his office, you know, so we can get a shot with diplomas and create an imposing intellectual atmosphere." His voice was flat and sarcastic.

Kate pulled down the visor and flipped open the mirror. Thankfully she did not look as bad as she felt. She grabbed a tube of lipstick from her bag and carefully applied it to her full lips. She smiled at her reflection for practice.

"You know, Kate, your looks are deceiving," commented Christopher, trying to liven up the somber mood.

She smiled. "I know. My granny used to say I looked like an angel and acted like the devil. It's helped me in a lot of interviews. People look at me and think I'm a dumb blonde. I like being underestimated. It works to my advantage."

They pulled into a parking lot, got out of the van, and gathered their gear. Kate was going to interview Dr. Benari about the newly dedicated Temple. He was one of the archaeologists the Israeli government had chosen to oversee the rebuilding. Dr. Benari had been instrumental in assuring the building would accommodate the needs of future archaeological teams to continue exploring the tunnels and chambers under the Temple Mount. Amazingly, all that had been destroyed by the meteor strike was the Dome of the Rock.

Christopher and Kate entered the building where Dr. Benari had his office. Kate opened the door for Christopher and they checked out the directory. The archaeologist's office was on the top floor. Once they got in the elevator, Kate punched the top button and grinned at Christopher. He hated confined spaces. On one assignment in Libya years ago, he had been trapped in an elevator for almost an entire day. He pulled a face back at her, which made her chuckle.

"Wow!" Kate exclaimed as the elevator doors opened to reveal the entire top floor. It was one open space, filled with artifacts on tables and placed in little piles all over the floor. There were people everywhere, and everyone seemed very busy. It reminded of Kate of what she always pictured the North Pole to be like, with elves bustling about.

Kate approached a young man working at a table near the elevators and tapped him on the shoulder. "Excuse me, I'm looking for Dr. Benari. Could you tell me where I might find him?"

The young man turned without looking at her. "He's at the

Temple Mount, of course, assessing the damage done by yesterday's terrorist attack."

Kate bit her lip and shook her head. "Damn, I forgot to call before we came. I am so sorry. I should have figured he would be called on to check out the damage from yesterday. Do you think we can get over there?" she asked Christopher. "I need to send something back to the station."

Christopher nodded, and they got back into the elevator.

22

HUMANITARIAN CENTER
WASHINGTON, DC

James sat in the cell and tried not to panic. Global Security officers had come into his church in the middle of the service and arrested him. Just him. They did not read him any rights or tell him why he was being arrested. They barely spoke to him at all.

He had been in the cell for hours now. He tried not to worry too much about David. Surely one of the women would care for him.

James tried praying but he could not think of the words. *Father, I can't even think of how to pray. Help me, please.* He rocked back and forth for a while.

The sound of a key scraping in the lock made him stop. The door opened slowly, revealing a tall, dark-haired man in his late fifties. He was wearing the uniform of a Capital Police officer and, by the number of medals on his shirt, he looked pretty important.

"Hello, Pastor Martin," he said quietly. "I am Sandra's father, Bernard. I'm the head of security for the Capital Police. Sandra called me and told me you were in here." His voice shook a bit as he spoke. He held out his hand and helped James up off the floor.

"I have to get you out of here right now, Pastor," Bernard said, turning toward the door.

"What do you mean? Am I free to go? Has there been some mistake?"

Bernard looked down at James. "I will explain when we are in the car, away from here. Let's go!"

The older man led the way through a maze of halls. There

were cells filled with men and women. Bernard and James passed guards. No one stopped them or questioned them. In fact, no one seemed to notice them.

They walked out of the front doors of the facility, and light blinded James's eyes. From the outside, he recognized it as the new detention center near the airport. He got into the passenger side of Bernard's car, and they drove in silence for a few minutes.

"I'm not sure what just happened," James remarked.

"When Sandra called me, I told her I couldn't get involved. There have been a lot of changes in the Capital Police force in the past few months. People have been transferred, or have just simply disappeared. Global Security personnel have been strategically filling the vacancies, and I didn't want to rock the boat and jeopardize my position. She begged me, but I still said no." Bernard turned his car onto the beltway and headed north.

"What changed your mind?" James asked.

"You won't believe it."

"We just walked out of a prison. How did you get me released?"

"That's just it, Pastor. I didn't. After I hung up the phone with Sandra, Jesus appeared to me in my office. I know it sounds crazy, but it wasn't a dream. He was just there, physically in the room with me. He told me to follow Him." Bernard's voice broke, tears running down his cheeks. "I never understood before. Sandra tried to tell me, but I was proud. What parent likes to listen to a child who says she knows something he doesn't? But all at once, I did understand. Something came over me—a warmth, a feeling, a presence. Instantly I knew He knew everything about me—everything—and yet I felt overwhelmingly loved and forgiven. I don't know how much time really passed—minutes maybe. Then He told me to walk into the prison and bring you out. He said He would make sure we were safe and to leave immediately . . . so I did."

As James stared at him incredulously, Bernard started laughing. "Do you realize I just walked out of a maximum-security prison with a prisoner? I don't think anyone even really saw us. There were no challenges—we walked right out!"

"You saw the Lord? He told you to lead me out of prison?" James was struggling to even find words to say. Even as a man of faith, he was still shocked.

"Yes! Isn't that amazing? Everything was just like He told me, right down to which cell you were being held in!"

"Do you know where my son David is?" James asked eagerly.

"I do. Sandra has him. She's headed up to the campground right now. We should be there in about nine hours or so."

"What campground?"

"The one the Lord told me to go to with you. It overlooks Lake George, in upstate New York. He has a place there for each one of us."

"Each one of us?"

"Yeah," Bernard grinned. "There's a place for each one He's called there. He wants me to help you with the community He's building there."

"What are we going to do there, Bernard?"

Bernard patted his shoulder. "We're going to prepare, Pastor."

New Babylon, Iraq

Stephen Amona shifted in his chair. The Italian ambassador's study was a picture of sleek modern style and simplicity, but it certainly did not fit Stephen's idea of comfort. He had been waiting for Luca for about twenty minutes, and the clear Lucite chair was not something anyone would want to sit in for long. He sighed and looked around the room. The designers had done a good job of conveying the ambassador's savvy, intelligent youthfulness. Big, bold paintings kept the light gray walls from looking institutional. Shades of red were prominent in all the paintings and in the other objects placed with perfect taste throughout the study.

He looked out the window at the birthday party going on outside. It was an extravagant affair for a one-year old. Clowns and performers strolled through the crowds of Babylon's social elite. The party was more of an opportunity to rub elbows than to truly celebrate a baby's birthday. *NewWorld*, a popular new online magazine, was covering the party hosted by the indulgent uncle and one of the world's most eligible bachelors—Luca Giamo. A cheetah Luca had ordered for the occasion was barely visible in the assembled menagerie.

A cheetah for a one-year old? Stephen thought it was all just too much.

He stood up and walked toward the window. There he caught a glimpse of Luca's brother-in-law, DC, and grimaced. There was no denying that the younger man was more than attractive. An old man like Stephen had no way to compete. He did not see Teo anywhere. He walked away from the window and sighed. *I suppose it is cliché for a man of my age to fall in love with a young, unattainable woman.* His thoughts were interrupted as Luca entered the room, closing the door behind him.

"Stephen, I'm sorry to have kept you waiting! The *NewWorld* reporter had a few questions for me. Have you been enjoying the party at all? Please, sit down." Luca took a seat on the divan across from the uncomfortable midcentury chairs. Stephen stifled a sigh and sat down again, too.

"No, I just arrived in time for our meeting. I have the test results right here. You know my first concern is you, Luca. You gave me quite a fright during the polo match last week." He pulled out a folder from the soft leather satchel beside his feet.

Stephen noted Luca's chart with approval. "Every test is perfect, Luca. It's amazing, in fact. It appears that your body heals incredibly. You broke that bone in your wrist just last week when you fell from your horse, and it is completely healed."

Luca shrugged. "It didn't even hurt after the first few hours, even without any of the pain medicine you prescribed for me. How are the rest of our plans coming along?"

"I've spoken to Smith, and we've reached an agreement. The AG terror group in North America will continue to cause major problems for Global Security, just as we planned. He will insure that the South American contingent joins in the rebellion in exchange for a seat at the table as leader over one sector. I believe the European group, under the oversight of our other friend, will also be able to escalate events over the next few months."

"Good, I am grateful for your help, Stephen." Luca rubbed his palms together slowly as he always did when he was pleased that things were working out the way he planned. "I believe that by next year, the World Union will be overwhelmed and will find the need to divide the world community into more manageable segments. I have enough support already to assure me of one of those segments for myself. In the next few months, I will garner a place for our friend, too." He smiled affably.

"The pro-faith law you put before the World Union ambassadors will be helpful in reigning in those new Christians." Stephen said the word *Christians* with a roll of his eyes. "Since it was passed into law, arrests have already been made. Leaders are being targeted first. Global Security is overseeing the process quietly." He glanced out the window and then back at Luca.

"Since the failed war in Israel, massive numbers of people have been converting to Christianity. Those new converts only go and make more converts. Underground churches are springing up all over the world and it is becoming a problem," Stephen explained. "These followers of Jesus refuse to join the 1Faith initiative instituted by the Interfaith Global Union. They will only continue to oppose you and must be taken out of the equation."

Luca nodded in agreement, silently encouraging Stephen in his tirade. Stephen went on ranting vehemently. "They must not be allowed to pollute the world with their pious allegiances to one god. They will only be a thorn in your side as you take your rightful place in this world, Luca."

"I hate them," Luca said. "Their unsophisticated religion and simple-minded ways. I do find it a bit exciting, thinking about them in the centers, though. Knowing that they are finally getting what they deserve . . . they must be destroyed. And Israel—you know the prophecies. I've been studying them in depth, and my Father has shown me the way to forestall their fulfillment. Israel is the key, which is why we must destroy the Christians and keep their 'faith' from infecting Israel." Luca poured himself a generous glass of wine and began to pace the room. "We have to make that nation bow before me. Once they accept me as the promised Messiah, I will destroy them just like those mealy-mouthed Christ-followers. Only then will my reign finally be secure."

"Your time is coming soon. Your plans are unfolding just as you detailed them. The world will become a better place once you are ruling it," Stephen said with admiration.

Outside, the sound of children's laughter erupted. Stephen looked out at the birthday party festivities, but he still could not see Teo.

"How kind of you to have a party for your niece, Luca!" The change of subject might have seemed abrupt to anyone who was unaware of the obsession Stephen had for Teo.

Luca continued to slowly pace the room. "Yes, I know. I hate those little snot-faced creatures, but I thought it would be good publicity to be seen as a man who cares about family. In fact, I was thinking it might make for even more public sympathy—and approval—if my dear niece were to become the victim of a terrible crime."

"What do you mean, Luca?" asked the older man, confused and alarmed. He and Teo had been working together quite a lot lately, and the young woman had become very important to him. Sometimes Luca could be quite cruel. He didn't like the loyalties of his followers divided, and Stephen was certain Luca knew the way the older man felt about his older sister.

Luca stopped his pacing and watched Stephen's face with veiled interest as he revealed his plans. "Well, how would it be if AG ter-rorists kidnapped and murdered my dear brother-in-law, and my little niece with him? My beautiful sister, Teo, would be inconsolable, wouldn't she? Why, she was practically an addict a while back. Do you remember? She is weak and dependent and would need some-one—someone like you, Stephen, my friend. You could have her as a reward."

"As a reward, Luca? I don't think she would . . ." but the thought of Teo, sorrowful and in need, appealed to Stephen. She did confide in him. They were already friends. Such a tragedy could bring them closer. His young master certainly could influence her. Stephen looked up as Luca began walking over to him, a wide grin deepening the dimples on either side of his face.

"Consider it done, my friend!" Luca said, clapping the older man on the back. "It's a winning situation for me. For both of us, re-ally. I will receive worldwide attention and empathy as I seek out the terrorists who viciously attacked my sister's family. You will receive Teo, who will be more than willing to be consoled by you. Now, let's go and enjoy the party, my friend!"

The two men walked out of the study. After a few minutes, the connecting door to the bathroom opened. Teo stood in the door-way, in shock. A vent in the bathroom adjacent to Luca's office had enabled her to hear every word spoken between the two men.

What on earth is going on here? What does this mean? She pondered Luca's words in mounting panic. The first part of their conversation had been very confusing. But the part about DC and Olivia was crystal clear. Teo could feel the fear rising in her throat and she felt like she was going to choke. Clutching her purse, she went back into the bathroom, shut the door to the office, and locked it. She opened her purse and looked at the small baggie inside.

She had dodged into the bathroom to take a pregnancy test. She'd heard Luca close his office door and greet someone, and had had to stifle her squeal of excitement as the word *pregnant* appeared on the little white stick. As the meeting went on in the adjoining

259

room, she was surprised to hear Stephen Amona's voice. And what she had heard had made her tremble.

A brown bottle lay next to the pregnancy test in her purse. She debated for a moment internally, then returned the positive pregnancy test stick to her purse before closing the bag. She would have to act as if nothing had happened for the remainder of Olivia's party. Then she had to find some way to communicate what she had heard to her husband. Would he believe her?

It was crazy. How could Luca, her own brother, talk about death camps and arranging the murder of her husband and daughter—his own family—to gain greater popularity? *He must be insane.* Maybe she should talk to her father instead. She looked at her pale reflection in the mirror and carefully practiced a smile. No one must suspect she was afraid . . . terrified, actually.

She returned to the party determined to keep her two big secrets, for the time being.

Jerusalem, Israel

It was only Kate's insistence that she had to see Dr. Benari to film a special for Israeli Network, and her coy charm, that got them through the security surrounding the Temple Mount. Both Kate and Christopher were surprised the damage was not as extensive as they had feared.

Kate tried not to look over the rail as she climbed up the stairs again and walked through the gate. Security was intense, and it took them a good thirty minutes to get through, even though the line of people was relatively small. Neither she nor Christopher made a comment or complaint. The Israeli Defense Force officers were just doing their jobs.

The two made their way along the Temple Mount. There was little observable damage, but Kate could make out a small crater ahead, just to the right of a walkway that led into the Temple itself. She could see the Levitical priests immediately inside the gates. A group of men stood looking down into the crater; their excitement was palpable.

"I wonder what's going on," she said. Christopher silently pulled out his camera and started walking quickly toward the group. She could see the red light indicating the recording mode as he put the camera on his shoulder. She smiled when he carefully shoved a couple of men to the side, saying, "Press, please stand aside." He could be so officious.

As Kate reached the group, the onlookers began exclaiming praises to God. Some of the men actually burst into tears. She pushed her way to the edge to peer over the side where the bomb detonation had opened up the crater, revealing a room underneath. A dark-haired man was standing on the edge of what looked like a well, yelling in Hebrew. Whatever he was saying was making the crowd wild. Men were jumping up and down, hugging each other, hooting and hollering with joy. Tears ran down most faces. Kate could see Christopher panning the camera, filming the emotional moment.

"Excuse me, sir, please excuse me," she said, pulling on the sleeve of the large man next to her. "Can you tell me what he is saying?"

Kate stifled a squeal as the smiling man picked her up off of her feet and swung her around like she weighed nothing. She grabbed onto his sleeves to steady herself.

The man put her down. "Praise the Maker of heaven and earth! Benari has found the Ark of the Covenant!"

Kate was astounded. "The real Ark? Like, *the Ark?* Is it down in that well?" She peered over the side, but she could not see inside the well where Dr. Michael Benari perched. She could see he was quite excited. There were other men with him in what looked like a room; one was a priest.

She turned to the man again. "Who is the priest down there

with him?" She had not seen one of the Temple priests up close before. The man below was wearing a strange hat and a vest-like garment covered with jewels. His bushy beard reminded her of some ancient prophet.

"That's the high priest, Aaron Katz. He and Dr. Benari are childhood friends." The man abruptly stopped speaking as Dr. Benari climbed off the ledge of the well and peered up at the group above him. Kate noted the keen intelligence evident in Benari's countenance; he was also strikingly handsome. He spoke to the group in Hebrew, so she had to wait until he was finished to ask her new friend what the archaeologist had said.

"Of course! Dr. Benari says that the poles to the blessed Ark of the Covenant have rotted away over the centuries. We must wait until the—" he stopped abruptly again. "Wait, the high priest is saying something to the doctor."

The group became silent as the two men conferred. Dr. Benari motioned to one of the men next to him and said something quietly. Then the man, a student by the look of him, clambered up the ladder. He did not stop to speak to anyone but hurried into the Temple compound. The men around Kate began to murmur. She caught Christopher's eye across from her, on the other side of the hole. He raised his eyebrows and shrugged his shoulders. They didn't know what was going on.

Dr. Benari addressed the group again. As he spoke, applause broke out from the men above him and next to him.

"What is it?" Kate asked.

"The high priest, bless him, had new poles made when he was the director of the Restoration Project. The young man went to get the poles from the storage facilities."

After about twenty minutes, Kate saw a large group of men and priests pour out of the Temple compound. She turned and saw IDF personnel coming toward them. The personnel ordered the group to stand back while they cordoned off the area around the crater. Kate looked toward the gate and saw that soldiers with guns were standing alert, looking for any sign of trouble. Christopher joined her.

"We are the only press here, Christopher," she whispered to him. "Do you know what this means?"

"Get your microphone out, Kate. I think we are both going to get the Pulitzer for this story," he whispered, leaning close to her and chuckling. "I just hope our faces don't melt off when they open that box!"

New Babylon, Iraq

DC sipped his morning coffee as he walked down the hallway to his small office in ComCenter Babylon. He still could not believe he worked here. Flipping on the light, he grinned when he saw a purple sticky note on his desk. Cassandra. She was the best tech in the building, and she had been helping him search for John Foster. Purple was her trademark. She either wrote in purple ink or on purple paper. She was a bit eccentric, but that was okay with DC. He liked eccentric, especially when it was combined with talent or skill.

He read the note quickly and picked up the phone to call Elena. John had been caught on video surveillance at a gas station in West Virginia. She didn't answer, so he called Teo.

"Hello?"

"Hey, honey, I'm trying to find your mom. We have John on video at a gas station in West Virginia." He smiled at his wife's response. "Do you know where she is?"

"I know she's been walking in the mornings by the park. I think she takes Olivia by the pond there to feed the ducks and swans. Look, I have to go into a meeting right now, but that is great news!"

DC said good-bye and hung up. It was nice to hear Teo excited for a change. For the last few days, she had been melancholy.

He had tried to draw her out, but she had put him off, saying she was just coming down with a bug.

He tried to call Elena's cell again, but there was no answer. She was in the habit of putting it on silent and then forgetting about it. He looked at the clock and saw he had only ten minutes before the morning briefing. He would have to wait until lunch to find Elena and tell her the good news. John Foster was alive and well, praise the Lord! DC could only guess that the violence in the area had kept him from contacting his wife or anyone else. Thousands of people had been killed in the past few months in North America. The World Union had just voted to send more troops into the former United States. It was quickly becoming a real civil war.

Alleghany County, Virginia

John Foster sat perched on a branch with his back against the tree trunk, about thirty feet up in the air. The last week had been very stressful. Hundreds, maybe thousands of people had fled the metropolitan areas of Baltimore and Washington, DC. At first, there had been no problems. But two days before, a group of men had driven up to the cabin while Blake and John were out hunting. The women had not been hurt, but the men had frightened them and taken most of the provisions in the house. Thankfully, Blake had the foresight to hide a lot more in the barn.

Blake. John thought about him. There was more to Blake than he had thought, more than Blake revealed. It amazed John how many things the man knew how to do. After the incident, he calmed his wife and mother, then gave John a rifle and told him to stay with the women. Blake was gone all night. When he came back, he was driving an eighteen-wheeler, and a teenage boy was following him in a pickup truck.

The boy, Billy Reynolds, had been left alone after the disappearances. He had worked hard alongside Blake and John for the last four days as they installed fences and gates across the long driveway. There was no way they could enclose the entire perimeter; however, they could at least extend a barrier along each side to the point where the tree line would impede anyone with a vehicle. Blake had insisted the first gate be away from the road. He thought that if those driving by saw a gated drive, they might be enticed to see what valuables were worth securing behind a fence. So John, Blake, and Billy had erected the barricade further up the hill. The initial gate was not clearly seen from the state highway leading to the property.

Billy had been helpful in setting up the other security devices Blake had procured. There were motion detectors and cameras set up along the perimeter, all with some sort of receiver devices inside the house. When they were finished, Blake had surprised them all with cold drinks from the cooler in the back of his pickup and told them to follow him into the barn.

"I found this the other day. I was in here looking through my tool chest when I noticed there was something odd about the panels on this wall. I pressed on the side of this one, and . . ." He touched the panel and it moved, opening a hidden door. Blake stepped through the doorway and flipped on a light switch revealing stairs leading downward.

"What is this, Blake?" John asked, excited and alarmed.

"I think it was intended as a panic room or something. But you have to see this, guys! It's unbelievable!"

They carefully went down the stairs and found themselves in front of a solid metal door. Blake opened it, revealing an attractive apartment. John and Billy spent a few minutes exploring it. There was a fully stocked kitchen, including a full refrigerator and freezer.

"How is this powered, Blake?"

"Remember those old solar panels we saw in the small field? We wondered why anyone would have them so far from the cabin if they wanted power. I think they're situated right above the bathroom back there. This apartment is only under the barn at the entrance. It runs behind the barn and ends right by that field where the solar panels are."

John pondered this apparently bombproof underground shelter. It seemed to him that Blake had a lot of "luck." He wondered if Blake's story about how he'd acquired the property was true. To John Foster, it seemed more likely that Blake had built this place himself. But why lie about it? He had already told John about working for the World Union undercover.

Whoever had built the subterranean apartment had included every technological advantage possible. There were even satellite phones and a portable satellite terminal they could use to get Internet access. The gear all looked like military grade.

John's attention snapped back to the present as a movement in the distance caught his eye, disrupting his thoughts. He had climbed up into the tree to try to get an idea of what was going on around them. He could make out the highway in the distance with his binoculars and noted a convoy of tanks and military vehicles rolling toward the southeast. Maybe they were headed to Charlotte? The report John had read last night indicated that the World Union had control of the major cities on the East Coast.

John leaned his head back against the tree trunk and shut his eyes. He had wanted to email Elena to let her know he was all right, but Blake had reacted strongly. He was afraid the e-mail could be somehow traced to their location, endangering them all.

Their group had moved into the bunker the night after jets had flown overhead, followed by the sounds of bombing in the distance. Somehow, Blake had been able to get Internet access and find a news website. If they weren't going to send messages out, at least they could get news in. Apparently, an official civil war was going on in North America. The AG terrorist groups, calling themselves "patriots," were fighting to take back America, and the World Union was fighting back.

John tried to picture what Elena would be doing in New

Babylon at this very moment. Probably putting Olivia down for a nap, he thought. She loved her granddaughter and was thrilled to get to care for her while Teo worked. John missed his wife deeply.

Opening his eyes, John looked at the blue sky, full of white clouds scattered into patterns that begged to be found. He remembered a picnic he and Elena had gone on before they married. Stuffed with fried chicken and potato salad, they had stretched out on the picnic blanket and looked at the sky. Elena found it amusing to search the sky for rabbits, angels, or whatever else she fancied. "Pareidolia," she had called it, like seeing an image of Jesus on a tortilla.

John smiled, remembering. That was the first time he had kissed Elena. Her lips were soft. *Damn! I have to find a way to get in touch with Elena.*

His thoughts were interrupted as an eagle soared overhead, and he watched as it circled in front of him. It was large and majestic, almost magical and ethereal. He could not fault those who wanted to restore America's national glory, of which this bird was a symbol. At one time, it was the greatest nation on earth. But right now, all he could think was that this war was destroying many lives and keeping him from getting home.

He packed the binoculars away in his sack and climbed carefully down the tree. As he headed back to the compound, he tried to think of ways he could contact Elena. Maybe if Blake were not around, he could use the satellite phone. He had to try.

New Babylon, Iraq

Arturo poured more coffee into his cup, listening carefully as Teo caught him up with the workings of the New Babylon Lifestyle Clinic. They were sitting at the conference table in Teo's ultramodern office at the clinic's main headquarters. Under Teo's direction, the clinic had added boutique offerings to their obstetrical, gynecological, and fertility services. After seeing the doctor, a woman could enjoy spa services and the exciting treatments now available for anti-aging skin care. Teo had done a great deal of research on this front. When she and DC lived in Israel, she had found a young Israeli dermatologist, Ari Turov, who had developed a truly effective anti-aging treatment.

Arturo smiled as Teo set a folder full of before and after photos in front of him.

"Teo, this is incredible!" he exclaimed. "And all of this change was achieved with no surgery?"

"That's correct. The best part of Ari's skin recovery treatment is that it doesn't require surgery of any kind. I've worked out a deal with him. He's willing to allow Giamo International to be the world-wide provider for his treatment. He'll train personnel for us, and we will provide all the marketing. We get 60 percent of sales; he gets 40." Teo couldn't help grinning. "Father, this is revolutionary! Do you know how many women we are going to get into our clinics for this beauty treatment alone?"

Arturo looked at the photo in front of him. The results were incredible. "How exactly did Ari make this discovery? I mean, large corporations have spent billions in research trying to find something similar."

"Ari is a Messianic Jew, and he believes every word of the Bible is true." She rushed on hurriedly. "I know how you feel about that," she assured her father, seeing the immediate displeasure on his face, "but you asked. He was quite intrigued by the story of Sarah, Abraham's wife. At the age of eighty, she was so beautiful that the king wanted to take her as one of his wives. So Abraham, afraid that he would be killed if it were known he was her husband, lied and said she was his sister. Ari wondered what it was that accounted for Sarah's beauty at such an advanced age.

"After the attempted invasion of Israel, an archaeologist found the place where Sarah had been buried centuries ago. There were human remains in the tomb. Ari was able to convince the archaeologist to allow him to take samples. They negotiated a deal where the archaeologist and the Israeli government would both get a percentage of any future earnings."

"What did he find?" The scientist in Arturo was interested.

"He found some genetic markers in the DNA of one of the tomb's occupants, a woman of advanced years, that was different from the others. As he experimented, he found something amazing. A sort of molecular 'machine' that seems to have the effect, once it is turned on, of renewing old or damaged cells. Once he found that, he was able to discover how to turn the machine on."

"So is this a one-time treatment?" Arturo asked, his curiosity peaked.

"No, the effects wear off, so the customer has to come in for treatments about twice a year."

Arturo picked up his coffee cup and toasted his daughter. "Teo, you have brokered a deal that has the potential to make us all even wealthier! Well done! I can't tell you how proud I am of you! We can leave a legacy that will extend through generations!"

"Thank you, Father. Listen, I wanted to talk to you about Luca—"

"Luca! Isn't my son something! Here you are making us even more fabulously wealthy, and Luca is about to change the world. He is a man of incredible gifts, isn't he, Teo?"

Teo was not sure what to say, but it did not matter. Her father continued on proudly about Luca, the paragon of virtue and virility, until Teo wanted to vomit. Literally. As Arturo relayed Luca's accomplishments, fear, her old friend, wrapped its paralyzing tentacles around her heart. Her head started pounding. She knew what she had overheard, but as Arturo droned on, she realized he would never believe her.

Say nothing, she thought she heard a voice say. *Smile and leave as soon as you can.* Teo almost dropped her coffee cup. The voice had not been audible, but someone else had just spoken to her.

"... don't you agree, Teo?" her father asked benevolently,

eyebrows raised.

Teo forced a smile and set her cup down carefully. "Indeed. Well, I'm afraid I have to go, Father. DC has just received his pilot's license and has asked me to go up with him. He wants to give me an aerial tour of New Babylon."

She got up and walked around the table. Arturo stood up and embraced his daughter enthusiastically. They said good-bye, and Teo hurried from the building, still trembling. As soon as she was safely in her car, she phoned DC and asked him to meet her at the airport. He had asked her yesterday about taking the plane up this afternoon. Hopefully, he would be able to get away from work.

Jerusalem, Israel

Kate sat in Dr. Michael Benari's office, looking around her curiously. There were a couple of framed diplomas leaning against the wall instead of on it. The only things actually nailed onto the walls were maps, diagrams, and photos of the Temple Mount, no personal items to tell her anything about the man she was about to interview. Christopher was moving a few things around. They had been waiting for the doctor for a while, so Christopher thought he would make the shot a bit tidier. Organization was obviously not a priority for Dr. Benari.

The door opened, and Kate stood up out of courtesy as Dr. Benari entered the room. From the moment their eyes met, Kate was mesmerized. She had been drawn to his intense good looks when she'd first seen him, but in person he was even more intriguing. As he drew closer, she tried to swallow unobtrusively. He was about five inches taller than she was, and she was a tall woman. Looking up at him, she felt her breath catch. He smiled warmly as he took her hand.

"It is a pleasure to meet you, Miss Havenstone. It is really such a privilege. You are one of the few Western reporters I know of who is truly unbiased toward my country. I appreciate that a great deal."

He turned and shook hands with Christopher as well. The two men chatted about where Christopher had traveled in Israel and the terror attack the two had both witnessed a couple of days ago.

Kate noted the doctor's slim build with approval. His dark looks were just the smoldering sort that had always appealed to her, but he lacked the bad boy aura of her past partners. This was a new sort of man for Kate Havenstone. She felt up to the challenge.

They sat down, and Christopher began filming as Kate asked question after question about Dr. Benari's latest find.

"I guess the question on everyone's mind, Doctor, is what is inside the famous Ark of the Covenant? We all grew up with the old adventure films that show the Ark having exceptional powers. Anyone who touches it, dies, or your face melts off . . ."she said, pausing, looking at him archly.

The handsome archaeologist chuckled. "I, too, loved those films as a child, Kate. But as with many things, Hollywood is entertainment, not reality. The Ark is without doubt one of the greatest archaeological finds in history. It also has significant implications for the Jewish people. It is not just a piece of history; it is part of our worship, of our faith. I haven't opened the Ark. I don't intend to open it."

"You've got to be kidding!" Kate exclaimed. "Surely the world deserves to know what is inside."

Something changed in Dr. Benari's expression. He became quite still and said quietly, "The Ark does not belong to the world. Please understand. The Ark is a Jewish treasure. We will not be making public any of our findings regarding the Ark, at least not in the immediate future."

Christopher framed the camera on Kate's beautiful face in a close-up. He knew her well enough to anticipate one of those moments that made her a star. Tears welled up in her stunning blue eyes

271

as she leaned winsomely toward the man before her. "Of course, Dr. Benari, please forgive my eagerness. I have admired the Israeli people since I was a young girl. The way that you as a people have survived centuries of Diaspora and yet retained your identity as a people, the way you survived the evil attempts of a madman to eradicate your race, the way you became a nation in a day against all odds, and the way you have stood against every attempt to annihilate you—it all makes me regard your people and your nation with the utmost respect. Of course, the Ark belongs to Israel." She smiled reassuringly.

"Would you share with us what we might hope to learn about the Ark?" she continued.

Christopher panned to Dr. Benari and stifled a smile. No one could resist Kate's appeal. She just had a knack for figuring out how to endear herself to almost anyone.

"Certainly, Kate," the good doctor responded. He explained that the high priest had responsibility for the national treasure. It was he who would decide when and how the Ark would be examined.

Kate finished the interview and shook the doctor's hand, thanking him sincerely, while Christopher packed away his gear. He saw Dr. Benari hold onto Kate's hand. Christopher leaned in and listened shamelessly.

"Would you have dinner with me tonight?"

She looked into the doctor's eyes. "I'd love to."

Christopher turned away and smiled. Score.

New Babylon, Iraq

Even from the sky, New Babylon was impressive. The city center alone had a population of almost two hundred thousand, and the surrounding areas were growing at a tremendous rate. Yet the view was the last thing on DC's mind right now as Teo revealed her secrets to him. DC was grateful for his experience as a Marine pilot. He had learned the importance of keeping his emotions in check and remaining calm when threatened.

He tried to keep his hands steady as Teo finished her revelation. He had been pretty certain about Luca's identity; now he knew for sure. To learn that he and his daughter's death warrants had been signed made him fiercely angry. He struggled to control himself.

"So, Luca has decided that Olivia's death can give him some good publicity?"

"And yours," Teo reminded him.

"No, mine is to make sure you are 'free' for that old freak, Stephen Amona."

"There's something else I have to tell you, DC." Teo turned in her seat to see his expression. "I was in that bathroom to take a pregnancy test. I'm pregnant."

DC took one of Teo's hands in his right hand. "I am happy about that, Teo, please believe me, but right now we have to make some plans—plans to get Olivia somewhere safe and to get you away from here. I just need to be quiet for a while and think, and pray. We need God's help to get out of this safely."

He squeezed her hand, hoping he was imparting to her the reassurance he was not feeling himself, and went back to flying and planning.

New Babylon, Iraq

Elena put Olivia's lunch down on the high chair just as her cell phone rang. "Hello?" There was static.

"Hello? Who's calling please?"

"Elena!" She recognized her husband's voice.

"John, where are you?" she asked excitedly. "Are you okay? Honey, it's been so long!"

"Listen, I only have a few minutes. I'm fine. I haven't had access to any communications before now. I'm stuck where I am now with the fighting that's going on here. We don't have much information about what is going on in North America."

"There are battles all over the East Coast, John. Most of the cities are under World Union control, but there are many portions of the countryside under control of the Interfaith Global Union. Where are you?"

"I can't say. This might not be a secure line. I want you to know I'm fine and I'm going to find a way to get back to you."

"I don't know how you can. AG isn't just a problem in North America, John. There are battles going on in cities in Europe and Asia, and in the Arab countries, too. GU forces are finding it a struggle to meet the challenge with rebellion going on in so many areas. There are curfews here and even travel bans." Elena tried to keep her voice calm and wished desperately there was a way to keep her husband's voice on the line. She drew strength from every second.

"Someone's coming. I have to go, Elena. I love you."

He was gone. Olivia looked on as her grandma knelt on the floor and began to pray.

24

LAKE GEORGE,
NEW YORK

The morning sun tinged the horizon with pinks and purples in spectacular array. James watched steam rise off the pond as he thoughtfully sipped his tea. The orchard to his left was in full bloom. The camp owner, a solidly built woman in her early sixties, Bess, had shown him around. She and her husband, Jack, had planted this orchard forty years ago. Upstate New York was hard on trees, and they'd had to replace the apple trees so often they had given up on them. There were a couple left still, but the fruit, according to Bess, was no good. They would have plenty of pears and plums at harvest, though.

James sat on the front porch of his cabin, his Bible in his lap. He had just finished his morning devotions and prayers. Again, he thanked God for rescuing him and bringing him and the others to Bess and Jack. They had been good people, had gone to church, had raised their children well, but they had never really believed they needed a savior. *Just like me,* James thought ruefully. The couple had shared their testimony with him the second night at the camp.

Bess and Jack had gone to church for a special Bible quiz event in which their grandson was competing. During the competition, they heard a loud noise.

"I thought a bolt of lightning had hit right next to the church," Jack had told him. "And in a single moment, most of the folks there were gone."

"Yes," continued Bess, "our daughter, son-in-law, and their

275

four children were gone. The pastor and most of the other folks, too. Just a handful of us were left."

"Did you know at the time what had happened?" James had asked.

"We did. Our son-in-law was very interested in Bible prophecy. He even got some author to come and speak at the church for a special 'end times' conference. We went to it, of course. We went to every church event. We thought we were good Christians, Pastor James."

"We all did," James agreed. "When did you come to believe?"

"Our daughter had a shelf in her bedroom full of journals she kept. I read through every one of them. It took me days. I think she started them as a teenager. At sixteen, she went up to the front at church to receive the Lord Jesus as her Savior. As I read through those journals, I saw there was a great difference between the relationship she had with God and my own. I encouraged Jack to read them, too. It was real hard for us. We missed our daughter and grandson. We were mourning them."

Bess had gone on to tell James how she and Jack had committed themselves to the Lord. They had seen some amazing things happen over the last year. A tornado had ripped through their small town, sparing the camp. They had joined together with other new believers to help those affected by the tornado. Strangely, the other people in town just left, even those who had not suffered property damage from the twister.

Over the last year, other people had made their way to this small town, nestled in the valley near Lake George. Amazingly, each one was a Christian.

"I think the Lord has designed this as some sort of refuge," Jack declared. "Things are getting bad with the fighting between the World Union and the AGs."

"And the increase in disasters, too, Jack," Bess added. "The floods that hit the Northwest drove whole communities out of those areas. The great earthquake in California . . . it's been awful. This year has seen record-breaking natural disasters. Somehow the Lord directed all the folks here. Almost every house is full now."

James looked over the campgrounds. There were about twenty cabins that now housed his congregation. David was asleep in the small cabin behind him. After his arrest and escape, James had sobbed at the first sight of his son. Bernard had assured the young father that David was safe, but until they arrived and he saw for himself, James had been anxious.

He turned his thoughts heavenward and prayed aloud, Bess agreeing with him in silence. "Lord, I know what we are facing. Thank You for what You are doing. The fact that You have obviously cleared this town and brought some of Your people to it gives me hope that You will see us through this next season. I am not sure when the Tribulation will begin, but I ask that You would guide me. Help me to equip these brothers and sisters for the time ahead. I pray that we would bring You glory, Lord. In Jesus's name, I do pray."

He finished praying, and he and Bess went their separate ways. There was a lot of work to do. He was grateful that Jack and Bess were so knowledgeable about farming and animals. James had joked that he could tell a cow from a sheep, but that was about it. That had prompted Jack to set up a work schedule, starting with training sessions for all the "city folk." Once the training was done, they were going to begin planting. Jack had stockpiles of seed stashed in various farms just outside of the small town. His wisdom in spreading out his resources was vindicated when armed men had converged on one of the farms. They had taken everything and burned the house and barn to the ground. Thankfully, the family living there had been helping a neighbor move in, and were spared.

James crept quietly into the small cabin, unsure if David was awake yet or not. The living area was comprised of one great room. There was a serviceable kitchen, a table with four chairs, and a couch that had seen better days. There were only two bedrooms. David's was just big enough for the twin-sized bed and nightstand. James opened the door and bent down to wake up his son.

"Hey, Buddy, it's time to get up!" he said, tousling David's hair and smiling as the young toddler opened his eyes.

"Daddy! Uppy!" David sat up and raised his arms to be picked up. James scooped him up and hugged him. He loved the eager way David awoke to greet each new day. The little boy thoroughly enjoyed being at the camp and had found a special friend in Jack, following him around to the point that James had worried his son was a pest. But Jack reassured James that he was happy to have David's "help."

"Hey, David, it's time to get breakfast, okay?" James carried David into the kitchen and set him in a booster seat on one of the chairs. He opened the small refrigerator and got out a bowl with eggs from the henhouse. Bess had assured him he could keep the eggs out on the counter as long as he did not wash them. Some substance on them would keep them fresh, even at room temperature. He believed her, but he could not bring himself to do it. Instead, he always washed the eggs and stored them into the refrigerator.

He flipped the switch on the stove and put a frying pan on it. "We're having eggs today, David. I'm not sure that it will not be eggs tomorrow, too, since we don't have any cereal. But God will provide, right?" He chuckled at the serious expression on his son's face. "Don't worry, David, He always does!"

New Babylon, Iraq

Teo pushed the stroller in front of her carefully. She did not want the blanket to blow away. Olivia was asleep inside, along with her special dolly. DC had given Olivia some medicine that made her sleep. Teo was worried about its effects on her daughter, but they couldn't take the chance of Olivia giving them away. She tried to control her fears. So much could go wrong! Methodically, she went through the steps of their plan. She looked ahead at her husband and marveled at his composure. Again, she thanked God that DC had served in the Marines and had completed missions much more difficult than the one they had planned. This had to work.

Elena walked next to her as they both followed DC through the small airport terminal. Teo had convinced Arturo to allow Elena to use his jet and his pilots to fly to Philadelphia. That city was firmly in the hands of World Union forces and was fairly safe.

Unknown to Elena, DC had put a tracing program on all her phones. He wanted to be able to follow up on any leads on John. He now had John's coordinates. One of his friends, Brant Hughes, was a member of the Babylon Security Forces. Teo had prevailed on her father's influence to assign the young man to accompany Elena on her search for her husband. Brant was also a member of the same underground church cell to which DC and Elena belonged. A single man in his early twenties, and intelligent, he rose quickly through the Babylon Security ranks. Not only that, Brant was a computer genius and an expert in hand-to-hand combat. When DC had confided his plans in him, the young man had been quick to volunteer his help.

Brant brought up the rear, pulling a suitcase filled with things he anticipated they might need. They got to the jet without incident. Teo was familiar to the jet's crew, so they made no fuss when she insisted that DC carry the small stroller up the stairs so as not to wake the child. Once inside the jet, Teo, DC, and Elena left Brant to get settled in and made their way to the bedroom. Closing the door, DC lifted the blanket off the stroller. Olivia was still sleeping. He unstrapped the large doll they had placed on her lap.

Teo picked up the little girl. Tears streamed down the mother's face as she stifled sobs. Her throat felt like it was going to explode. Elena put an arm around her shoulder and kissed her cheek. "I will take good care of her, Teo," Elena whispered. "DC will get you back home to us safely."

DC interrupted their good-byes. "Elena, I'm sure Brant will be very helpful in tracking down John for you. Teo has you booked into the Ritz-Carlton. You can be nearby, but safe, while he searches," DC chose his words carefully. He didn't know if Arturo's plane was bugged and did not want to take any chances. "Promise you won't do anything foolish, okay? It's a war zone."

Elena followed his cue. "DC, I'm so thankful for all you've done. You're like a son to me. You watch after my girls while I'm gone, okay?"

Teo cried softly as she stroked her little girl's hair away from her face. The room became quiet, so Teo turned. She saw her mother and DC praying silently on their knees.

Teo stopped crying. She felt warmth fill her as she watched her husband and her mother. They looked beautiful—no, that wasn't the word—*noble*. Noble and strong. Watching them, Teo felt like she too, became stronger. She could do this. She could choose to trust God. DC trusted Him. Her mother did. Couldn't she?

They finished their silent prayer. DC strapped the doll in the stroller and covered it with the blanket again. He picked up the bag he had brought onboard the aircraft and placed it on the bed.

"Here's your bag, Elena." Without a word, he opened the bag and removed the contents. The bag was just big enough to put the toddler inside when they landed. Netting hid the many small, strategically placed holes punched in the sides. Brant would carry the bag out of the plane and through security, most of which they would be able to bypass, thanks to Arturo's status. DC pulled a syringe out of his pocket and carefully handed it to Elena. She nodded at him and put it into the drawer next to the bed.

Elena drew Teo into an embrace. Neither of them spoke. DC also hugged Elena and then opened the door to the cabin. Teo pushed the stroller out of the bedroom and dried her eyes. DC shook hands with Brant and then picked up the stroller, careful to give the illusion of weight as he went down the stairs with his precious load. Teo followed him.

Inside the terminal, they watched out the window as the jet was readied for takeoff. Teo allowed tears to stream down her face as she waved. The jet took off safely. The terminal area was mildly busy, so for the benefit of any onlookers, DC hugged his wife and asked, "How about I take you and Olivia up for a ride? You know how much she loves it, and it always cheers you up to see New Babylon from the air. What do you think, honey?"

Teo smiled up at him. "I would love that. Thanks, babe."

"I'll get the plane ready. Why don't you wait here?" he said. She sat down to wait, carefully pulling the stroller right in front of her and adjusting the blanket.

Rome, Italy

"How in the world could this happen!" Arturo Giamo shouted. "What do you mean, it exploded?" He listened for a few minutes and then threw his phone across the room with a curse. Judith heard the noise and came back into the bedroom.

"What is it Arturo? Has something happened?" She was very concerned when she saw the expression on his face. "Is Luca all right?"

He looked at her desperately. "Luca? Yes, Luca is well." He collapsed into a chair. She rushed over to him.

"What has happened, darling?"

"It is Teo. Olivia, too. DC took them both up in his plane this morning and crashed southwest of the city." His voice cracked. "The rescue crews could not even attempt a rescue. The plane exploded on impact. The fire was too intense for emergency workers to get close to the wreckage."

Arturo Giamo sobbed, grieving over the loss of his daughter and his grandchild. Judith sat on the floor next to him, an arm around his shoulder, murmuring words of consolation, stifling a sigh of relief.

ONE WILL BE TAKEN

New Babylon, Iraq

Stephen Amona sat in his office, stunned, the phone pressed to his right ear. Luca continued speaking, heedless of his mentor's pain.

"I think this will make an even better opportunity to capture the sympathy of the world, Stephen. My family, all gone. In one tragic moment, I lose everyone I care about. We can make sure the press plays it up; we can garner a lot of attention with this. We can play up the angle of AG terrorists targeting my family—and the subsequent, heartbreaking death of my father."

"Wait," Stephen stuttered, "your father is still alive. You haven't lost all of your family, Luca."

"Oh, didn't I tell you? He had a massive stroke when he heard the news. He died in Judith's arms just an hour ago. She didn't even have time to call for the ambulance. He was gone that quickly," Luca chuckled. "I will be leaving here in a few minutes to console her."

Although he thought Arturo Giamo was a pretentious fool, Stephen was shocked at Luca's response to the death of his father. *I'm sure it is the shock*, Stephen told himself, though deep inside he did not believe the lie. He had seen things in the past year—awful things that made it not quite possible to believe Luca suffered shock of any kind. Stephen quickly shoved that thought aside. Luca was sensitive to any criticism, even unspoken criticism.

"I will contact the media myself, Luca, on your behalf. Everyone will understand your need to grieve," he offered.

"That will be fine, Stephen. I think Judith and I will be grieving together in private for the next few days. Once you have made the funeral arrangements, I will make my public appearance. Make sure that Billings is overseeing the funeral of my family. He is my special friend, after all, and the one who healed my dear sister so she could conceive my precious niece. I believe he was her godfather, wasn't he?"

"Yes, he was, Luca."

"The stage is set, Stephen. This tragedy, and my amazing response to it, will pave the way for my entrance onto the world stage—not just as a politician but also as a world celebrity. Everything is going well, Stephen. Soon I will take my rightful place. One step at a time, eh?"

"Yes, Luca," Stephen answered dutifully, but Luca had already hung up.

West of New Babylon, Iraq

DC drove the jeep across the desert to the west. Teo wrapped the scarf around her mouth and nose to block out some of the dust. She could not believe they had made it. Once DC had the plane ready, she had pushed the stroller out onto the tarmac. DC had parked the plane with the passenger door facing away from the terminal. She'd taken the large doll out of the stroller and put it onto the passenger seat, being careful to fasten the seatbelt just as she would if Olivia were there.

DC had rolled the stroller back to the terminal and left it stored by the counter, after asking one of his acquaintances to watch after it for him. "We're just going on a quick flight to cheer up my wife. Her mom just left for North America. Can I leave this here for a bit?" he had said. He gave a quick thanks and hurried back to the plane.

Once they were far enough away from the monitoring radar, DC landed his plane on a deserted dirt road. Teo got out quickly with the doll. DC took off again as soon as he saw Teo race to the jeep he and Brant had hidden in the bushes on the side of the field a few days before.

He quickly gained altitude, heading west. When he was high enough, he put the plane on autopilot and donned his parachute. He thanked God for the training he had received years ago, then he opened the hatch and jumped out.

Teo had a pair of binoculars trained on the plane and so was able to follow him as he drifted back down to earth. A minute later, she pulled out a radio detonator from the seat next to her and pushed the trigger. The plane exploded. She quickly drove the jeep to meet her husband, arriving just as he was rolling up the parachute.

DC looked intensely at his wife. "Are you okay, Teo?"

"Yes, I am just thinking about Olivia. I wonder if we are ever going to see her again," she said, tears filling her eyes. DC did not know what to say. The only way he could think of to get the toddler safely away from New Babylon was on that jet with Elena. There was no way, given the plans Luca had, that they all would have been allowed to leave New Babylon.

"I think I can get us both there, Teo. The way we are going would be too hard on Olivia."

"I know, DC."

They drove along for miles in silence.

"What are you thinking about?" Teo finally asked.

"I was thinking about a song my mom used to sing. Something about being ready, one being taken and one being left. That song's been on my mind a lot lately. I was not ready, Teo. I should have been, but I was not ready. If I had been, maybe we would have avoided this mess." His voice cracked.

Teo looked at her husband—really looked at him, for the first time in months. He was strong.

"DC, if you had been ready, I would have been here alone with Olivia. The way I see it, God is using you to get us out of this mess. Where are we going first?"

"Jordan." He didn't want to tell Teo, but he did not have any plans for after that. He prayed God did.

Coming Soon!

ONE WILL BE LEFT

New Babylon, Iraq

Arturo heard a soft whirring noise. Turning his head, he tried to open his eyes, but the effort was too much.

"I think he is waking. Should we call the ambassador?"

"Not yet. He wants to be called when his father is more cognizant."

Arturo could hear the words being spoken and wondered, confused, what they meant. He could tell he was lying on a bed, but where was he? He struggled to open his eyes again and caught a glimpse of a woman dressed in scrubs. Was he in the hospital? He saw her come closer and bend toward him.

"Well, hello! We've been wondering when you would wake up! I'm Jean. Your son has hired a private medical team to see to your needs. You're in his home."

Arturo tried to move his hands to push himself up but could not. Panic began to wash over him as he pulled against the restraints.

CPSIA information can be obtained
at www.ICGtesting.com
Printed in the USA
LVHW111501100220
646416LV00001B/174

9 780985 457884